Crown Hunt

R. M. MORGAN

3rd Coast Books, LLC

Montgomery, Texas 77356

2018

3rd Coast Books, LLC

19790 Hwy. 105 W. Ste. 1318

Montgomery, TX 77356

www.3rd CoastBooks.com

ISBNs

Perfect Binding-978-1-946743-22-0

Project Coordinator-Ron Mumford

Editor-Faye Walker, Ph.D.

Cover Artist-Fiona Jayde

Cover Coordinator- James Price

Text Designer-James Price

Printed in the United States of America Copyright © 2018 R. M. MORGAN

READER TESTIMONIALS

"After reading R.M. Morgan's fast-paced *Crown Hunt*, I felt he had taken me with him on an adventure of international intrigue. Not until Don, the main character, and Roth completed the hunt, and the antagonist is put to rest to solve the mystery could I breathe easier." L.L. Carpenter.

"Suspenseful story and colorful characters; couldn't wait to see how it turned out. I highly recommend *Crown Hunt* for mystery lovers." Sheila Larson

"The *Crown Hunt* is a riveting detective mystery written by a talented storyteller who incites readers to sleuth for the truth." Leonard Szymczak, Award-winning author of *Kookaburra's Last Laugh*.

"R.M. Morgan's first book in his series of detective novels introduces Don Gannon, a likeable P.I. who works for an interesting lady, Harriett Roth. The story takes Don to South Korea and back to North Carolina, blending the two cultures in a search for missing historical artifacts…and a killer." Jacquelyn Hanson, author of *Matilda's Story*.

"Author R. M. Morgan weaves a tale of theft, murder and intrigue in his debut novel, the *Crown Hunt*. The mystery reader will certainly enjoy finding out about how Roth Security earned its well-earned reputation in this newly established series." David Eugene Andrews, Author and storyteller.

CONTENTS

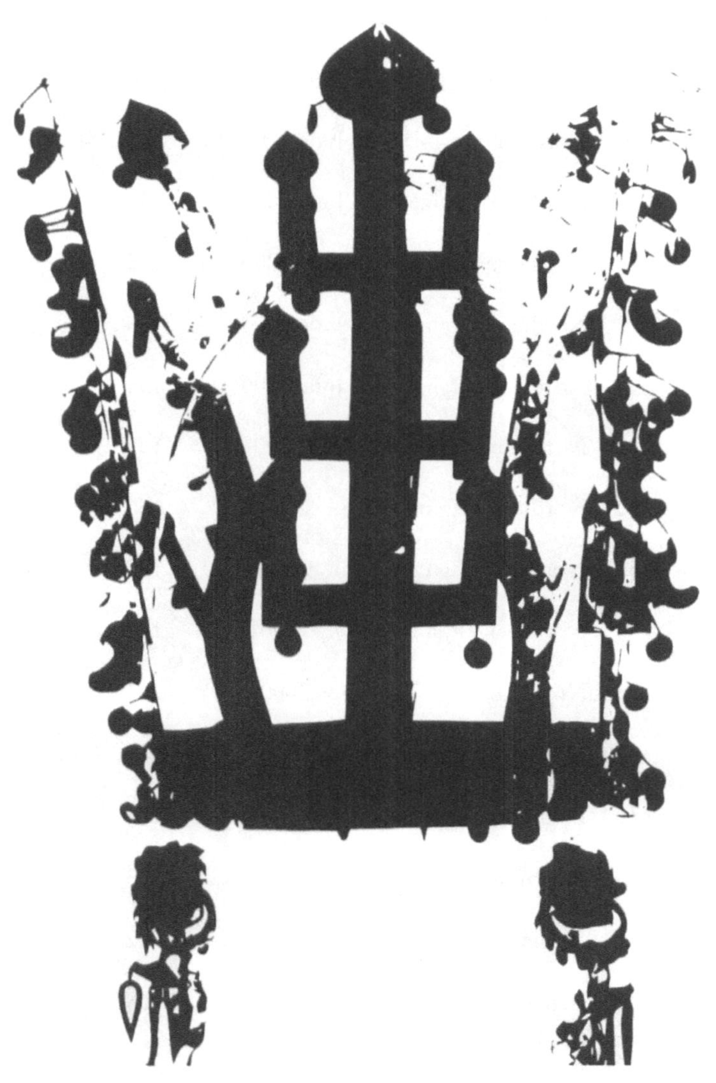

ACKNOWLEDGMENTS

This tale of the Appalachian Mountains and the scenes depicted in the Korean War are a work of fiction. But I read many books diving into the background for this story. For readers wishing to peruse historical fact, I suggest the following books as a starting point:

Shin, Hyung Kyu. *Remembering Korea 1950: a boy soldier's story.* Reno and Las Vegas, Nevada: University of Nevada Press, 2001.

Sloan, Bill. *The Darkest Summer: Pusan and Inchon 1950: the battles that saved South Korea—and the Marines—from extinction.* New York: Simon and Schuster, 2009.

Sohn, Mark F. *Mountain Country Cooking.* New York: St. Martin's Press, 1996.

Yup, Gen. Paik Sun. *From Pusan to Panmunjom.* Washington, D.C.: Potomac Books, Inc., 2000.

I am grateful to my writing coach, Leonard Szymczak, who good-naturedly showed me how to awaken my prose and who made writing fun.

I thank the Morgan family: Ida, who taught me how to use and love my native language, and Travis, Debbie, and Tyler, who read many pages and enhanced the book with sharp-edged suggestions. I also thank my bright beta readers, Barbara Hennessey and Linda Rosenberg, who took the time to read the manuscript and tell me what worked and what didn't.

I had a support team, who critiqued my writings for countless months, helping me finish my manuscript. They are Mel Zimmerman, Jacki Hanson, David Andrews, Craig Wells, Sheila Larson, Mary Keown-Watkins, Kim Hudson, Kathe Caldwell, Jan Mannino, and the late Joy Young.

Big thanks go to Ron Mumford and the group at 3rd Coast Books: editor Faye Walker, Ph.D., and text designer/ cover designer James Price. Enormous thanks go to Fiona Jayde for her ideas for the cover design.

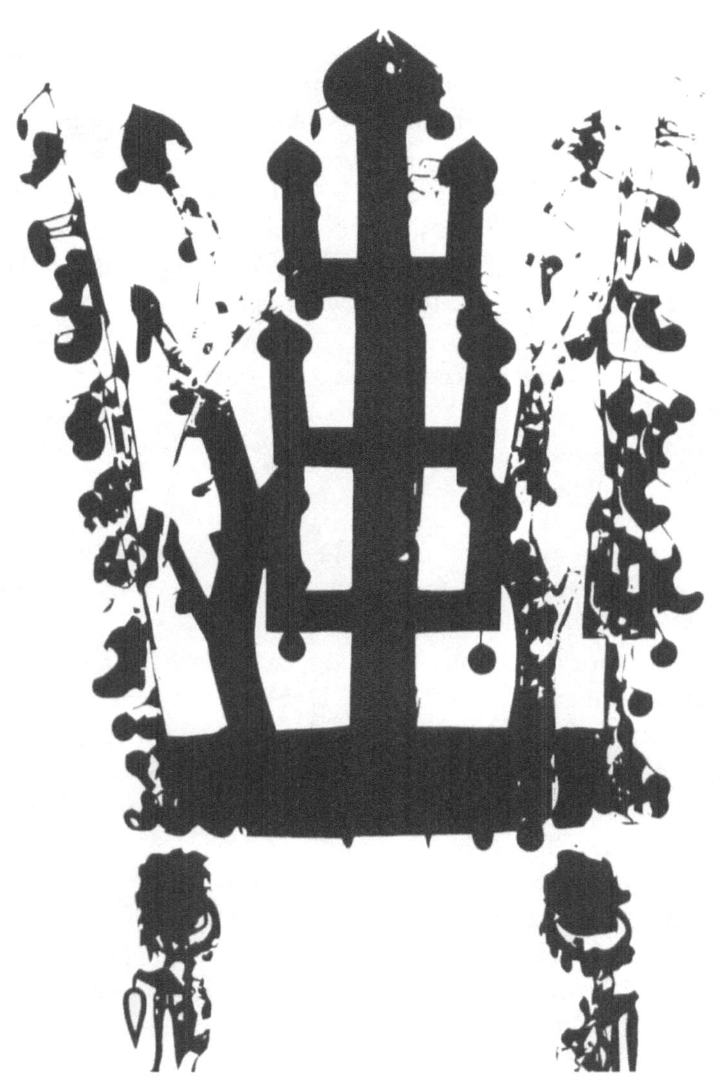

"Pray for us, for we are sure that we have a clear conscience, desiring to act honorably in all things." – **Hebrews 13:18**

SOUTH KOREA—17 MAY 2000

Seong-gi Kim, a brooding man, believed life is good, and then evil pulls back the curtain into darkness.

He had this dim view because he had become a man of advanced years and entered the frosty winter of his life. But his past had been pleasurable, his life's work satisfactory. In his traditional Korean home, with its gently sloping eaves, he sat on the floor in front of his TV at night and finished watching a Korean variety show. He thought about his family, his upbringing, and his years of hard work. His mind reminisced over his youth, at a time before the terrible war fifty years before. He had grown up in a poor farming family, without TV.

He sighed and continued watching the television program, *Happy Together*, a favorite South Korean variety show. He was alone while his wife and mother were away visiting his son. At times like this, Seong-gi caught up with the programs he enjoyed. As he watched, he heard a sharp noise—Clang!—Clang! He ignored it, believing one never regrets putting off a task to watch TV. At a commercial break, the noise continued. The old man, his curiosity aroused, rose and checked his set, but the metallic sound came from outside, behind his home. He knew an animal such as a dog or a wild boar might've found its way into his yard, but neither could make this sound.

Seong-gi slipped on shoes and pushed past a sliding door at the rear of his house. He saw nothing but shadows outside. Stepping into his yard and facing the source of the clanging, he walked toward a vine-covered concrete wall stretching across the rear of his garden. Treading bit by bit into the shadows, he discovered the noise maker.

A toy bunny, standing about a foot tall, with its head tilted backwards, whacked little cymbals together with its paws. Seong-gi stared at the toy—a joke?

He bent over the robotic rabbit.

Strong arms grabbed his right shoulder and the left side of his neck. A forearm squeezed his neck, putting pressure on his carotid artery, cutting off blood circulation to his brain. Another assailant, also from behind, seized his lower torso and left arm. Seong-gi's mind cried out to run, to escape. His vision dropped out of focus and flip-flopped like successive scenes from an old-style movie film. Gradually, his awareness slipped into blackness.

# # #

Seong-gi awoke. He lay supine and stared at an unlit light bulb high above his feet. The seventy-year-old man felt the ache in his arms and legs—limbs crying out to move, to flex. His back rested on a wooden rack, his wrists and ankles seized firmly by rope, his head secured to the frame by a rubber-like mask. Though limber for his age, he could barely move.

He rotated his eyes sideways and studied his surroundings. The rack was level like a table, set in a room with brown-gray walls of mud brick. The high-ceilinged room contained a single door to his right. Dust coated the four windows high on the wall to his left, and a metal funnel hung three feet directly over his face. Where was he? Seong-gi seethed with frustration, with anger. A tight sensation roiled his viscera as when a roller coaster drops abruptly from a height. He cursed silently, then shouted, "Help me! Somebody! Help!" No answer. Seong-gi closed his eyes. *Remain calm.*

Later, he pushed aside his agony and anger and glanced around the room again. Daylight came in under one of the slanting windows, its white radiance illuminating the motes dancing in the air and shining on a section of the opposite wall. He heard birds, their sound broken by the occasional slap of river swales or the whistle of the wind. Once, the horn of a ferry wailed. He guessed he lay near the Han River, a major waterway near the border between North and South Korea.

Seong-gi's stomach quivered in a chill dread in the dark room. Someone had brought him here; somebody had to be near. He bellowed out curses and called for relief. Again, no answer. He tried stringing together more thoughts. Try as he might, Seong-gi could no longer concentrate, collapsing into thick, black oblivion.

# # #

Seong-gi felt a sharp pain in his chest and recovered consciousness a second time.

A man, his face covered by a close-fitting knitted cap—a black balaclava—stood above Seong-gi and struck him again with the heel of his hand.

Seong-gi cried out. The overhead light bulb had been turned on and illuminated his tormentor's barren eyes, eyes showing no interest in the old man's cry of agony. Seong-gi studied the black-clad figure, his captor. A full outbreak of anger galvanized his body. He shouted, "Who are you? Damn you!" He threw curse after curse at his captor, who neither moved nor replied. Finally, Seong-gi gave up and stared blood-red animus at the man beside the rack.

"Answer one question," his tormentor began, "and you go free. Never see me again."

Seong-gi realized the individual in the balaclava spoke with a cold voice, without feeling. "Cut me loose. I hurt."

"Your pain interests me not. Reply to my question."

Tilting his eyes to the right, Seong-gi made out the ridged weave of the black balaclava close to his face. He smelled the faint scent of lemon, the odor of a detergent used to wash clothes. He recoiled from his captor's voice with its frozen, condescending timbre. Anyone who would capture an old man and lash him to a table had to be evil. *Don't trust him.*

But Seong-gi had to find a way off the rack. He had to get this mystery man to release him. "What question?"

The man thumped Seong-gi's chest with stiff fingers. "Fifty years ago, you stole objects. Where are they?"

Seong-gi gazed at the windows high on the sidewall. The falling-plunge feeling returned to his gut. He thought maybe the continuation of his life hung on his answer and his existence had grown darker. He had to figure out his captor: who was he?

How had the man in black found out about a long-ago event? Through his pain, he visualized an earthen mound in a valley, a small hill covered in vegetation by the passing years. Seong-gi must keep his knowledge from the man in black.

"Do not know . . . about the objects you seek." Seong-gi's eyes dropped under the intense stare of his tormentor's eyes, unable to conceal the lie. He began pleading with his tormentor. "Let me go."

The captor's dead eyes held steady on the old man. "Time is not ripe. I want you to want to speak. Meet my persuader." Seong-gi heard a wooden box being pulled up to the rack. The man in the black balaclava stepped up and fiddled with the funnel above the old man's face.

A liquid drop fell onto Seong-gi's forehead, a region not covered by the rubber mask.

Plop!

He focused on the funnel above his head; a few seconds later another drop fell onto the same spot.

Plop!

Because Seong-gi's restraints immobilized his head on the wooden rack, the funnel targeted all the drops into the middle of his brow. His tormentor disappeared. The overhead light bulb had darkened.

An hour passed. The old man grew frantic. The tingling in his bound limbs continued, and the dripping drops bounced onto his skull like non-stop drilling by a dentist. He watched each liquid drop form on the tip of the tap, pause, then fall onto the identical site on his forehead. His mind created the image of a tunnel growing in the middle of his skull.

Stay calm. Find a way to escape.

#

Seong-gi woke a third time. Looking up at the windows, he viewed soft moonlight illuminating the tilted window, giving a blue hue to the frame holding the glass.

A drop hit his forehead. He sensed wetness over his face. The droplets cascaded like a column of ants. He rotated his eyes to see if the man in the black balaclava had returned. Seong-gi was alone.

Then his abductor turned on the overhead light bulb. The man in black stood next to him, with his unblinking, emotionless eyes. Another droplet dripped. He waited to bluff his tormentor. He would deny knowing about stolen objects.

"Where are the items you took?"

Would this devil ever let him go? Exhausted, he wondered, *How much longer can I go on?* His captor just watched him through the eye holes in his face covering, unmoving, maybe waiting for the old man to give up. "Can't tell you . . . I know nothing."

The tormentor remained motionless. "Tell me. Then you can go. Your suffering stops."

"Stop the water pounding my head."

"Answer me. I will loosen your ropes and stop the drips."

Seong-gi wanted to believe him. Perhaps his captor would be faithful to his words and not trick him. His captor hadn't shown his face or said who he was. If released, Seong-gi did not know him, couldn't point him out to the police. However, his intuition continued to distrust the man in black.

"Yes, loosen my bonds—I will talk." Seong-gi rotated his body as best he could to stretch his limbs. He had to get feeling back.

"I am in charge. You will suffer until you give me what I want."

Through his pain-driven stupor and overwhelming frustration, the old man saw the overhead bulb go dark and heard his tormentor leave.

# # #

Days passed. The old man grew weak. He began to feel defeated, caring less and less about withholding his knowledge. His pain-numbed brain struggled to register when one day ended, and another started. One night, the sound of constant rain meant clouds cut off moonlight and starlight. He felt an impacting droplet. Then he caught the lemon scent. The balaclava man stood near.

"Where are the objects?" his captor said, switching on the light.

"I do not . . . do not trust you."

His captor's head nodded as if he had been waiting. "Give me what I want. I will not hurt you. You do not know who I am."

Seong-gi's brain had fallen into sluggish inactivity, into near total exhaustion. His head ached when he tried to think. Eager to stop his crushing pain, anxious to rest, he whispered, "I will tell you . . . what we took."

"And where?"

Seong-gi faltered and then responded, "And where."

For hours, Seong-gi described the house holding the objects. He gave a detailed account of how to enter a locked room.

The old man ignored another liquid splash. "Let me go. Told you all."

"Tell me once more," his captor demanded. "I have to make sure you keep telling the same story again and again."

Seong-gi blacked out.

When he regained consciousness, his captor said, "We will pick up where you left off."

After more hours of interrogation, Seong-gi said, "I told you everything. Release me."

Maybe satisfied he had his answer, the tormentor seemed to relent. "You did well. I set you free." He unfastened the cords around Seong-gi's feet. While standing on the box, he reached to the funnel overhead and closed the tap.

"I feel . . . nothing in my legs," Seong-gi gasped.

His captor released his arms. "Your feeling will return. Flex your ankles."

Seong-gi rotated into a fetal position and emitted soft groans.

# # #

Watching the old man bend in evident relief, the captor moved behind Seong-gi and pulled a .22 pistol out of his waistband. He held the barrel near the old man's head and squeezed the trigger twice. Bullets tore through the center of Seong-gi's brain.

The assassin removed his balaclava and chuckled, pleased with his work. "See, I told you I would set you free—you will never see me again."

He turned off the light and went into the next room where his accomplice sat at a desk. "Clean up the mess and wrap the body in plastic. Tonight, we drop it into the Han River."

"I wanted to kill him," the man at the desk said.

The assassin stopped, frowned. "I don't care. Remember, follow my orders." He left the room.

ASHEVILLE, NORTH CAROLINA—14 JUNE 2000

My brain roiled in waves of agony and noisome vertigo—payback for overindulgence. Last night, I drank too much beer with my best friends, Bruce Seeker and Mickey Ploughman. I went to bed late and slept even later in one of the nine bedrooms in my boss's two-story mansion, the headquarters for Roth Security. I had slumbered in an inert ball like an ancient mangy dog. Ordinarily, I would have bolted out of bed at sunrise and jogged around the gray brick house with its ten-acre grounds and surrounding woodlands. This morning, I woke two hours late at nine.

Like a squirrel exiting hibernation, I opened an eye and peeked out my open window. A pleasant June morning; Asheville daybreaks seemed either heavenly or shrouded in the rain like a monsoon in Southeast Asia. Through the window, I sniffed cloves, a smell coming from rhododendron shrubs with the white flowers. I padded across the hardwood floor to my bathroom, one of seven in our mansion, where I took an Alka-Seltzer—my preferred cure for a combined headache and upset stomach. After a shower, I dressed and ambled downstairs for breakfast.

I heard the faint sounds of Taylor Ploughman—cook extraordinaire and strange hillbilly lady—preparing our meal. A spoon clinked against a ceramic bowl and plates clanged together. Most mornings, our chef served food in a combined kitchen and dining area. This room had long been my favorite in the mansion, an elegant-looking structure built in the fifties.

Stepping into the breakfast room, I sniffed fresh polish on the wooden floor and the heavenly smell of eggs, apples, and biscuits. I dropped into a chair and listened to the sounds of percolating coffee and crackling and sputtering oil. Bruce sat at the long dining table. Roth's computer expert, he possessed an in-depth understanding of geek stuff, like search techniques and databases.

Bruce sported a silly grin like an ugly Cheshire Cat. After a brutal night of drinking at the Naughty Hops pub, he had arrived at the breakfast table before I did; his smirk seemed to match his delight at beating me.

"Good morning all," I said.

"Howdy Donnell," Taylor replied, as she flipped the eggs on the stove across the room.

I turned to find Taylor bringing me a mug of coffee. Caffeine, my favorite morning drug.

Bruce ceased grinning and sipped his hot coffee. "No morning run to greet the rising sun? Just drop out of bed to feed your face? You peaked at twenty-eight and are now fading swiftly—sad."

Bruce and I had been close friends for over a decade. An African American of average height, he had the body of a bull.

"More's the pity," I teased him back. "Quick as I am, I find you already entrenched at this table, shoveling grub into your face."

Bruce took some of the grits off his plate. "You have the skin color of a mackerel. Go back to bed. You shouldn't be impersonating an investigator today."

"I may not be Sherlock Holmes, but I'm a damn good private investigator. Though our boss, Harriett Roth, hasn't said it, I'm sure deep down, she'd agree. Maybe one day, she'll tell me, 'Donnell Gannon, your skills of observation are so insightful, I'm giving you a raise.'"

He snorted at me.

"Oh dear! Are we having an unhappy-hangover morning?" Taylor asked as she brought a platter of food to our table. Petite with red hair and blue eyes, she had grown up deep in the mountains around Asheville, where her parents instilled a deep appreciation of Appalachia. Sort of a female Huckleberry Finn. As an old saying goes, she is "as different as chalk from cheese."

She positioned the serving in the middle of the table. "This here is crispy fried apple. Hep yourself to biscuits and gravy, fried eggs, and pork chops. I also made country grits and fresh-squeezed orange juice. Eat up.”

“Yum,” Bruce responded.

“I appreciate you’ns, Bruce. When I was a-growin’ up, my people always a-fixin’ up a big breakfast. For my grits, I boil water and slowly whisk in a cup of old-fashioned grits . . . old-fashioned grits are stone-ground, whole kernel grits.”

As she turned back to her cooking, he whispered, “She’s a treasure, and I’m beginning to understand what she’s saying.”

I spooned food onto my plate. “Bruce pal, you see the transforming power of Harriett Roth. She has taken Taylor under her wing and is upgrading her phraseology. Think of Cockney flower girl Eliza Doolittle.”

“Works both ways,” Bruce noted. “Our buddy, Mickey, changed after he married Taylor—what is it now, roughly two years past? Now he sounds like he’s chewing tobacco when he talks.”

“Because I love you like a brother, Bruce, I will not breathe a word—to Taylor or Mickey—of what you just said.” I glanced around the table for the newspaper. “Do I remember right? We’re meeting some Korean-American guys this morning?”

“You do. What’s the topic?” my partner asked.

“No idea. Roth told me these guys were in a rush to see us.”

Bruce wolfed down the remaining grits. “Is this . . . the same company we do security for in Northern Virginia?”

I grabbed the newspaper off the table. “Yeah. We installed the security system in their building a year ago.”

Bruce pushed his plate aside and sat back with a mug of coffee. “Pass me the sports section.”

I tossed part of the paper at him. “I’ve got sports just now. Here’s the front section.”

He frowned at me. “You always hog the paper.”

“No, I don’t. You’re too slow.”

My partner began reading the front page. “This is interesting. There’s news about divers finding the ancient port of Alexandria.”

That caught my attention. Most often we discuss TV and sports, not the newspaper.

“Alexandria, Virginia?”

“No. Alexandria, Egypt, you dummy.”

I put down my sports section. “Are you saying divers discovered the ancient city of Alexandria?”

"Yep."

"The one created by Alexander the Great? As in Cleopatra and Mark Antony's time?"

My friend had piqued my interest; I read history books and watched history programs on TV. On many nights, I dropped off to sleep reading about ancient times.

Bruce continued to read the paper. "The old town is underwater. No one has seen it for roughly 1,200 years."

"Alexandria had the world's oldest university complex and one of the Seven Wonders of the World, the Pharos," I said. "I read about the Pharos, a 440-foot-high lighthouse."

Bruce frowned. "Thank you, amateur historian."

I gazed around to see if Taylor would bring more coffee. "If you'd read more, you'd know such things."

Bruce ignored me. "Paper says divers found the ancient city sunk about thirty feet under the water surface."

I dreamed of finding an ancient statue or holding old pottery. "Maybe Egypt will open old Alexandria to exploration—so we could scuba-dive down to see those ruins." To dive down into the Mediterranean waters and hold a Greek vase or a wine drinking cup in my hands would swamp me with adrenalin, skyrocketing my heart rate. Wiping the vessel's grime away to expose its original texture and color would be my dream. Afterwards, would I give the receptacle to the authorities or steal it away? Not me. Faced with a practical choice of keeping a historical object or turning it in, I would do the right thing. If I am anything, I am ethical.

I glanced up at the old-fashioned clock on the wall. "Hey, nearly time for Roth's guests to arrive."

ASHEVILLE—14 JUNE 2000

Shortly before ten o'clock, a black Lincoln Town Car parked in front of the mansion. Three Koreans in dark-blue suits, white shirts, and light-blue ties exited the vehicle, walked up the stone stairs, and stopped at the front door. Our visitors appeared similar in age: late sixties or early seventies. They smiled to greet me but—apparently eager to move into the house and meet Roth—they walked around me to the open door.

The shortest Korean acted as their spokesperson, advancing before the other two. "My name Sook Park."

I turned to the second man, the tallest of the three. He introduced himself. "My name Bin Bie."

Unlike Sook and Bin, who were thin and frowned a lot, the third man wore a slightly rumpled suit, carried extra weight, and smiled a lot. "Hi, I Yeong-ho Park." He projected the relaxed comedian, a chubby funnyman who smirked and waved his hand at me from three feet away.

I, in my outfit of a mid-gray, classic-fit Burberry suit, light-gray tie, white dress shirt, and brown Gucci moccasin shoes, led them through the glass-paneled front door and onto the polished oak floor of the foyer. I pressed a button on the intercom. "Ms. Roth, your visitors are here."

"Escort them to my office," she replied.

Walking through the hallway, Sook Park glanced up at the chandelier with its electric candles and sideways at the landscape paintings along the wall to our right. "Grand house."

"Just a house," I said. "It's exciting because it's crawling with remarkable individuals."

Roth is mostly an enigma to me. I talk with her daily but have little idea who she is. However, I don't fret because I am gradually learning. Several times, she has refused to tell me where she grew up; I think she's from the north. She went to college at a prestigious college for women and married a medical doctor. I dug that out of her one evening when she drank too much wine at dinner. Harriett Roth loved her husband and depended on him extensively. A single tragic event defines Harriett's life: her loss of her beloved husband by suicide, following a slide into abject poverty. From that moment forth, Harriett became determined never to be sans large sums of money. Rumor has it she sank everything she owned into her start-up detective agency. Roth leads us, her group of investigators, from the headquarters in Asheville, NC. She guides us with wisdom, compassion, and craftiness. Her character is complicated at times: cranky, agoraphobic, and greedy.

I steered them into Roth's office at the rear of the mansion, an airy room with a row of windows along one wall, a room filled with a red leather couch and lots of chairs. Positioned to the right of the fireplace, Harriett Roth, clad in a black, full-length dress of luxurious satin, stood at her desk. Her alabaster white hair fell to the top of her shoulders. A vase of purple cornflowers sat on her desk, and she had potted plants on the mantle and in crocks in two corners.

Her intense black eyes looked the Koreans full in the face. Taylor, Bruce, and Mickey rose from the sofa. My boss shook hands with Sook Park. "You came to complain?"

"You did good work for us," Sook Park responded stiffly. "Now, I need you for different job."

She pointed to the chairs facing her desk. "Be seated."

Our guests scanned the office and the bookshelves lining the front wall. Sook Park and Bin Bie sat in leather chairs while Yeong-ho searched for the roomiest chair and moved it in front of Roth's desk.

Roth glanced at Taylor. "Can Mrs. Ploughman offer you fresh-brewed coffee, tea, or fruit juice?" A cool breeze came through the open windows as she served drinks. When she had finished, Roth gestured for her to leave the room.

I sat in front of and to the side of Roth's desk. Our visitors shifted in their seats and glanced at each other with vacant looks, like students waiting to take an examination. Sook Park clicked a ballpoint pen in his left hand. Otherwise, silence settled in the chamber. My boss waited for them to speak.

Sook Park ceased snapping the retractor of his pen. "I discuss awkward topic. May we speak in private, without others present?"

Roth remained still as if contemplating Sook's words. Then, my boss raised both hands, pointing her palms toward Sook Park. "These three men—Mr. Gannon, Mr. Seeker, and Mr. Ploughman— are my confidants. They will keep our discussion confidential. They stay."

Upon Roth's pronouncement, Sook emitted a low exhalation. "I wish them leave room."

She kept an expressionless visage. "Each of these men has a unique forte. Collectively, they've learned to work together and get the job done. Take me; take my team."

Our three visitors whispered back and forth in Korean. I would need a Korean phrase book if I ended up working with them. The whispering stopped, and they nodded at each other. Sook Park turned to Roth. "We agree to your condition. Keep my words private. Tell no one."

Sook Park hesitated again. Roth impatiently tapped the index finger of her right hand on her desk. Mr. Park seemingly wanted to go the slow-boat-to-Korea route; she appeared to want to cut to the chase. I studied my moccasin shoes, expecting an eruption from Roth.

"I heard you always reach your goal," Sook Park began. "You, hmm, solve problems, even if you have to break a rule."

Roth appeared cautious, pursing her lips, and squinting at him. She interrupted. "I assume you aren't planning to commit a crime. If you are, do not tell me, as I must inform the police."

She tapped her finger waiting for Sook Park's response. Bruce and I had learned that the longer a client kept our boss waiting, the more irritated she became. I fingered a crease on the left leg of my pants.

Finally, he spoke again. "Two days ago, Monday, burglars stole priceless relics from our house in Northern Virginia."

She ceased tapping. "Have the police taped off your house as a crime scene?"

"We have difficulty. Cannot go to police because of legalities."

He and my boss stared at each other until Roth asked, "And?"

"You find artifacts—bring back to us."

Sook's words puzzled me. Burglars stole property from him. Why didn't he call the cops? Did he have a lawful right to the objects?

My boss frowned at him. "Does this legality concern your involvement in homicide or a robbery in the United States?"

"No."

Roth paused half a minute to purse her lips and rubbed her nose as if she worried. "Very well, continue—no wait—we need to establish a client privilege between my company and yourself. Pay me a dollar and retain me as your consultant."

Sook had a puzzled expression. "This is binding? We have confidential relationship?"

"A private investigator may not release information acquired during an investigation, other than to the client. However, if criminal offenses are involved—" Roth raised her eyebrows in concern.

Sook Park took out his wallet and handed her a dollar. He settled back in his chair. "Fifty years ago, we—Bin, Yeong-ho, a fourth person presently in South Korea, and I—fought the North Koreans as they invaded my country. We were young. We struggled against tanks and soldiers with guns.

"We battled all the way from Han River in the north, down roads in middle of our country, and to Pusan farther south. Our brains harbor dark memories from those times. At night, our memories emerge in ungodly nightmares."

Sook Park paused like he had lost his way through his lengthy discourse. I waited. When he continued, I thought of a character in a Shakespeare tragedy delivering a monologue.

"In course of fighting, we unearthed buried riches from old Silla Kingdom."

He paused, possibly to let his words sink in. No one moved. No one spoke. No one breathed. "We removed gold crown and other relics from earth. We smuggled wealth into America—fifty years ago."

I glanced at Bruce and Mickey. They showed blank expressions. They didn't know what the Silla Kingdom meant.

Roth also noticed their befuddlement. "Do you know about the Korean kingdom of Silla?"

The two of them—Mickey and Bruce—shook their heads.

Roth glanced at me. "You're our amateur historian. Tell them."

I walked to one of the bookcases, grabbed a book, and flipped through several pages. "The Silla kingdom emerged in what is now South Korea in the first century B.C. It grew to control what is now the southeast portion of the Korean peninsula."

"That's a big area," Bruce said.

"The Silla kingdom fell apart sometime in the tenth century A.D.," I continued.

Sook smiled. "Our artists built marvelous artwork of gold."

"Ancient Silla made unique pottery with surface like slate," Bin Bie added.

Roth pursed her lips. "Describe what you found and did."

"We took Silla treasure to America," Sook said. "Carried gold crown with antler-like decoration, six bracelets, four rings, three sets of earrings, three swords with ornate handles, a chest-lace, and smaller items."

"You branded all those objects into your memory," Roth said.

Sook glanced around the room to ensure we followed his tale. "We sold some smaller pieces. We kept rest of treasure in safe house in Great Falls, Virginia. This past Monday, thieves broke into house and took relics."

Bruce glanced at me and raised his eyebrows. Our visitors had arrived at what they wanted.

Sook began clicking his ballpoint pen again. "Must recover artifacts."

"The artifacts you initially seized in Korea fifty years previously?" Roth asked.

"Those relics."

For a minute, my boss appeared to be thinking. Then she said, "If we recovered the stolen items, knowing you had purloined them, the authorities would likely revoke our P.I. licenses. Such an undertaking carries extraordinary risk."

Sook Park traded glances with his two companions. They both nodded. He turned back to Roth. "I propose exceptional approach. You recover Silla pieces from thieves, without involving the police. We split treasure with you."

I stared at Sook with my mouth open.

He waited several seconds before continuing. "Rather than you return stolen items to us, you salvage lost items. Rescue lost property. Because you had no knowledge of goods before past Monday, you not responsible for property snatched fifty years ago in Korea."

Roth tapped her fingers without speaking. No doubt, she was calculating profits. Mercenary, thy name is Harriett Roth. Bruce, always cautious, signaled his disapproval by shaking his head. Our three visitors sat frozen, waiting for her answer. Sook Park chewed on his lower lip. My boss pursed her lips again.

Sook Park stood up. "We lost everything, and we lack skill to search and recover. You are our road back. Half better than nothing." Sook nodded to his companions, then sat down on the edge of his chair.

No one spoke. Outside, the robins broke the silence, their whistles rising and falling in pitch. My boss stared at Sook Park. I suspected visions of a vault filled with her gold pranced through her head.

"We would not be paid to recover property you stole," Roth muttered to herself. "But we would locate and take back lost items— and split those salvaged items with you, is that right?"

The way she spoke indicated to me what she would do: she had shown her hand.

Sook Park eased back in his chair. "Together, we can recover lost wealth we never could separately."

Roth tapped her fingers and stared aimlessly at the ceiling. "It would be a finder's split," she mused to herself. She lowered her gaze to Sook Park. "Do you have information to jumpstart a search? Where to look? Do you have any theories about who did it?"

Park traded glances with his two colleagues. They shook their heads. "I know nothing of relics' location. I not sure where search."

Roth tapped her fingers and stared at the ceiling again. "Surely you have a clue?"

"We had hidden in America for fifty years. No idea how a mystery man found us."

"Do you have video cameras around your house?"

"None."

"Were the robbers seen?"

"No."

Roth frowned, wrinkling her nose. I suspected she wanted the three Korean-Americans out of the mansion while she decided what to do. "I am intrigued by your stratagem, your deception. I will discuss your proposition with my three associates and give you my response later. I'll tell you by four o'clock this afternoon."

The three whispered among themselves and ended by nodding at her.

The three men's bodies perceptively loosened a little, perhaps relieved that Roth had not rejected their proposition at once. "All right," Sook answered. "We wait in Asheville and return here at four for your decision."

Roth furrowed her brow. "Go back to northern Virginia—await my decision there."

Sook Park grew agitated, and his eyes opened wide. "No! We anxious. We wish hear your choice directly."

Roth shook her head from side to side. "If you come back to the mansion and aren't satisfied, you will want to debate my decision."

She turned to me and pointed her finger at the door out of the room. "I will give you my final decision at four. Mr. Gannon will show you out. Go back to Virginia." I walked the three men to their car and returned to my boss's office.

Roth seemed to pause on a precipice. "I need counsel," she said. "Let me take a few minutes and call him."

As Roth dialed Mr. Otis Quayle, Mickey turned his head to me and whispered, "Her oily lawyer."

Roth put the conversation on speakerphone. She gave Otis a long narrative and then asked if a salvage operation along the lines suggested by Mr. Park had legal standing. Her phrasing left no doubt she wanted the money.

Quayle's voice came over the speakerphone. "Can your clients overhear our consultation?"

Roth leaned over the speakerphone. "They are gone."

"I know about salvage operations," Quayle began. "You did not take part in the acquisition of the items fifty years ago, or know of them until they were, shall we say, lost to the owners."

"I told you that. Get to the point."

"I have read the Supreme Court ruling on the British ship Blackwall, which caught fire in San Francisco harbor. Let me discuss this decision with my assistant."

Bruce whispered, "Quayle doesn't have an assistant. He's searching for the book with the Blackwall ruling." Over the speakerphone, I heard the rustling of pages turning. "He'll charge Roth time for the assistant."

Quayle resumed his account. "Any award amount—and I think

this is what we seek—does not depend on the ship's prior history. Award depends on the labor and skill of the salvagers, the danger to the rescuer's property and person, and the property saved and damaged.

"Therefore, the award amount did not hinge on whether the owners stole the Blackwall or not. In the situation you described, I can legally defend you if you salvage the missing items."

Roth smiled. "Thank you, Mr. Quayle. Goodbye." She terminated the call.

Bruce and I giggled. All that for a substantial lawyer's fee!

She faced us, Bruce, Mickey, and myself. "We'll discuss at two o'clock this afternoon. I need time to assimilate Mr. Park's salvage offer. Opportunity comes to us each one but, when all is done, we remember most our lost opportunity."

I reasoned it best not to argue with her for now. I guessed the odds as nineteen to one that Roth would accept Park's proposition and lead us through a door into a knotty mystery: who took the crown?

ASHEVILLE—14 JUNE 2000

Two o'clock that afternoon, Bruce, Mickey, and I met Roth in her office. Bruce had always avoided high-risk cases and would push for dropping the Koreans' offer of a job based on a vague salvage claim. He inched forward in his chair, maybe anxious to argue his opposition. Roth sat back, appearing lethargic as a cat. However, she had a way of getting her will once she sniffed gold.

All was quiet except for the hum of the AC, recently turned on to battle the afternoon heat. Then, in a sharp tone like the bang of a starter's pistol, Roth began. "Let's start. We're here to discuss the salvage plan proposed by Mr. Park."

Bruce raised his hand.

"You may begin," she said.

Bruce shook his head. "Guys, we reject this salvage hunt because the North Carolina License Board will discover the four Koreans stole the goods. Cuz, our P.I. licenses be toast when the Board learns Mr. Park and colleagues took the items from South Korea."

Mr. Park's brainchild stumped me. The cost might be high, but then the benefit could be significant. I judged the salvage argument shaky, but we were not going to broadcast our intentions to the police. "We could investigate the Great Falls crime scene. Maybe the CSI folks could dig up a clue—who burglarized the home. Little pain; could be a big gain."

"I agree," Roth said. "We have a skilled crime scene investigation crew at our disposal."

"Begin the case," I continued. "If we learn the artifacts have left the U.S., going who knows where on this planet, then we pull out."

"Why we look, Sherlock?" Bruce asked. "I can tell you da treasure done bolted out of the country."

This discussion would take a while. I leaned back in my chair to get comfortable. "You don't know this."

Bruce shook his head and glared at me. "You named Don after Don Quixote? What you suggest is we run out and tilt at windmills? How we recover a crown without getting ourselves killed?"

He reminded me of a hound who had a bone in its mouth and wouldn't let go. "You can believe I'm Don Quixote or not. I believe in half a Silla treasure."

Roth slammed her hand on her desk. *Crack!* Her face rotated between Bruce and me, a bobblehead that yawed instead of pitching. "You two can squeeze the most argument into a discussion better than any other human beings I ever met."

She pointed at Mickey who hadn't spoken. "Mickey is practical. Why can't you two be more like him?"

Mickey didn't acknowledge Roth's remark, possibly because he had just stuffed a donut, brought from the kitchen, into his mouth. Powdered sugar coated his chin.

Bruce opened his mouth as if to give a rebuttal to Roth. I shook my head—*leave it alone*. He saw me and shut his mouth.

Mickey too kept quiet as he finished his donut.

"Let us continue without clowning," Roth leaned forward in her seat and turned toward me. "Would undertaking this endeavor be manifestly dangerous?"

"No, ma'am. Don't need to carry guns to search for clues, to interview people. It could turn ugly afterwards, but we don't know that in advance."

Roth grinned and rotated herself to Bruce. "With additional information, can we better estimate our chances of locating the robbers?"

He ran a hand through his corkscrew hair. "Yes, Boss. We know more about risk after going over the Great Falls house. Can't rule out the possibility of salvaging the relics."

She had asked if we dealt with a known evil. Could we better understand our chances of success if we investigated a little further? She had decided to do the job, pulled in by her lust for anything gilded. She just hadn't told us yet.

Roth nodded and returned to me. "Were we to be successful in recovering the crown and other artifacts, would Sook Park honor our agreement to split the salvaged goods in half?"

"Yes, ma'am. Bruce will vet our three Korean-Americans by doing a background check on them. If Sook Park were to renege on our agreement, we would tell the police he stole national artifacts from South Korea."

Roth settled back in her chair and issued her directions in rapid-fire. "Don, you take the lead in investigating the theft. Bruce, run your background checks on our clients and any suspects Don uncovers. For now, I'll keep Mickey working here on other surveillance tasks in Asheville."

Roth turned to Mickey who had yet to open his mouth, except to put a donut in it. "Are you in?"

"Yes, Ms. Roth." Mickey had spoken only those three words during the discussion. Our chubby Hercules had the spine of a jellyfish when around Roth.

"I'll call Sook Park and confirm our agreement," Roth said. "I'll ask for a complete description of the stolen articles."

She grinned. "That way we'll know we have the right relics when we find them."

She pursed her lips and seemed to contemplate her next decision. "Don, go to Fairfax County, Virginia, and investigate the house. North Carolina and Virginia have a reciprocity agreement for a P.I.'s license. Your North Carolina license will be sufficient.

"Bruce, arrange with Porter Radar's company to perform a crime scene investigation at the Virginia house and grounds."

Roth added her usual pithy comment. "None know the future. We'll jump into the ring, and we'll observe. That's investigation. Dismissed."

Out in the hall, Bruce scowled. "Guys, she never listens to me. Why am I the only one to whine when we've got to do something awful? Isn't right."

"She has her eyes on the shiny object," I said. "We investigate for a few days. If no headway, we talk Roth into pulling back.

"I'll fly up to Virginia in the morning. Bruce, find what you can about stolen Silla relics."

"Do my best," Bruce said. "Guys, stay in touch by cell phone."

"We're still going out for grub and brews tonight?" I asked. "Right?"

They agreed. When it came to beers, we don't argue.

# # #

That evening, Bruce and Mickey argued, in the front row of Mickey's Ford Explorer, about the Washington Wizards' changes in the upcoming basketball season. In the rear seat, I sat back and watched the office blocks slip past on Patton Avenue. Asheville's buildings are a testament to the charm of America in the first half of the twentieth century. Turning my gaze from modern architecture to those old buildings affected me, like watching the scene in *The Wizard of Oz* where the color goes from black-and-white to all the colors of the rainbow. A lot of Asheville's structures went up before the Great Depression and remain standing today, enclosing businesses and condos, housing living people.

Mickey parked across from the Naughty Hops pub. The pub occupied a cream-yellow stucco building, with outdoor and indoor seating. It consisted of a brewery and a restaurant. We sat indoors at a wooden table and ordered a round of beers. I pointed at a picture of Henry VIII's head, covering an entire wall. "I love that drawing." Bruce nodded while Mickey munched on the pretzels with mustard.

I nudged Bruce's arm. "Get the CSI team up to Northern Virginia—tomorrow."

"They be there." He nudged my shoulder back. "Guy, don't push me. I didn't want to take this gig."

"Don't have a choice, do we?" I said. "Roth says jump, we jump."

Mickey glanced around for more pretzels. A waitress served our beers. Hops represented an early evil weed, before marijuana. Back in 1519—my idea of ancient history—Henry the VIII of England declared hops would ruin the beer. He lost that first beer fight. Wonder which side Henry the VIII would have taken in the Taste-Better-Less-Filling beer battle of the late nineteen hundreds? Bruce gulped at his beer. "Two days are gone since the thieves took the artifacts. We be looking for a needle in a field of haystacks."

I put down my beer glass on the table, a little harder than I intended. "If there's a loose end, I'll find it."

Bruce grimaced and took another big gulp. "Guys, we don't know what we're doing."

I had grown tired of Bruce's complaining. "When we don't know, we hunt for clues. I call that investigating. Stop whining."

"Consider this," Bruce said. "Given your need for endless research help, I be the one who untangles your loose ends."

Bruce had a university degree, but he tended to slip into a slight vernacular when he got angry or nervous. To catch the waitress's eyes for another pitcher of beer, Mickey flapped his arms high in the air, like a goose drying its wet wings. Bruce and I glared at each other and drank.

Mickey said nothing. On occasions like this, when Bruce and I bellowed, we ignored Mickey, and he stayed quiet.

Somehow Bruce felt someone had wronged him. "Is it something I did?" I asked.

Bruce changed his expression from glare to introspection. "Why can't I go to Virginia? You always get to go."

Bruce's voice grew loud. He seemed to think we had neglected him. One moment he wanted nothing to do with a salvage case; next, he tried to lead. I didn't know how to respond. "Indoor voice, Bruce. You've always done the computer search. You're good at it."

"It ain't right. When I do good on the computer, I am a magician. When I ask to be a gumshoe, I can't go because I be a computer expert."

I felt uneasy; I brushed my cowlick. "Have you told Roth?"

Bruce ran his hand through his corkscrew. "No, but I always talk about the cases. Roth doesn't pay attention—neglects me."

"Maybe you should tell Roth?"

"Why I need to say anything? You don't tell her, and you lead the investigation every time."

"Talk to her. You do the computer stuff because you do a marvelous job."

"Maybe I'm assigned to the computer cuz I'm black," Bruce objected.

I could hear Bruce's voice getting louder than usual. I signaled him to lower his intonation. "What are you saying? The black guy gets assigned to the computer?"

"Yes, why does the computer guy always have to be the black man?" Bruce asked.

We weren't going to resolve Bruce's concern without talking with

Roth. "What have you found out about Mr. Park and his two colleagues?" I asked.

"Still digging," Bruce replied. "You're the exalted history buff. How much stealing of Korean artifacts take place?"

I sipped my beer. "Lots of people removed cultural relics from South Korea between 1910 and 1945, when the Japanese occupied Korea. Collectors took cultural objects from 1950 to 1953—throughout the Korean War."

"Our clients weren't the first?"

"Nope."

I began to feel woozy and a little anxious about our task. Where had the burglars taken the treasure and how would we retrieve it? Needed to get to bed. I always read history books at bedtime. Puts me to sleep.

"Let's call it a night," I said. "I'll clean my M1911 pistol before going to bed. Should one of you need to bring it to me in Virginia, you'll find it locked in the gun box in my room."

Soon, I would be on my way. My stomach felt queasy. It always felt that way before a case but would calm when I started investigating tomorrow.

NORTHERN VIRGINIA—15 JUNE 2000

Bright midmorning—mild sun rays and dry air touch my skin. A lawn of short grass borders a stream bank—an embankment gently slopes down to the creek. I step in water—shallow, covering my sneakers and soaking my white socks. Rocks in the stream, gray, small—I pick up a stick—turn over rock after rock. Find a crayfish, gray, long as my finger—grab at it with my hands, miss, it swims away downstream, escaping. I step purposely down the creek, turning over rocks, looking for the crayfish. Nothing is under the stones. I keep moving downstream—stream stretches far into the distance. Rotating rock after rock—so many.

I had awakened from my dream. I reclined in my bed, in the cozy backdrop of my bedroom. It was dark outside and too early to rise. I lay in darkness and got up when the alarm clock wailed. Early Thursday morning, I left Roth mansion for the Asheville airport. Water poured from the sky, not surprising as rain often gushes on Asheville in June. I smelled fresh, dirt-free air with an aroma of ozone. After landing at Dulles Airport in Virginia, I rented a red GT Mustang and drove to the Residence Inn in Herndon, Virginia, close to the house where the burglary occurred.

Checking in, I ogled a striking woman, about my age, sitting on a couch near the front desk. She watched the news on a wall-mounted TV. She had an inviting smile, mischievous and direct eyes, a short but full-bodied figure, and was just my type—female. I hesitated to approach strange women, but this ponytailed brunette was cute. I tried to overcome my nervousness. It would have been rude to be unfriendly.

I strolled to a spot beside the couch and struggled to speak a greeting. I froze, staring at the side of her head.

She turned her head from the screen. "Hi, I'm Carla Diaz."

She waited, but I remained tongue-tied.

"I'm here for a few weeks," she continued. "I'm doing the internal design for a new building."

My tongue finally began to move. "N-n-name's Donnell Gannon. I'm staying in Virginia for a few days." I sneaked a peek at her blue slacks, which fit her curves snugly. "Great seeing you." I explored her curvatures again.

"I'm a little bored when I get off work." She spoke slowly with a sexy, distinctive voice. "I'm always on the lookout for a friend around here."

I hesitated, needing to get to the burglarized house. Except I wanted to keep talking with her.

She eyed me from head to toe. "I hope your room fits you, Mr. Donnell Gannon. You're big."

"Yeah, I get that a lot." I kicked myself for the hoary cliché. Why couldn't I talk cool in front of females?

The man behind the check-in counter interrupted us. "You can use our gym. It's complimentary."

"You need a gym?" Carla eyed my biceps. "You're already strong."

Carla's penetrating gaze and broad sunny smile made me melt like a snowman in spring.

The clerk handed me my passkey. "The fire department has been conducting fire drills. If your alarm sounds, leave your building and wait in the courtyard."

I nodded and took the room key.

"What do you do, Donnell?" Carla asked.

"I'm a private investigator."

Her eyes grew wide. "Wow. No kidding?"

Few had said "Wow," when I told them I was a P.I. "No kidding. And you're an interior decorator?"

"Yes. I speak Spanish. Helps because we have both English- and Spanish-speaking workers."

I had become mesmerized by this shapely, Hispanic brunette, but I had to get to the crime scene. "I-I'm late for an appointment, Ms.

Diaz. Have a good day."

"Call me, Carla. Hope to see you again—soon." She winked.

I stumbled out of the registration area. I had to correct my tongue-tied-tendency around females. Maybe, I could write pithy one-liners and memorize them, like, "I'm an investigator. Want to investigate with me?"

After dropping my bags in my suite, I drove down a two-lane road to the burglary-site house in Great Falls. A bucolic area glided past my windows. Slowing the Mustang, I gazed toward the Potomac River, dividing Virginia from Maryland. Expensive homes peeked through the trees.

I pulled into 1224 Potomac Drive, finding a two-storied building set back in the woods away from neighbors. I noted two white vans parked in front of the white wood-sided house. When I left the car's AC, I felt a high humidity, the moist air of Northern Virginia in June—like stepping into a greenhouse. My long-sleeved, gray cotton turtleneck stuck to my back. I shed my sports jacket and left it in the Mustang.

Sook Park exited the front door and greeted me. He pointed at the vehicles. "They belong to crime scene team. They in house." Roth routinely rented a CSI team when she needed to comb for telltale signs at a crime scene.

"Mr. Park. Tell me what happened?"

"Oh, like what?"

"The night of the break-in, what security existed?" I asked.

"House had electronic alarm system. System would set off a loud alarm . . . send a signal to the security company?"

I had my notepad out. "System tied to twenty-four-hour service?"

"It was."

I walked into the shade of the house. "Just the electronic system? No one in the house?"

As Sook Park talked, he paced in a circle. "Had live-in caretaker. You talk with him. He college student."

"I'll speak with him later. Show me the house."

# # #

The burglar-alarm wiring snaked through the window frames. Were a window to be opened or broken, the event would have triggered a break in the electric circuit, causing the local security company to rush to the house. At the rear of the house, I craned my neck to peer at a single dormer window, located just under the roof. Then I checked the ground and noticed two holes in the mulched soil under the window. The holes were spaced apart about the width of the bottom two feet of a ladder. The footprint of a big boot, maybe size eleven, lay beside the two impressions.

I grimaced and faced Sook. "That high window—does the electric wiring cover it?"

The edges of Sook's lips drooped. "No. It went unnoticed when wiring installed."

How had the burglars known? Had they spotted the dormer window had no wires around the edges? "You had a dormer window as open as a Sunday morning church door?"

Sook frowned. "Yes. An oversight."

"How did the burglars get to that window?"

"A ladder."

"The thieves brought a ladder?"

The Korean nodded.

"Did you find a discarded ladder?"

"No. Burglars took it."

We stayed back in the shade while I absorbed what Sook had told me. "Your burglars carried away a ladder and artifacts. Maybe more than one perpetrator? Must have used a car or truck."

I stopped studying the high window and turned to Sook, "So, where did they park it?"

Sook paused to rub his left eyebrow. "People park on main road through Great Falls and carry picnic baskets through woods to Potomac River. Easy to park without being noticed."

The robbers had estimated the height of the dormer window and brought the correct-length ladder. They knew the caretaker did not have a guard dog at night. In the days before the burglary, they had to have built a shelter in the woods to spy on the house.

"Let's explore the woods."

Walking to the tree line, Sook and I searched for a hideaway. I wore a long-sleeved shirt, blue jeans, and slip-on boots topped in heavyweight leather, all suitable for slogging through the thick bushes. The CSI team had wrapped yellow caution tape around a dense clump of shrubs and trees. Impressions lay in the matted leaves and grass at the back of the stand.

The thieves had been careful. They left nothing that might lead us to them: no cigarettes, no chewing gum, no candy wrappers, no clothing threads, and no discards of any kind. The tamped-down area was about four feet wide, room for two watchers.

We left the woods and entered the front door. I passed a living room and kitchen, stopping before a sturdy steel door with faux wood exterior and a numbered keypad.

I examined the keypad. "Show me how you enter."

Sook punched in the combination. "This door to exhibit room." When the door opened, we stepped into a room with overhead lighting and no windows. Empty shelves and display cases lined the walls, like a grocery store stripped of food before a blizzard.

Sook nervously pulled out a pen and started clicking it. "We kept artifacts here."

"Did you leave the door open?"

Sook shook his head. "Always locked chamber—needed numerical combination to open door into exhibit room."

"To display the artifacts, you transformed a room into a secluded museum?" I asked.

Sook closed the door. "We viewed the treasures here."

Sook and I stood among the empty shelves and cases, their shiny surfaces blackened with fingerprint powder spread by the CSI team.

"When was the last time you saw the relics?"

"Artifacts were here all-day Monday," Sook said.

"Tell me what the college student did Monday."

"Caretaker went to his pharmacy class Monday evening. Before leaving, he armed alarm system using keypad beside front door."

Sook bent to peer at one of the empty shelves. "He returned Monday night and locked house before going to bed."

"Who discovered the theft?"

"I did. Early Tuesday. I came here—find artifacts missing."

"Does the caretaker know the combination?" I asked.

"Caretaker, Emmanuel Jackson, not know combination to exhibit room."

"Did he observe anything unusual Monday night or Tuesday morning?"

"Say he slept soundly."

I scanned the exhibit room one more time and then walked out.

"Let's inspect the dormer-window room."

We went up to the chamber and examined the window. One pane had a circular section missing where the burglars had cut out the glass. They had unlocked the window and entered the treasure house, like Ali Baba shouting the old saying, Open Sesame.

"Where was the student when the burglars came through the window?"

"Student slept in room on opposite side of the building."

"Didn't hear anything?"

"Caretaker didn't hear the burglars coming through this window."

I studied the window. "Isn't that odd?"

"No. Door to this room closed Monday night. Maybe interior walls muffled any sounds thieves made?"

I turned to leave. "Let's talk to the crime scene investigation people."

Park led me. "They been working two hours."

# # #

Not all CSI teams work for police departments; many examine crime scenes for private investigation firms like Porter Radar's company. Back when I worked there for Porter, I met his head CSI technician, Allen Brasher. He stood before me now, at the rear of the Virginia house. He had an overly competitive alpha-male complex that tainted his character. For example, when Porter Radar had a company softball game, Allen turned the festivities into an athletic competition to prove he was top dog. I always had to put him in his place—sitting down with the losers.

He turned, saw me, and shouted—in a loud bark—"Don." He strode toward me, swinging his right arm back over his shoulder, ready to give me a high five.

Not to be outdone, I yelled "Allen" at full volume and strode toward him, raising my right arm over my shoulder. We both rotated our arms forward, like throwing a ball overhand. Our hands met, emitting a loud smacking sound, like a watermelon dropping on a floor. Allen tried to crush my hand, but I outdid him and squashed his. Our greeting was more like overhead arm wrestling than shaking hands.

Once we finished our macho greeting, Allen told me he found

fingerprints belonging to the caretaker and the three Korean Americans. No other prints—perpetrators had worn gloves.

He tapped my shoulder and spoke in his helter-skelter cadence. "The burglars are professionals. Came through woods. In through the dormer window."

"Of course—I knew that," I snapped back.

He rubbed a white scar on his chin. "Well, did you now? They didn't track dirt or debris. In from the outside. Guess they wore shoe covers."

"Yeah, that's what I concluded."

He kept rubbing a scar on his chin. "They likely taped their pants to their shoes. Taped sleeves to their gloves. Probably had soft-sole shoes. No noise."

"Couldn't the student have heard them?" I asked. "Maybe he was in on it?"

"The student sleeps in a front room. Keeps his door closed, eh. The stairs down to the first floor. Are at the back of the house. Say the intruders had the combination to open the exhibit room. Wouldn't have made much noise."

I brushed my cowlick. "Yeah, that's what I figured."

Allen shifted his weight from foot to foot as he talked. "If they had the keypad code. How'd they get it? The student could've just been sleeping. On the other hand, he could be an inside person. Don't know."

I didn't know either, but I figured we had finished inside the house. "Show me the thieves' hiding place."

We went to the thieves' cover in the bushes behind the house.

"Shelter concealed two individuals," Allen said. "Guess they spread a cloth on the ground. Like a painter's drop cloth. Took the fabric away with them. When they left with the heist, eh."

I let him know I hadn't missed a beat. "That's what I thought."

Allen jerked his head around to me. "Did you see the holes in the mulch? Under the dormer window?"

"Course I did."

Allen walked back to the house and stood under the dormer window. "Two indentations. Consistent with the bottom feet of an extendable aluminum ladder, eh. Find at any hardware store."

I smirked at him. "An aluminum ladder makes a loud noise when extended. Did you think of that?"

Allen shrugged. "Maybe the burglars set up the ladder when the AC switched on. The AC could've masked the sound of extending the ladder. Covered any noise removing the window pane, eh."

As Allen and I tried to outshine one another, Sook looked back and forth between us.

I pointed to the footprint below the dormer window. "I'd say a new boot, approximately size eleven. We have pros with new shoes, with taped openings in pants and shirts, and with covered-up feet, hands, and face." I folded my arms and grinned smugly.

Allen never stopped hopping, always moving his feet. "These robbers. Carried out a well-planned operation. Not an impulsive snatch. You'll get that in my report."

"I'll check the neighbors," I said. "Did they see anything unusual Monday night? Do they have a video system covering their yard?"

A smug grin appeared on Allen's face. "Good luck with that. These woods are dense. I'll finish inside. Call me. I can help you, eh."

With relief, I watched Allen depart back to the house. Having him around was like carrying a nervous nanny on my shoulders.

# # #

The land near Sook's house overflowed with foliage, swarmed with wildlife, and held few homes. Sook and I knocked on the door of each neighboring household, interviewing every adult and child who had been home Monday evening. No one had seen men going through the woods with a ladder.

One individual had noticed an activity near her house. Sook's neighbor, a senior citizen, wore a pink housecoat, had on wire-rim glasses and a frown, had stringy auburn hair done in curlers on top of her hair and didn't want to talk with him. "I heard noises in the woods at night, but I don't want to get involved," the woman said. "Go away."

"Please ma'am, I am neighbor," Sook said. "We had theft. When was this commotion? What took place?"

She glared at Sook. "I'll give you five minutes, and then I shut my door. A week ago—around midnight—our dog barked at a noise behind our house. Something was back there."

Sook had rushed in front of me and started interrogating the old biddy. He didn't have an inkling how to approach this woman. She didn't want to be bothered, intended to get back to her TV show. She ignored his please-help-me interview tactic because she couldn't care less about him. Faced with the "wolf at the door" approach, she would have spewed everything she knew about noises in her backyard. I would have fibbed about men peeking in neighbor's windows and stalking women in their homes. Then, her words would have gushed forth, like vehicles rushing down an interstate highway at high speed. If Sook had let me lead, things would have gone differently.

Through the open door, the sound on her TV heralded a commercial about vacuum cleaners. "It wasn't a deer. Because of the dog, the deer avoid my house."

The TV blared another commercial, this time about installing new windows. Before closing her door, she said, "The dog stopped barking after two nights. Now, go away!"

My client kept pushing. "Did other neighbors hear anything?"

"No!" She slammed her door.

Throughout the neighborhood, I found lots of squirrels up high, but no surveillance cameras. In most communities, I usually found an individual dying to know what was going on during the day. Why was there never an insufferable busybody when you needed one?

We had reached midday, sweating as we walked in the June heat. Sook seemed disappointed and weary. "I think we spoke with every neighbor," he said.

There had to be someone who saw the burglars coming or going. "Does a cleaning crew come to your house?"

"No cleaning crew. We agreed pay house sitter little extra. He vacuums and does stuff like that."

Back at the house, Sook had his head down, as if in thought. "Our gardener comes weekly, Monday morning, but he never inside house."

"Hmm, we might find a clue talking to your gardener."

"I call him. Arrange to meet."

"I want to question you, Bin Bie, and Yeong-ho Park. You need to tell me everything and everyone connected with bringing your Korean artifacts to America."

He nodded. "We tell you about mortar squad and what happened in Korean War?"

"Yeah."

Sook took me to the dining room. "I call my two friends to come over now." He hesitated a moment, then continued. "Over years, we wrote journal about mortar squad in 1950. An account in English."

# # #

After I returned to the house in the afternoon, I concluded this investigation would be a slog. I had unearthed only a few clues and had no witness to the theft. A meticulous planner had organized the burglary. Like a high-school student who prepares for his exam but flounders, I had failed to unearth a lead to the burglar. As Taylor, our Appalachian-Mountains cook would say, "My cake was dough."

"I have examined the crime scene, investigating for the elusive Eureka," I said to Sook. "My Greek muses had told me solving this case will not be easy."

"This your first day," Sook said and patted my arm. "Don't judge yourself so harshly. Be patient."

I pulled my arm back from Sook. Great, I had been crying on our client's shoulder. I glowered at Sook. "I get irritated when someone tells me to be patient."

I turned my back, slowed my breathing, and calmed myself. Behind me, Sook said, "Do not worry about this morning. Old saying goes, 'Don't cry over guilt milk.'"

"That's *spilt milk*."

We were quiet for a moment. Maybe to calm his nerves, Sook took out his pen and began clicking it in his left hand. "Bin, Yeong-ho, and I went through house on Tuesday after theft. We too made no progress. Like headless chickens running in circle." Sook sat at the table with his head down. He then glanced up past my shoulder.

I turned to find Allen Brasher in the doorway, filling the space with his height and bulk.

"Finished?" I asked.

"Eh!"

"Good to see you again," I fibbed. "I'll tell Roth you arrived at work early."

Allen locked eyes with me. It didn't appear like he planned to leave right away. "Hmm, got a little time. Could help you. Got a good head for investigation, eh."

Oh, good grief, the hot dog had started to sniff around my job. I stood slack-jawed. "Thanks, Allen, but I've got this one. You should start back. You'll want to have daylight to see the road."

"You sure? Don't mind helping. Make a good team. You and me."

Typical alpha male, his idea of the team consisted of collecting a band of toadies around him. "No thanks. I prefer to work alone. Excuse me, got work to do."

Allen swayed, shifting his weight from foot to foot. "Eh, on my way. Tell Ms. Roth I enjoy working for her. Might give her a call. Be in touch."

When he left, I had a bad feeling. Allen didn't give up easily. Roth had a saying: if you have two skilled cooks in the kitchen, you have one cook too many.

I glanced at Sook. "Let's get started. Tell me how you found the treasure."

"Tale is long. Events occurred during my youthful years. Cannot tell story quickly."

I stood up to find a cup of coffee. I had the feeling this was going to be quite a story. "When your two comrades arrive, we'll start the tale."

SOUTH KOREA—25 JUNE 1950

Fifty years before, Seong-gi had commanded a mortar squad. In his journal, a book I held in my hand, he joined us at the table in the Great Falls dining room.

He had chronicled his team's experience in the war from late June through August 1950. Seong-gi wrote most pages, but—when he had not witnessed an event—Sook Park, Bin Bie, and Yeong-ho Park added activities they had seen.

I expected my review of the wartime squad would move sluggishly, like an antique farm tractor on a two-lane country road. I hunted a suspect, a unique individual who had lived in 1950 and popped up again in the year 2000 to conspire and steal a crown.

The three Korean-Americans sat around the table staring at me with blank expressions. "Why do you think we're here?" I began.

They glanced, each at the other, and then shook their heads.

I held up the thumb and forefinger in my left hand and counted off them. "First, how did you get the Silla relics? Second, can you identify someone you knew in 1950 who could have stolen the crown in the year 2000?"

Bin raised his arms in the air, in a gesture of surrender. "This waste of time. You should consider today's clues—find suspect we know today."

I brushed my cowlick to give Bin time to cool down. "Someone discovered your safe house. Do you agree?"

Bin pursed his lips. "Yes. But theft occurred three days ago, Monday. Not fifty years."

"Do you know for sure the thief is a recent acquaintance?"

He looked at Sook and Yeong-ho, but they returned blank expressions. He turned back to me. "I not know how thief found treasure, but why hunt going back to 1950?"

"Why not? If we can't identify someone you knew back in the war as a suspect, then we focus our search on people you've met lately."

Yeong-ho giggled. "Mr. Gannon cunning detective like Charlie Chan." Sook chuckled along with him. We had begun to develop trust.

Sook Park coughed to signal he wanted to interrupt. "I set up time for you to interview housekeeper. It getting late. We should start reviewing."

"When?" I asked.

"Hour from now."

I needed to learn how the mortar squad found the relics back in the Korean War, but any suspect interview came first. "Let's start our mortar-team review. I'll stop when it's time to cross-examine the student caretaker. Sook, you want to start?"

"You lead us," he answered. "You read from the journal. Is in English. We speak when you want us make a passage clear."

I flipped through several pages reading Seong-gi's words. "Why didn't Seong-gi write his journal in Korean?"

Sook took out his pen and began clicking it as if to collect his thoughts. "He started writing journal in Korean, ten years after we left South Korea. Someday, we tell our children what we did in the Six-Two-Five War, our name for Korean War. South Korea called war for day it started."

"Other than you four, who has read the journal?" I asked.

"No one."

"Why English?"

"Seong-gi recorded what he remembered doing and saying. He wrote first in Korean, and then we translated into English. English because of three of us now Americans."

I glanced over more pages and noticed Sook Park's name. "Did you change your names when you arrived in the U.S.?"

Sook answered immediately. "I always took name Sook Park. Bin Bie used his same name in Korea and America."

"I called Yeong-ho or Ho-ho," Yeong-ho added with a chuckle.

Sook and Bin groaned.

I turned a few pages. "Where's a good place to start?"

"Begin morning of twenty-five June 1950," Sook replied.

I found the page and read Seong-gi's words aloud:

25 June 1950 - Shifting under the canvas shelter protecting me from the rain, I, a Republic of Korea (ROK) soldier, awoke and rose. My name is Seong-gi Kim, and I led a mortar squad. I sniffed the air, smelling the scent of earth and wet evergreen. Dressed in my drab army uniform, I listened for the sound that woke me.

Over the rain's patter, I heard a growl, coming from the north, the border with North Korea. Low-hanging clouds in shades of black and dark gray increased the darkness, darkness broken by broad slashes of white light flaring among the clouds and then disappearing. I saw the blaze of artillery bursts reflecting off the clouds and then vanishing to make the horizon black again.

I discontinued reading. "Tell me what kind of journal this is. A diary has short, hastily written sentences—no frills. This document— the one I'm reading—sounds like a novel. It's polished."

"Seong-gi wrote most of account," Bin said. "He wrote years after fighting. Not diary was written during fighting—his tale based on memory."

"Okay," I said. I began reading again:

Looking toward a big strip of flashes, I imagined raw power beyond anything used by ROK soldiers. That explosive force frightened me. My mortar squad and I were farmer sons forming a ragged militia. I woke my second-in-command, carefully, like a woman telling her husband of noise in the house. Yeong-ho, my squad gunner, grumbled at me but rose.

I asked Yeong-ho if he heard the sound.

He heard the noise and then wanted to know what made the crash noise.

I told him artillery thud—coming from the north.

Taking no notice of the rain running off our steel helmets and ponchos, we listened. We stood in a mortar trench and stared over the top in the direction of a road stretching far to the north, not yet visible in the coming sunrise.

The noise had gotten louder—closer.

Yeong-ho grinned, put his hand on my shoulder, and told me to be calm. He said not to act like an old lady. Said it was another border raid from North Korea.

I replied the attack had to be big—not small squads.

Yeong-ho's grin faded. He suggested we wake rest of team.

At the rear of shelter, Sook Park, appearing more like a youth than a soldier, slept with his frame rolled up into a ball. I told him to wake up. There was great fighting to the north.

Sook awoke with a start, maybe thinking he had neglected some task. He checked his equipment. He told me his gear okay, just damp. Yeong-ho and I moved on, paying no more attention to him.

We five soldiers stood together, leaning on the trench embankment, watching over the top toward the thudding sounds and the flashes reflecting off the clouds. The mound before us was on the downslope side of a hill covered by a thick forest of green pine trees. The slope dropped down to the road. We waited.

I closed the journal, using my thumb to mark the stopping place. "I count four soldiers: Seong-gi, Sook, Bin, and Yeong-ho. Who's this fifth soldier?"

"Originally, we five-man squad," Yeong-ho explained. "Fifth soldier killed our last battle in August. He named Sang-hun Lee."

I returned to the journal.

As the sun rose higher, its dim light coming through the overcast sky and the rain, I made out the checkpoint on the road directly below our hill, a lane empty of traffic.

ROK soldiers manned the roadblock, men without powerful weapons, only M1 Garand rifles, Browning Automatic Rifles, and grenades.

At our table in the dining room, Sook Park squirmed and held his head in his hands. "I remember moment well."

I discontinued reading and waited for Sook to continue. "What do you remember?"

"Feeling abandoned and frightened. I had arrived as fresh conscript, new add-on to mortar squad, wishing I back with parents in snug farmhouse."

He raised his head, stared out a window, and then continued. "I knew something had gone wrong: my team leader and gunner, each older by few years, were intense as if they had death in family. When they had trained me, they might have been stern and grim, but the morning of the attack they scared."

I nodded and went back to reading the journal:

Sook asked what we would do. I told him to be quiet—not ask a stupid question.

I felt my heart beating faster and realized I had been holding my breath. We stayed motionless in the rain, continued to watch far-off flashes, and listened to battle sounds. Yeong-ho said he could see something moving. I saw gray shapes far up the road.

Sook took deep breaths, seemed to be choking, and whimpered he was terrified. Bin told him to be quiet. Yeong-ho, our squad comedian, said Sook's heart pounded like a frog croaking in the water. We laughed at poor Sook and smacked his back in encouragement.

I told my squad to take the cover off our mortar. We had set the base and bipod to lob shells up the road. I shouted at them to move.

Gray T-34 tanks rolled down the road, moving in single file toward the roadblock, making a clamor with machinery and diesel engines. Death came at us through the cleansing rain.

I told Yeong-ho we faced a significant force. We had to fight but be ready to pull back to our fortified lines farther south.

Sook said he had never seen a tank. Again, he asked what to do. Bin shouted at him to shut his mouth. I told Sook to get ready to fight. Directed him to do his job as ammunition bearer. Bring us shells.

My squad grouped around the mortar. Earlier, we had bore-sighted the mortar at a distant point up the road in front of the ROK roadblock. As one of the two ammo carriers, Sook worked behind the mortar.

Yeong-ho told Sook to fetch him a shell.

Sook seemed panicked as if he feared he would make a mistake. He struggled to open ammunition box and pull out a mortar round. He inspected the shell for rust, wetness, or something put together wrong. Sook sheltered the round with his body to keep the rain off the shell and handed it to Bin Bie, my assistant gunner.

The assistant gunner held the round in a vertical position with the fuse end up. After withdrawing the safety wire, Bin Bie released the shell into the muzzle of the mortar at the *fire* command from my gunner, Yeong-ho.

The shell blasted out of the mortar barrel.

Just as the North Korean tanks reached a point a mile away, our first 60-mm mortar shell detonated wide to the side of the road. I corrected elevation and transverse mechanism, and my squad lobbed continuous shells that exploded close to the line of tanks. The mortar shells were only a danger to troops and not to the long line of tanks, now over a dozen. At half a mile distance, the first T-34 fired at the roadblock, breaking up the barricade and scattering the ROK troops down the road toward Seoul.

Sook shouted we had used all our mortar shells.

Yeong-ho said the tanks had destroyed the barrier and nothing could stop them. He stated the squad should run. I yelled at them to wait for my order.

Up in our mortar position, I smelled smoke and burnt powder. The sound of explosions and shooting continued unbroken. I didn't understand how we could be facing so many tanks.

What I did not know then was those tanks formed the spearhead of a big surge of the North Korean Army, crossing with roughly 90,000 soldiers over the 38th parallel. The attack wave came just before expected monsoon rains. ROK headquarters had given out fifteen-day leaves to thousands of our troops, to allow our peasant soldiers to help their families in rice paddies. A smaller ROK Army remained to resist the onslaught.

I shouted at my team to pack up our mortar and withdraw.

Sook gave the impression of wanting to turn and run. Maybe he feared he would disgrace his family by sobbing like a child. He was not a warrior who could stop tanks. I knew he didn't want to be a soldier, but a student who studied in high school. That day he did his duty for his country.

The rest of my crew grabbed pieces of the mortar: the bipod legs, the baseplate, the cannon barrel, and the sight unit. Leaving our canvas tents behind, we five ran, rushing to keep up with the ROK Army retreating to planned defensive positions farther south.

As I ran, I turned my head. Behind me, an endless line of tanks from the north clanked down the road.

NORTHERN VIRGINIA—15 JUNE 2000

I dropped the Seong-gi journal on the dining room table and faced our clients: Sook, Bin, and Yeong-ho. "I'm going to interview everyone who knew about the treasure and the combination to the exhibit-room door. When you left South Korea, who knew you carried treasure?"

Bin spoke first. "My uncle gave us a way out. Took us out of Korea on his ship."

"Your uncle knew about the treasure?"

Sook stirred in his chair and played with his ballpoint pen. "Bin's uncle, Seong-woo Bie, is a smuggler. Fifty years ago, he smuggled us away from the fighting.

"He knew about treasure but kept it secret from his ship's crew. He told them his nephew and two friends were deserters. We departed carrying two canvas bags."

"Has the uncle seen the secure Virginia room?" I asked. "Knows the combination?"

"He viewed artifacts few times a year, but he could not enter exhibit room alone."

"Where is he now?"

"He splits his time between Baltimore, Maryland, and South Korea. Long ago, the uncle sold his one-fifth portion of the treasure to a man named Isaac Hunter."

"Who knew the combination?"

"Three people besides me. Bin Bie and Yeong-ho Park, and Seong-gi Kim, who lives in Seoul. We all swore not to tell our families."

I scanned the three Korean faces. "No one can keep a treasure a secret. Someone must have brought a wife or son to see the relics."

The three men shook their heads.

"No," Sook said. "We pledged keep safe house a secret."

"You all knew the combination. It could have been one of you."

They stared at me.

"Isaac Hunter knew about exhibit room but not know combination," volunteered Bin. "When we arrived United States, he cashed in smaller pieces for us. He is antiquities fence."

I wrote Isaac's name in my notepad. "How did you find Hunter?"

"My uncle knew him. We used the money get started in United States."

"I'll talk with Hunter. Who else goes on my interview list?"

"I gave you name of each person who knew about relics," Sook said.

"Are you sure?

Sook stared at his pen. "A stranger found us. He learned about artifacts. He not tell how he find us."

"Who is he?"

"Wang Gang. Without warning, he called me and asked to meet. It was . . . let me think . . . some time ago, maybe two years."

"And?" I asked.

"Bin's uncle knew Mr. Gang. Suggested we avoid him like disease. But we met him, and he brought giant bodyguard with him—guard as big as you, Don."

I flexed the muscles in my arms. "Hmm. Did Bin's uncle know Mr. Gang's business?"

"Mr. Gang's enterprise is illegal immigration and smuggling."

I entered Gang's name in my notepad. "What happened at your meeting with Gang and his behemoth?"

"Mr. Gang said we had rare Silla relics. He wanted to buy artifacts for his private collection. We denied having them."

"What did he say to that?"

"Said we mislead him. Gave me business card and asked me to call him when I changed my mind. His office and home in Leesburg, Virginia."

Sook paused and chewed on his lower lip. "He said he had outstanding Asian art collection in his home. I haven't spoken with

Mr. Gang since meeting two years ago."

"Did he steal the treasure?" I asked.

Sook waited before answering, clicking a retractor on his ballpoint pen up and down. "Maybe."

I had four suspects: the house caretaker, Bin's uncle, the fence Isaac Hunter, and a gangster named Wang Gang. And possibly the four Koreans. I asked Sook to hunt down Gang's address and arrange a meeting.

"Tell me about Seong-gi. How often does he visit the U.S.?"

"When he leaves South Korea and visits U.S., he spends long hours in exhibit room. My former squad leader not come to the U.S. for year now."

"Does he need money?"

"He began with monies we got from selling the minor artifacts. Money has not been a problem for us. We worked hard—got ahead."

"You phoned Seong-gi after the theft?"

"Yes, I rang him. But as you know, he not there."

"We need to call him ASAP and find out what he knows about the theft."

"Time different in Seoul. We call when it's morning there—our evening here."

# # #

The housekeeper, Emmanuel Jackson, was sitting at a desk in his bedroom when Sook and I visited him upstairs. Two windows, with sheer drapes and shades, looked out on the front yard. The furnishings were an uncluttered wood desk with built-in drawers, a desk lamp with a blue shade, and a twin bed with a nightstand and reading light.

The African-American had an average height with a slender build, wore glasses with thick lenses, and sported a thin mustache over his upper lip. He smelled of lilac, like Clubman aftershave.

Sook and I sat on the bed. "Do you prefer Emmanuel or Manny?" I asked, trying to set him at ease.

He concentrated on his sneakers. "Manny."

Sook had told me a little about his background. "You grew up locally? You attended Cardoza High School in D.C.?"

"Yes."

I pointed to his gray tee shirt with Howard School of Pharmacy across the front. "You're pursuing a pharmacy degree?"

He raised his head and gave me a defiant expression, like an angry teenager. "Yes." He acted more like a grumpy bill collector than a friendly pharmacist.

"What do you do here at the house?"

"Watch the house. I keep it orderly and clean for the two Mr. Parks and Mr. Bie."

"Tell me how you manage security."

He avoided my gaze. "When I go to bed, and when I go out, I activate the alarm system. A few times a day, I walk around the property."

"Do you know the combination to get into the exhibit room?" I asked.

Manny raised his head and locked eyes with me. "No, I don't."

"Are you ever in the exhibit room alone?"

Manny waited for several beats before answering. "No."

"Do you ever go into the exhibit room?"

"Only with Mr. Park."

I brushed my cowlick down with my hand. "And what did you do to keep things orderly and clean for Mr. Park?"

"Clean, vacuum, rearrange things per Mr. Park's direction." Manny tapped his left foot on the floor.

"Could you see the combination as Mr. Park keyed it in?"

Manny scrunched up his face in a mean-looking frown. "You're askin' me if I peeked over Mr. Park's shoulder? No, cuz I am not a thief. Don't badmouth me—didn't spy on nobody." Trembling with anger, he rose and turned toward the door as if to walk out of the room.

I spoke in a small voice, trying to melt the icy shell he kept around him. "Sit down, Manny. Take it easy. No one said you watched over Mr. Park's shoulder."

Perhaps Manny feared Sook blamed him for the theft. Or maybe he dreaded he would lose his funding source if he had nothing to guard. Maybe he envisioned his life crumbling around him. I waited for him to cool down and then continued.

"The evening of the theft, you went to class at Howard University?"

He moved back to his desk but remained standing. "Yes."

"When leaving this house, and returning that night, you saw nothing? Nothing out of the ordinary?"

"Nothing. After I had gotten back, I walked around and checked the windows and doors before going to bed. I turned in just after I got home."

"How do you handle your tuition and living expenses?"

"I . . . I get my room from Mr. Park. My pay covers my tuition, clothes, and food. My financial package at school is from a partial scholarship."

"You get by adequately with your job?" I asked.

"Do okay. I spend my free time studying for my pharmacy degree. Just because I'm not rich doesn't make me a criminal."

"Do you have contact with offenders?"

Manny paused. "What you mean?"

"Any family members charged with a felony?" I asked.

Manny turned toward the window and stared into the yard.

"Manny, did you hear me?"

"Why? You say I is a criminal?"

"Please answer the question."

He turned around, his mouth twisted into a grimace. "My two brothers convicted of felonies. My mother proud of me and doesn't want me to be a criminal, so I avoid my brothers."

I learned nothing of value during our talk. It was like two actors reading unrelated scripts: I acted out the lawyer, and he acted out the hostile witness in a courtroom. Before finishing, Manny provided the names of some students in his class and his Monday-night pharmacy teacher at Howard University.

"Thank you, Manny. I can't think of another question just now, maybe later."

Manny turned to Sook. "Mr. Park, I still have a job?"

Sook patted Manny's arm. "We try to find burglar. You continue to have job. We busy figuring out how burglars got numbers to open door."

Sook and I left Manny's room. Sook said that when he keyed in the numbers to open the door, he hid the digits he punched by holding his left hand over the pad. But sometimes he forgot. Manny remained a suspect.

It had been a long day. I headed for my motel and sleep.

Tomorrow I'd start again by reading Seong-gi's journal.

SOUTH KOREA—JUNE AND JULY 1950

The next morning Yeong-ho grinned at me. "You surprised I once lean soldier."

Settled beside him, Bin replied. "Stop clowning. You were fattest assistant gunner in ROK Army. Your family sent you off to military so they wouldn't have to feed you."

Yeong-ho giggled. "Papa tell me kind words come from dear friends. Now know he mistaken."

We sat in Sook's conference room on the top floor of his five-story office building. His conference room featured a long, beige-colored table with metal and fabric chairs all set on a rug with a variety of brown swatches. He walked in with a cup of tea, glanced out the floor-to-ceiling windows along one wall, and sat at the table. "How review going?"

I turned a page in the journal. "I'm getting an education."

Sook sipped tea. "What you mean?"

"When the North Koreans crossed the border, your peaceful world fell apart."

The three former soldiers exchanged glances and talked in Korean. I kept hearing the words *ilbon* and *roshia*, which I later learned meant Japan and Russia.

Bin spoke. "For long time, traumatic events had shaped our world. Painful period in Korea spanned 1910 through 1945. Much of time we three not born."

Sook nodded. "Before we were soldiers, we were schoolchildren. We taught Japan left Korea August 15, 1945, after thirty-five years of occupation."

"While Japan ran Korea, and fought World War II, you lived in Korea as a student," I said to Sook. "What was it like?"

"Korean people forced to work for Japanese army in World War II. Along with other schoolchildren, I divided my time between school and war effort: building airfields, harvesting rice, and collecting scrap metal. My shoes had soles made by cutting rubber from old automobile tires."

"At least we weren't getting bombed," Yeong-ho added.

Sook snorted and interrupted him. "But Japan dictated Korea's policies. They occupied and ruled us."

Ignoring Sook and Yeong-ho, Bin continued. "End of World War II, Soviet Union accepted surrender of Japan in northern portion of Korea. Japanese forces in southern part surrendered to U.S. forces. In July 1948, South Korea elected a president and created constitution."

"That's when Korea split into two countries?" I asked.

"Yes," Sook answered. He pointed at the journal. "We should start reading again—how we found the old Silla treasure."

"One more question. What were your ages in July nineteen hundred and fifty?"

"Seong-gi, son of a farmer, as were the rest of us, was nineteen," Sook answered. "Being most experienced, he led the squad. I youngest at seventeen and others were eighteen."

I turned a page of the journal and began reading Seong-gi's words:

After falling back from skirmish at roadblock, along with the ROK Army, my five-man mortar squad set up on the south bank of Imjin River. Not deep river, it had cliffs and a muddy or rocky bottom, making fording difficult. By 27 June, the enemy attacked and forced our troops back from Imjin line to new defensive line halfway between 38th Parallel and Han River. We obtained shells for our mortar; my squad fought and then retreated south.

# # #

After fleeing the firefight at the roadblock and abandoning the defense on the south bank of the Imjin River, my team marched through rain, heat, and humidity to the newest defensive line of the

ROK Army. I watched two members of my squad dig into water-saturated ground to set up our mortar. Our uniforms were dirty and sweat-stained.

The mortar baseplate wobbled. Yeong-ho, my gunner, and Bin Bie, my assistant gunner, shoveled dirt around to make ground level. We had twelve mortar shells. Our army had little ammunition for mortars and artillery. Yeong-ho, my funny man, picked up a rock and threw it northward.

Later in afternoon, I joined platoon meeting with Lieutenant. When I returned to the squad's dugout, I told my team happy news: Lieutenant had said Americans had entered the war against the North Koreans.

Yeong-ho informed me he had seen American planes. Bin had heard an American aircraft bombed ROK units by mistake. Things had become disorganized. We didn't have enough supplies and the Americans sometimes confused the two sides.

Bin Bie asked when we would get more ammunition. The Lieutenant had told me shells were scarce for 105-mm howitzers. We could not depend on trucks to bring fresh supplies. My squad had our 60-mm mortar shells, and we would slow down our enemy's onrush for as many days as possible, but we were to pull back when our path of retreat about to be cut off. Kept doing the same thing: stand, fight, and drop back. We had to give our forces time to bring fresh troops and supplies to the front.

The toil seemed endless: dig in, get rained on, be attacked by the North Koreans, and retreat. The enemy led its attack with clustered armor and followed with troops. While our ROK antitank guns and 105-mm howitzers could not destroy a T-34 one-on-one, I had seen our ROK soldiers group their weapons to pour intense fire on a single tank. Off in the distance, artillery firing started anew. Soon my mortar team would fight again, escape again, and retreat south to the Han River.

# # #

29 June 1950 - My mortar team, along with the remnants of the 1st ROK Division, crossed to the south bank of the Han River. Most of the Division's trucks, big guns, and other heavyweight gear lay abandoned on the north bank of the Han. Because South Korea

demolished Han's main bridge, the 1st ROK Division crossed on ferry boats and rafts, obliging me to lead my mortar team in paddling to the south bank.

Beginning in July, we continued marching southward with our mortar and what shells we had on our shoulders. Refugees clogged the road, refugees who had piled their belongings on carts, refugees often wearing white. The road went through deserted rice paddies, over a dirt highway slightly raised and stretching like a ribbon into the distance. The women walked with bundles on their heads, and many strode in shoes soled in rubber from tires.

I urged my squad on and told them we would survive if we kept moving—no relaxing on side of road. We would find our unit. MPs would know where our division had stopped.

Bin, trudging beside me, said he had seen our soldiers fight fiercely—if only our artillery could stop the tanks. I had seen our troops, carrying dynamite in a canvas bag with a trigger, charge tanks. I had viewed them through my binoculars. They hurled themselves under the tanks and detonated the explosives.

Some ROK soldiers attacked a tank with demolition charge on end of a four- to six-foot-long pole. Rushing a tank with bombs worked if enemy troops didn't lay down covering fire for their armored vehicles. Still, I could not assault a tank knowing I would lose my life.

Sook, walking behind squad, seemed to be willing all his strength on putting one foot in front of other. He appeared to be recoiling from horror of killing and endless exhaustion of lugging mortar shells.

Bin, next to me, complained we always retreated. If retreat continued, we would walk into South China Sea and drown. We were not running like dogs. They had great firepower, but we knew our terrain well. We held them at Imjin for three days, and we held them at Han River for six days.

Bin continued to protest we were not winning. Except, we were winning. We were giving the Americans and the United Nations time to get their armies to Korea.

The two shells and mortar parts on my back grew heavier and heavier. A mortar is not that massive and is transportable by a single soldier, but the weapon gradually becomes weighty when carried long distance. Each shell I lugged weighed about five pounds.

We moved with jerky steps to keep our balance on uneven ground. A modern army, to transport mortar shells, had individual soldiers of entire company carry single round. Before setting up to repulse the enemy soldiers, each trooper dropped his projectile next to our mortar.

Although I marched among many soldiers and refugees, I felt alone and homesick. To keep me moving among the retreating surge of troops and refugees, I thought of happier times, of my youth. I remembered returning home from elementary school; at same time, the sun began its evening descent over Korean hills. The hills orange-brown, the low-lying clouds yellow, the sun a pale white. Further beneath the hills and gradually shrouded in darkness, the houses of my beautiful town clustered beside the river.

When the river froze in winter, my classmates built skates, of any metal with a blade-like shape, skates bound to a slender platform and tied to their shoes. My fellow students and I raced in the cold. If I did my chores and homework, my parents let me play, knowing I would be home to eat when the sky grew dark.

I awoke from my trance when I bumped into soldier in front of me, regaining my balance, and starting forward again.

I went back to thinking of home, remembering the garden plot in the front yard of my parent's house, giving family a plentiful supply of vegetables. My mother fixed meals of steamed rice, fish, vegetables, and *kimchi* during the summer. In cold Korean winters, heat traveled from our stove to an adjoining room through horizontal air passages under the floor.

We marched south. I left behind memories of childhood. The ROK Army tramped toward the port of Pusan, at very southern edge of South Korea.

#

As days passed, we got help delaying tide of enemy forces. Some army reinforcements, hastily assembled, arrived to fight the North Koreans. On July 5, 1950, Americans battled near Osan, about 30 miles south of Seoul, a site near our withdrawal route. U.S. Army dug in on line of mountains across main road, mountains affording cover for U.S. troops and elevated position for artillery.

Through my binoculars, I saw about five-hundred Americans dig trenches around the road, with 105-mm howitzers on a slight rise behind front-line American troops.

Leading with column of tanks, the North Koreans attacked in early morning. American armament bounced off the North Korean tanks without penetration. One lone 105-mm howitzer had anti-tank rounds, which enabled it to destroy a few tanks. The column of leading tanks charged past the dug-in Americans and sped down the road, going south. Enemy troops and trucks followed the tanks. Americans ran out of ammunition and pulled back.

Along with Americans and ROK Army, my mortar squad steadily moved south, farther down the Korean peninsula. We marched in the heat of summer. Torrential rains of June had given way to a lack of rain in July and August. By late July, I had led my squad roughly 180 miles south of Han River.

In early August, my unit stopped retreating. We defended a position above Gyeongju, on the east coast near the Sea of Japan. The city of Gyeongju was small but well known as capital of ancient Silla Empire. The battle area around the old town was relatively quiet because it near coastline. Naval units off coast would pour shells down on any enemy forces, like raining down a curtain of fire on enemy.

To our west, the U.S. and ROK had combined forces on defensive line called Pusan Perimeter. It covered 100-by-50-mile rectangle in the southeast corner of South Korea. No fortified sites existed between the Pusan Perimeter and the city of Pusan on the lower coast, giving Americans and ROK Army option of standing firm or retreating and swimming in South China Sea.

We had heard endless chain of ships now unloaded at Pusan. The ROK and American forces had built up reinforcements and supplies. In contrast, the North Korean supply line stretched from 38th parallel to our defensive positions around Pusan. Tactically, our forces pounded the enemy armies with nonstop air and naval bombardment. Enemy hid tanks, artillery, and large troop concentrations in tunnels or under numerous apple trees in the region. The enemy left their cover and attacked with all their forces at night or in rain.

All through August, the Americans and our ROK forces—now outnumbering the enemy in troops, tanks, and artillery, and having total control of the air—turned back enemy attacks trying to break through the Pusan Perimeter.

I stopped reading the journal and faced the Koreans. "Seong-gi explained all five of you came from a farming background."

"We shared similar upbringing," Sook replied.

"Even you?"

Sook nodded. "I was born into farming family, near a town of 20,000, in the middle of South Korea. Most children finished elementary school and went to middle school, studying farming. My parents paid extra to send me away to liberal-arts middle school."

"But you started the war in Seong-gi's mortar squad."

"After three years of middle school, my family could no longer pay for high school. Back at farm, I wanted to continue education, not burden my family. I volunteered for ROK Army, planning to serve until I could go back to school."

"You were a rookie under Seong-gi and Yeong-ho?"

"I was the youngest soldier in basic training. Had much difficulty. Army times so different from my school days. After basic training, the military assigned me to Seong-gi's mortar squad, as one of two ammunition carriers."

Sook grimaced and nibbled his lower lip. "Instead of being in high school, I dragged mortar shells and suffered taunts of my squad. I failed at everything in the army."

"Well, you didn't fail at finding the artifacts. Worked out okay." I placed the journal on the table. "I have to leave now and interview Bin's uncle. We'll continue reading after the interview."

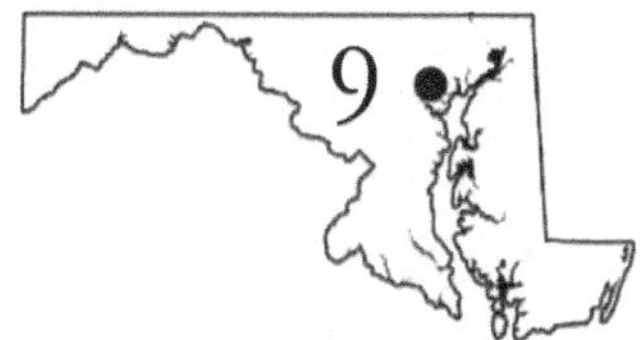

BALTIMORE—16 JUNE 2000

Sook took two hours to get to Baltimore. We went through hot and humid Washington, D.C., reminiscent of a swamp. Thankfully, the AC in Sook's BMW pumped out cold air. He drove, and I reviewed the comments I had made in my case notepad.

"When we go over what squad did fifty years ago,' Sook said, "to find suspect. What you search for?"

I stopped scribbling in my notepad and pondered what I listened to as Seong-gi and the three Koreans spoke; how did I connect some events and ignore others? "Roth taught me to seek the crossover between two events. A criminal, when they talk behind their disguise, is not what they appear. Get behind their mask—hunt for the hidden truth."

"What you mean?"

Sook had asked about an unknown reason explaining the way an event happened, not the way it seemed. How could I describe an obscure reason, underlying cause, in an understandable way? My mind struggled to find an explanation. My eyes spotted the AC controls in Sook's car.

"Hypothetically, say we sought the birth of the AC. The first air-conditioner."

Sook turned to gaze at me with half-closed eyes and a frozen face, his statue stare. He twisted back to watch the road. "And?"

"Where do we search for the origin?"

Sook's appearance changed to puzzlement "Don't know. Electronics store? Furnace supply store?"

"A book publisher!"

Sook pursed his lips and focused on the road. "You joking?"

"Nineteen hundred and two, in Brooklyn, an engineer named Willis Carrier began work at a publishing company. During his summer's high humidity, the paper would wrinkle, causing the ink to go cockeyed on the book pages."

Sook closed his eyelids to a narrow slit and stared at me, like gamblers rechecking their dealt cards.

"So," I continued, "the company tasked Carrier with figuring out how to print books during the muggy summers. To reduce temperature and humidity in the printing room, Carrier built a machine to blow humid air over cold coils.

"Carrier's device eliminated the printing errors in the pressroom. The sweaty plant workers began to spend their free time in the chamber housing the printing presses. That's the hidden connection: keeping the paper from wrinkling birthed the AC industry.

"Like the relationship between book publishing and the AC, we're scanning for a mysterious link between the past and the present, a connection leading us to the thieves."

Sook focused on his driving. "You believe hidden connection exists? Cloaked in my past?"

I went back to scribbling in my notepad. "Maybe. Maybe not. If it's there, Roth will find it."

We parked at the uncle's warehouse next to the Patapsco River in Baltimore Harbor.

Baltimore is the thirteenth to sixteenth busiest water port in the U. S. for tonnage of waterborne trade. We stood in front of a dark-brick, three-story warehouse. It was old, large, with two cargo doors in back facing the water. A rusted chain-link fence enclosed the area around the building; the enclosed area abounded with discarded wooden pallets, overgrown grass, and crumbling pavement. A product of gentrification it was not.

Bin's uncle, Seong-woo, waited for us in front of the warehouse. The eighty-year-old man was six feet tall and weighed maybe two hundred pounds. Bin's uncle had a vacant expression and a receding hairline, emphasizing the patch of long, horizontal wrinkles across his forehead. He dressed in a dirty jersey and long pants, as did most of his dock workers, and carried a clipboard.

Leading into an area just inside the sliding door at the front of the structure, Seong-woo took a seat and talked with us around a pitted-wood table with folding chairs. Bricks made up the inner wall. My nostrils detected a musty mold odor, reinforcing my sense of the warehouse as bare bones.

"My nephew told me about theft," the uncle said in unhurried but raspy English. He shifted his face close to mine as if he had poor vision.

"You know about the treasure?" I began.

"Long ago, I helped my brother's son a-a-a-nd made small profit same time. You say, buy one, get one free. When I remo-o-o-ved three men and treasure from South Korea, I no tell my ship's crew about treasure." As he talked, the old smuggler continued to put his head close to me and spoke in his grating speech rhythm.

"Did others on your ship know your nephew carried artifacts?"

"I ma-a-a-de it clear Bin and his two friends were cargo. I said they pay me with last of their meager funds. Back then, many Koreans moved about to avoid the fighting."

As we talked, the uncle continued to place his face close to me and stutter. To block this distraction, I rotated my head back, staring at the ceiling while I developed my next questions.

"When your nephew found you near the coast—the first time—was anyone with you when he told you about the relics?"

"No-o-o," the uncle replied. "Two of us wa-a-a-lked along beach. No one close enough to hear."

"By helping your nephew and his friends, you got a fifth of the artifacts. How did you sell the items? How many people knew you sold your share of the Korean treasure?"

"One other person knew I go-o-o-t relics from nephew. Isaac Hunter sold my fifth of Silla relics. I know Isaac for decades."

"Does he keep secrets?" I asked.

"He keeps secrets. I tr-r-r-ust him."

"From time to time, did you view the gold exhibit in the Great Falls house?"

My question appeared to alarm him. The uncle jerked away from my face and stared blankly at me, perhaps wondering if I sought to pin the burglary on him. He waited several moments before responding. "Rarely."

"Did you know the combination to open the door into the exhibit room?"

Before responding, Seong-woo stroked his scraggly white beard. "I not kno-o-o-w combination. Someti-i-i-mes I visited house as guest of Bin. Because Bin or Sook brought me into exhibit room, I no need know combination."

I had begun to run out of questions for the uncle. "So, Seong-woo, who do you think took the treasure?"

"Didn't do it. If Bin or one his three friends did it, they would have done it year-r-r-s ago. Consider other suspects."

"Like whom?"

"I-I-I don't know. Do not have good idea what to do. From what Bin told me, someone passed security measure details to thieves."

"I heard the Korean Cultural Heritage Association and the FBI questioned Sook about the Silla relics," I said.

The uncle stared at me impassively. "I hear, too."

"Have you talked with KCA or FBI?"

"No," Bin's uncle replied in his croaky voice. "If CHA heard rumor, then they likely heard in South Korea. Ma-a-a-ybe burglars came from Korea, not America."

I thought about the uncle's suggestion to search for the robbers in South Korea. Or maybe he was sending me on a wild goose chase. He might show the world a vacant facial expression, but he struck me as shrewd.

# # #

I walked outside and strolled to the shady side of the warehouse, where a cooling breeze wafted off the river.

Roth answered my cell-phone call. "Report."

I filled her in on my interview with Bin's uncle. I then said, "If the rumors—about Sook having Silla relics—originated in South Korea, maybe the burglars found out—about the treasure—there."

She didn't speak for a moment. "Finish your interview with the three Koreans. Then we'll discuss what to do about Korea."

I rubbed down my cowlick and waited for Roth to continue. "What about the stranger who learned about the Silla treasure?"

"Wang Gang. I am going now to interview him."

"Let me get Bruce," Roth said.

He joined our call. "Guy, do I need to get up to Northern Virginia and pull your investigation out of its quagmire?"

"Bruce, you're a superb drinking buddy, but I am quite capable of directing an inquiry without bringing my support staff up here."

"Don, you couldn't lead a kindergarten class with a bucket of ice cream."

Roth interrupted Bruce. "Find out about a Wang Gang, living in Leesburg, Virginia. Two years before the thieves stole the Silla artifacts, he approached Mr. Park to buy them. Don's on his way to interview Gang now."

"Okay, Boss."

I terminated the call and got in Sook's car to leave Baltimore. He drove toward Northern Virginia, went over the upper portion of the D.C. beltway, and headed for Leesburg.

# # #

Using a road atlas, Sook and I found Wang Gang's house in the middle of old Leesburg. The building had a two-story construction, with its siding split between red brick and white paneled wood. Approaching the front door, I spied exterior video cameras, outdoor spotlights, and security wires around the inside edges of the windows. To the left of the front door, a bronze plaque proclaimed the house a historical building.

I rapped the bronze knocker. A large man in a grey turtleneck shirt, a navy hopsack blazer, and khaki pants filled the door. He had the visage of a haughty goliath. Mr. Gang's bodyguard had my size but nowhere near my style.

"Mr. Park and Mr. Gannon to see Mr. Gang," Sook announced. "I have appointment."

The big guy allowed Sook to pass him into the hallway and then said to me, "Sir, may I pat you down?"

I would not be allowed entrance otherwise, so I nodded. I would soon learn about the professionalism of the tough employed by Gang.

"Sir, please empty your pockets on the table," Big Guy said. "Please raise your arms to your sides." I emptied my pockets, took off my sports coat, and raised my arms as he asked.

Within fifteen seconds, he patted me down quickly, non-intrusively, and thoroughly. Gang's well-trained bodyguard did not pat down our client.

Big Guy led us down a hallway with solid wood flooring and old-style radiators to a comfortable study. Along the way through the hall, I passed stairs going up to the second floor. An open door revealed a stairway down to the basement. The study had the same wood flooring as the hallway and boasted a fireplace. We sat on a couch; Big Guy stood in a corner; our host took a leather chair beside the hearth. Gang had an elliptical mouth like a guppy, long white hair down to his collar, and droopy eyelids that made him appear like he viewed the world through two slits; he was dressed in a lightweight blue suit.

I took the lead. "Your house is beautiful. And old."

He didn't smile. "What can I do for you?"

"About a year ago, you asked Mr. Park if he had Silla artifacts. Who gave you this information?"

The gangster stared at me, seemingly absorbing what he had just heard. He remained motionless for a while. Either he had no idea why we were in his house, or he was doing a superb acting job to hide the fact that he had already stolen the Silla gold.

"Two years ago, I heard a rumor Mr. Park had Silla relics," Gang finally answered. "When we talked, he said he did not. Now you've made a special trip to ask me who passed me these rumors of . . . nonexistent relics."

We sat in silence, each waiting for the other to offer up information. "Yes," I replied. "We're asking for the name of the person who said Mr. Park possessed Silla pieces."

"Why?"

Both Gang and I applied silence in hopes the interviewee would feel inadequate and start to blabber. Since both of us used matching schemes, we wound up with not much jabber but lots of quiet. I brushed my cowlick down before answering. "Thieves attempted a burglary at Mr. Park's property. We wish to speak with the person who told you about the relics—to see if he might have told other people."

Gang remained quiet, seeming to absorb what I had said. "For years, vague anecdotes have circulated among suppliers of high-end antiquities: Mr. Park might have access to a superb set of Silla art. I merely asked Mr. Park, based on those elusive ambiguities. By the way, what did the burglars take?"

"I only mentioned an attempted burglary," I said.

"So you did," Gang replied. "I find it odd you would come all this way to investigate an attempted burglary. If you wish, I can give you the names of the brokerage companies I use to buy antiques, but I don't think they can help you solve a burglary—an attempted burglary."

I pressed. "You don't recall the name of the individual who alleged Mr. Park had Silla relics?"

Gang stared at me like a guppy viewing me through the glass wall of an aquarium. "I don't remember."

We went through another period in which neither of us spoke. I fiddled with my college ring. Finally, he resumed talking, "I reiterate that I would be genuinely interested in buying individual works of art that Mr. Park might have."

Sook nodded his head at Gang. "I'll keep that in mind."

Gang got up from his couch. "If you change your mind and have something to discuss, you have my number."

Sook also rose and said, "Thank you for your time."

Big Guy walked us down the hall and out the door. In the car, Sook said, "What do you make of him?"

I brushed down my cowlick again and thought about Gang's demeanor and his questions. "He appeared interested in figuring out if you have or don't have the relics. Then again, I place him high on our suspect list."

"I agree," Sook said. "Well, let's start back to Great Falls house and call my old squad leader, Seong-gi."

Before departing, I swiveled in my passenger seat and scouted the building. Wide-open space surrounded it. In this section of Leesburg, the power and telephone cabling came in on overhead wires. Diagonally across the street, a church stretched over an entire block. I saw no convenient place to hide and observe.

SOUTH KOREA—10 AUGUST 1950

Sitting at the long table in Sook's conference room with Yeong-ho and Bin, I checked my notes while waiting to continue reading Seong-gi's journal. Then Sook entered the room, and I resumed our review. "When did you depart South Korea?"

"Middle of August," he replied.

"You haven't told me about finding the crown."

He gave me his frozen face. "Patience."

"Soon, I'm going to hear about the gold crown, right?"

He nodded.

"Sook and I plan to call Seong-gi later tonight," I said. "I want to finish the journal before we call South Korea."

Bin Bie had been staring out the row of windows on one wall. Now he turned to me. "You had us meet with you and read journal. Do you now know who planned theft?"

"Not yet."

"Then you wasted our time?"

"We'll see. I haven't finished reading all the events."

Bin faced Sook. "You okay with this?"

"Yes," Sook answered. "Let us continue reading."

I nodded at Sook, glanced back at the journal, and read Seong-gi's words:

Preparing part of a defensive line slightly north of Gyeongju, I had Sook and Yeong-ho dig a trench. Under hot midday sun, my uniform stuck to my back. My feet ached, their underside exhibiting large blisters with thick patches of dry, red skin and calluses. We had not marched previous day, but my feet needed more than one day to recover.

Using T-handle entrenching shovels, Sook and Yeong-ho dug a ditch about six feet by four feet, piling up brown dirt facing toward the north, the enemy, leaving grass along south-facing rear side of the trench. I had positioned the mortar behind a large mound, a small hill topped by dense growth of trees and underbrush. Everywhere else around us, the land had flat contour.

Near the top of the mound, I knelt and gazed out through the line of trees toward the front. The ROK soldiers in the frontline talked back and forth, waiting for enemy attack. The sound of shovels— digging trenches and piling up dirt in mounds facing north—echoed over the ground. Killed in artillery barrage earlier in week, our platoon's lieutenant no longer directed us, but I guessed the enemy would attack our company—a unit reduced to thirty or forty men— before day ended. The enemy would precede any attack with artillery barrage.

I paused in my reading of Seong-gi's words. Glancing at my notepad, I saw I had put down the lieutenant as an individual of interest. "Is this the officer who directed you from the beginning? Always knew what you did?"

"Yes," Sook replied.

"How did you know he died?"

"Seong-gi saw his mangled body," Sook said. "A corpse."

"New lieutenant appeared to lead you?"

"No replacement. Seong-gi took on more command."

I resumed reading the journal:

Once they finished the dugout, Sook and Yeong-ho sat on the edge of the trench with their legs hanging into the hole. Based on the intensity of the fighting and withdrawing over the past month, I worried whether we would get out of this struggle alive. Gazing around during the successive withdrawals, I had seen retreating soldiers, in disarray, with killing on both sides.

My former lieutenant kept saying ROK Army stood and fought as it withdrew. Someday, after we reorganized, our forces would return to these battlefields and drive the enemy back north. A question kept occurring to me: would we stop North Koreans first or would enemy kill me first?

As he sat resting alongside new dugout, Sook told Yeong-ho he remained scared after month of firing mortar and marching. But Sook noted he no longer froze with fear before attack.

Sook had learned to do his job as one of our two ammo carriers. I trusted him to hand us shells to keep mortar firing.

Yeong-ho lay down with his back toward the mound. He said he had worried about Sook when North Koreans first attacked. I praised Sook on how he now kept up with rest of us.

Yeong-ho smiled, patted Sook on his shoulder, and told him he remained our little brother.

Sook pointed out we were unique in company. We had not lost anyone from our original squad. The enemy had killed many friends in initial group—gone forever.

I suggested we had survived because we set up in rear. As a mortar crew, we had entrenched soldiers in front, our troops with guns in forward defensive line.

Sook responded many shells had exploded near us. The enemy seemed always to have explosives. No—Sook knew our mortar team had been lucky.

I walked over and sat next to my two soldiers. We had positioned ourselves in proper defensive position, among trees with mortar concealed behind this embankment. I looked at the mortar's barrel. The cannon stood beside us and had become our reason for being.

Sook talked about when I first taught him to fire mortar. He enjoyed my tale of weapon's history as much as the practical details of operation; namely, the mortar squad came into being in World War I, created to heave a projectile in a large-angle arc so it would come down in enemy's trench.

I viewed the level ground around our mound and hoped it would stay quiet all day. Beside me, Sook continued talking about his training. Heavy artillery had a flat trajectory that flew over the top of the enemy's trenches. Mortars, with a shell that went nearly straight up and came almost straight down, could rain down explosives from directly above. Back when I trained Sook, I showed him the steep arc of the mortar shell streaming through the sky.

Because a mortar round has a steep upward arc when fired, my mortar crew set up behind a protective mound like this one. For mortars to function best, a forward soldier, me, sighted the enemy and signaled back to the rearward mortar team how to adjust their fire to land on the enemy. During the numerous skirmishes since the invasion began, my squad followed this approach.

Late in afternoon, whistle of enemy artillery shells started, growing louder and louder, building to an ear-piercing volume just before the beginning of explosions, eruptions ripping up earth in front of company's trenches and progressing through the front lines back toward us in our trench. I crouched down, pressing my face into the side of the dugout and my curled-up legs against Yeong-ho. The dirt sides of the trench shook, the air had compressed, and soil scattered down around me. Again, and again, and again.

Silence.

I waited. Felt no pain. A minute had passed without further explosions; hence, the attack had finished its opening artillery barrage, and now the troops would come. Yeong-ho stirred.

I jumped out of foxhole, ran forward, and yelled for squad to work the mortar.

Behind me, Sook got up, grabbed his first shell, and carried it to the assistant gunner. On my order, they lobbed the explosive at North Korean troops charging our company's front line. The second ammo bearer, Sang-hun Lee, had not arisen to carry shells.

Sook called for Sang-hun, my fifth squad member. Why didn't he bring the next round?

Yeong-ho had seen him go down, wounded. Yeong-ho shouted for Sook to bring more rounds.

Sook ran back and forth carrying ammunition to the squad. I heard firing in front of us, the noise increasing in loudness like a train coming nearer. To offer lower target, Sook ran hunched over with the shell he carried.

Close to the mortar, giving off a high-pitched whistle, bullets tore through the air.

The enemy had overrun us.

I screamed at the team to grab their rifles.

A North Korean soldier came running through the trees in front of our position. He charged closer, in a tan uniform, carrying a burp gun.

Sook froze and stared, appeared to be searching for his rifle.

Both Bin and I fired our M1 Garand rifles at the North Korean soldier.

He staggered, leaned back, and fell face up, a dead warrior wearing baggy pants, a canvas jacket, felt hat with a brim, and canvas shoes.

Louder noises.

Ten miles away at sea, naval ships off the coast targeted the attacking troops. As cruel raindrops falling from sky, portions of the earth around attacking enemy sprouted up, like short-lived water fountains appearing and falling back to earth. Some shells strayed and landed near our mortar position.

I saw enemy had begun to pull back.

The North Koreans withdrew, leaving heaved-up earth, torn-down trees, sprawled bodies of soldiers, broken equipment, and a slight sulfur smell. My team slumped down, stunned, resembling a group of frozen carcasses. We were exhausted, our food and now our mortar shells depleted.

Yeong-ho pleaded for help with the injured ammo carrier, Sang-hun, who had been wounded and bled badly. Bin ran to assist the fallen soldier.

Again, Yeong-ho called for medical help, for a medic.

Peering over the mound, I saw no medical aid. I realized the enemy had destroyed remainder of the company. Farther off where the front line had once been, a few survivors wandered about, seemingly confused and soundless. This attack had been one of the worst yet; after all, our company had crumbled, but we had beaten the enemy back, inflicting horrible loss on them. We searched but found no medic to treat Sang-hun. Yeong-ho and I tried to examine his injury.

Blood covered Sang-hun's face and uniform. Bin and Yeong-ho shifted him to examine the wound. The injured man screamed and then lay motionless in supine posture.

I organized my team, assigning Yeong-ho to explore for food and medical help for fallen ammunition bearer.

When Yeong-ho went off by himself to search for food and a medic, he made remarkable discovery. The next few pages of my journal tell his story as he later said to me.

I shut Seong-gi's chronicle and directed a question at Yeong-ho. "At this point in your search for supplies and medical help, you encountered the Silla tomb?"

"I did," Yeong-ho said. "I help Seong-gi write next part of his journal. I see things he no sees. I told him what I unearthed."

"We're not going to read from the journal. I want you to tell me, in your words, what you did."

Yeong-ho hesitated.

"Start just after Seong-gi sent you to search for food. Omit nothing."

Yeong-ho sat frozen at the conference table, twitching his left foot on the floor, maybe composing his words. "I remember moving over shredded ground like ghost, warily, as now only the moon lit my way. The noise of our company had vanished. I just heard nighttime buzz of crickets and occasional snap of distant gunfire—from the north.

"I zig-zagged around the blast craters on the mound, its previously smooth contour now chewed-up by the pounding from naval shells. Coming close to a large hole, I glanced downward."

I had scribbled down Yeong-ho's narrative in my notepad. The room had grown dark. I stood up and flipped on the overhead fluorescent lights.

Yeong-ho glanced out the windows along the outer wall of the conference room. "The rubble glowed, giving off a white glow. What glowed there? By crawling and crab walking, I dropped down the slope of the crater."

"Let me be sure I understand," I said. "You were in darkness, except for moonglow?"

"Yes."

"And you saw no one; you were alone?"

"No one."

I wrote his words down on paper. "Okay, continue with your account."

"Stone formed the shimmering rubble in crater, a pile of white stones stacked up like pile of onions in grocery store, glowing because moonbeams reflected off the white surface. I guessed ancient builders had quarried rocks, piled them up, and then placed soil over stones. Over time, trees and brush had risen on the mound, as Mother Nature rebuilt her forest.

"Clustered among the stones were wooden beams and planks, splintered and scattered."

"Did you realize what you had found?" I asked.

"I understood then. My thoughts jumbled to recognize each new item I saw. I stood in an old tomb.

"Among the scattered wood, I saw gleam of metal and ceramic objects. I pawed through the timber and dirt down to the objects. My fingers pulled away a tangle of beads: a chest-lace of glass, gold, and jade.

"The chest-lace appeared like assortment of necklaces that went around the neck and hung down, covering the chest. More digging uncovered a gold earring."

"You were pretty excited?" I asked.

"The recognition staggered me, stunned me. I had resigned myself to die soon, maybe this day; instead, this day gave me this wonderful tomb, old vault from times past."

"Yeong-ho found items by himself," Sook said. "We were back by the mortar and did not know what he had found."

"I thought about what I should do," Yeong-ho replied. "Had uncovered ancient burial site. Had not spotted food or medical help, and I did not know if I had found valuable objects or pieces worthless as sand on a beach.

"I believed I should return to the squad and ask Seong-gi to examine objects. Wanted his guidance. He would know what to do.

"Confused, I forgot my purpose to explore for supplies. Using illumination from the moon and holding tightly to the beads and earring, I scrambled up crater wall and stumbled back toward mortar squad."

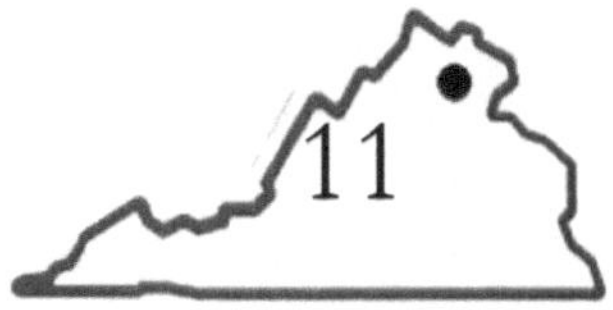

NORTHERN VIRGINIA—16 JUNE 2000

Yeong-ho, sitting at the conference room table with Sook, Bin, and me, suddenly jumped up and shouted, "Need bathroom—now!" He, Yeong-ho, rolled his metal chair back on the rug, away from the table, and rushed out of the room, to the laughter of Sook and Bin.

"Such a clown," Sook exclaimed. "Always joking."

While our joker relieved himself, Sook and Bin took a break from telling their account of the North Korean invasion.

I had been exploring for a clue about the theft, digging like a blind pig rooting for an acorn. So far, I did not have a hunch about who planned the robbery.

Bin went to the kitchenette for tea, but Sook remained seated. He spoke solemnly. "Seong-gi, Bin, Yeong-ho, and I ashamed of what we did. For past fifty years, we hadn't told our families about stealing Silla artifacts when we left Korea."

There were four soldiers. I had been talking face-to-face with three. I needed to speak with the fourth. "Why didn't your corporal leave Korea with you?"

Sook stood up and gazed out the windows, appearing to watch the geese in the pond behind his office building. He folded one arm behind his back. In the hand of his other arm, he grasped his ballpoint pen and clicked the retractor. "When we tell rest of our tale, we explain why he remained in South Korea."

Because Seong-gi led the mortar squad fifty years back in time, he knew about the treasure and was a suspect. "Have you talked with him about the theft?"

"Day after robbery, I called him in Seoul, but he wasn't home. I meant to call him back. Slipped my mind."

"I need to talk with him."

Sook nodded. "Okay, I call again tonight."

"In the meantime, don't be ashamed of your past."

"What you mean?" Sook replied.

"You saw your friends killed in large numbers. A Prussian general, von Clausewitz, said, 'War is an area of uncertainty.'"

He continued to stare out the windows and punch his pen's retractor. "Uncertainty," he whispered.

I saw Sook's head slump and his mouth sag. "Are you okay?"

"At battle of Gyeongju, I scared and exhausted. Command chain in ruins—no one tells us what to do. I felt fear enemy might destroy us."

I thought back to my war-time experience, ten years in the past. "My partner, Bruce Seeker, and I were MPs in Desert Storm. We learned to drift with the tide, and the flow always changed.

"We directed traffic at crucial crossroads where stragglers returned to their units. I heard about the looting of antiquities in 1991 as the Gulf War wound down. You and your colleagues were not the last to take artifacts, and I'm sure soldiers had taken spoils before you did."

Sook frowned and lowered his head again. "Still, I not proud of what I did."

"During your endless firefights, your lieutenant was the individual most in contact with you, the person who knew what you were doing, day by day. Am I correct?"

Sook glanced at me and then nodded.

"And the lieutenant was killed in battle about the time you got to your position above Gyeongju?"

Sook grimaced, moved back to the table, and slumped down in his chair. "I saw him. He was dead. We lost the one person who kept track of us."

"Any other individual who knew what you were doing?"

He shook his head. "On our own."

People from the past who knew about the Silla treasure remained few. I needed to confirm my clients kept their actions and findings a closely-held secret. My intuition told me that Seong-gi was an essential piece of the puzzle. "I have to talk to the author of this journal."

Sook checked his watch. "Soon is a good time to call Korea. When Bin and Yeong-ho return, we place the call."

NORTHERN VIRGINIA—16 JUNE 2000

It was 6 p.m. Friday. With the thirteen-hour difference in time, it was 7 a.m. in Seoul on Saturday when Sook placed the call to his old squad leader. Since Seong-gi knew the combination to the exhibit room, he was a suspect.

Seong-gi could speak English so I would be able to question him directly. I asked Sook to start the call in Korean and then switch to English.

Sook told me most Koreans began studying English in the third grade. Throughout the late twentieth century, South Koreans had found if they spoke English, they increased their job skills. Money talked.

Sook—using my cell phone—called Seong-gi in Seoul and began speaking in Korean. After a minute of chitchat, both parties switched to English.

Frowning and whispering curses under his breath, Sook turned to me. "I can't speak with Seong-gi. No one knows where he is. His son on phone."

"His English sounds fine," I said.

"English is excellent. Attended American college. Has agreed to speak with you."

"The doc gave my mom sleeping pills," the son said. "She's in bed. We haven't seen Dad for a month."

Sook glared at my cell phone as if it were a cat clawing a cherished table. "He been missing a month?"

"Police have searched all over Seoul for him. I have been

nauseous with fear. Why didn't he leave a note?"

Sook bit his lower lip. "Your father missing a month, and you didn't call me?"

"Been a creepy time. Two detectives always searching for him. I meant to call Dad's friends in America but kept putting it off—my bad."

Sook pushed mute on the cell phone, whispered, "Son not know about the artifacts," and returned to an open line.

"I called to ask your father about burglary here in America. I have private investigator helping solve this crime. Would you answer few questions for him?"

"Sure. Put P.I. on the call."

"Which day did you realize something was wrong?" I asked.

"Hmm . . . May 15. Mom stayed at my home night before. My dad remained in his home alone."

"Did you detect a struggle?" I asked.

"Nothing pointed to a scuffle. TV stayed on all night. Father never leaves it on when not watching."

"Before he went missing, did anyone approach him regarding his old mortar crew in the Korean War?"

"I don't live with my parents, so didn't see him talking with anyone. Mom said a government agent visited the house. He wanted to know about my dad's war years."

Sook and I locked eyes. I might have stumbled on a clue. "What agency?" I asked. "Who did he represent?"

"The Korean Cultural Heritage Administration."

"The CHA?"

"Yes."

"Did this official leave his business card?"

"He did."

"Can you find it?"

"Does it matter?"

"Yeah. Could you get it?"

The call went silent until the son returned. "The dude is named Ji-hun Cho."

Beside me, Sook snapped his fingers in recognition and pushed mute on the phone. "Ji-hun Cho! The CHA investigator with the FBI at the Washington, D.C. office."

"When did the CHA representative talk to your father?" I asked when we returned to an open line.

"Mom said visit took place two weeks before his disappearance. The police contacted agent, but he said he had no further contact with my father."

I brushed down my cowlick before asking. "Is money missing? Does your mother know?"

"Mom confirmed nothing missing at home or his business."

"Is your father's passport at the house?" I asked.

"Wait, hang on." After a few minutes, the son returned and said, "His passport's here."

"Did he pack a bag? Did he plan to travel?" I asked.

"Dad's clothes and luggage are here."

"Sorry to hear about your father. When you get news about him, please call Sook Park immediately." I let Sook finish the call.

"I will give you the number for my new cell phone when I get it," he said.

After we had disconnected, Sook told me, "Do you think my old squad leader kidnapped?"

"It isn't good he's been missing so long," I said. "I hope he's alive. Whether the thieves snatched him or not, we have to assume they got the combination for the door keypad from your old friend.

"Do you have a photograph of Seong-gi?"

Sook had to think a moment. "Yes, from when he visited us little over year ago."

"Please make copies for me."

Had someone kidnapped the former squad leader? Or had he stolen the treasure? If a kidnapping, it took place in South Korea and the criminals planned their theft there, not in America.

# # #

Later that night, I returned to my suite at the Residence Inn. I ate a deli sandwich, drank a beer, replayed the day's events in my mind, and watched TV. Phil Jackson, the Los Angeles Lakers coach, gave an interview, saying a successful person must integrate the spiritual, mental, and physical into one.

After writing up our phone call to Korea, I rang Roth and recounted our conversation with the son.

"Someone kidnapped Seong-gi and forced him to reveal the

combination to the security door in Virginia," Roth said. "Or is he the burglar? What do you think?"

I sipped my beer. "I think the burglars kidnapped Seong-gi in Korea and forced him to reveal the code."

"It's very tricky to solve a burglary in our business," Roth said, "and even harder to solve a homicide."

I crushed my beer can and tossed it toward the kitchen where the trashcan resided. "On the other hand, I'll work faster as I'm more alert with the strong anxiety of my death."

We ended the call. I thought of Phil Jackson. When his team lost, he consulted with his advisors and decided on a strategy. The time had come to take care of the mental, change my approach.

NORTHERN VIRGINIA—17 JUNE 2000

Motivated to learn how the Silla relics got to America, I arrived at Sook's office building in the early morning. The three Koreans waited for me in the conference room, standing together and staring out the wall-length windows overlooking the pond at the back of the building.

I sat at the conference-room table. "The Seoul police are busy finding your old corporal. I need to learn what you did following the Gyeongju battle. Let's get started."

The three turned from the windows. Sook sat down first. "Ask away."

"Yesterday, Yeong-ho told me he had found two pieces of jewelry in the crater, and then went to inform Seong-gi, your squad leader. What happened next?"

Yeong-ho sat with his elbows propped on the long table with its beige top. He bowed his head, letting his left foot tap nervously against the chair's metal support. "I remember early morning 11 August. I scamper back to mortar. Found Sook and Bin eating rice."

I got out my notepad and began making notes. "Did you see other ROK soldiers around you?"

Yeong-ho shook his head. "Sook and Bin had small fire burning at bottom of trench. Seong-gi had been staring north for enemy infiltrators. I told him I had no food and held out my hands with two objects from crater."

I stopped scribbling in my notepad and glanced up. Had anyone spotted Yeong-ho leaving the hole with those objects? "Yeong-ho, how could you be alone? What happened to the other soldiers? How many men in a company, a hundred—two hundred?"

"They were dead, missing in action, or lost and trying to find company. We had fought almost two months. Only our squad left alive on battlefield."

My brain struggled to absorb the stark reality of the chaos and killing depicted by Yeong-ho. "What did you do next?"

"I jumped down into trench and held objects—beads and earring—in light from fire. My friends might have preferred food to fill their empty stomachs. Seong-gi squeezed into the dugout, crouched next to me, and stared at objects in my hands.

"I glanced over trench top and make out Sang-hun, our fifth squad member, motionless on the ground where he had lain for some time, still as in coma or death. Bin, Sook, and Seong-gi gathered around me. They couldn't see the relics well in firelight, so Bin shined the beam of his army flashlight on items."

Yeong-ho had ceased speaking. I gazed up. He watched two geese lumber in flight past the conference-room windows. They flew but appeared awkward. He continued his tale from fifty years in the past. "My three friends stared at chest lace and earring."

"I remember instant," Bin interrupted. "Items were old and metal gold. The four of us passed the two objects around, hand to hand— clumsily."

"I told them," Sook added, "had seen similar things in school book. Pieces were Silla Empire jewelry."

Yeong-ho grinned. "I felt relieved: they had forgotten I had not brought food. I explained mound, the one we stood behind, must be large tomb. Navy ships had blown the hilltop away with their artillery explosions.

"Found two jewelry pieces, at bottom of big crater dug out by the naval blasts. Told them my guess was more jewelry existed, under debris. Before digging further to find more relics, I had left the tomb to come tell friends."

Our three clients turned to me. "What?" I realized I had interrupted them, tapping the conference-room table with my class ring from college, on my left hand. My mind had been stampeding to organize the whole shebang of Yeong-ho's account. "Sorry. I didn't realize—"

Yeong-ho resumed. "I told Seong-gi, Sook, and Bin we should go back to crater. Explore for more objects."

"Seong-gi told us keep watch for stragglers," Sook added. "We left Sang-hun, thought him dead. Yeong-ho led us to crater."

# # #

"We four soldiers collected branches for torches and lit them," Yeong-ho continued. "We gathered T-handle army shovels and descended into dark hole."

All along, Sook had been nodding his head, agreeing with Yeong-ho. "I remember we planted our lights on sides of the pit. We were far enough below ground level so no one would see lights. We dug with short shovel strokes."

"Our Silla relic hunt like your Easter egg hunt, but with pricey eggs," Yeong-ho quipped. Sook and Bin rolled their eyes.

"After a few minutes, I turned over little bells," Bin said. "We put what we found in a pile off to side. We dug with gentle strokes because didn't want to destroy treasure with shovel thrust.

"We dug in silence broken only by shovels entering the dirt. I found a ceremonial sword and Sook found gold rings. To hold items, Seong-gi told Sook to go and bring back two canvas equipment bags."

I flipped back through my notes on Yeong-ho's narrative. "You found wooden beams and planks situated at the crater bottom?"

"Yes," he answered.

"The wood in the crater had enclosed a final resting place for members of the Silla royal family?"

Yeong-ho nodded at me. He waited half a minute before continuing. "Digging like badgers, we kept finding artifacts under timber and dirt. We uncovered ancient treasure: a gold crown, a bronze Buddha, gold belts, earrings, necklaces, bracelets, rings, and decorative swords of gold and silver.

"We finished and sat down side of crater and talked about what we do next. Before I joined the ROK Army, I lived as dirt-poor student. Once war began, I had endured an endless nightmare.

"That night, I had seen riches. Maybe we had been the first to see tomb in a thousand years."

I realized they were brave soldiers. They had begun to think, "Why risk existence and body to explosion and projectile?" They could run away with this treasure and be wealthy for the remainder of their lives.

"I replied we needed to keep wealth away from North Koreans and tell someone in ROK Army," Bin said. "No one agreed with my words."

I leaned back in my chair and brushed my cowlick. "Your company had been decimated. In normal times, what would you have done?"

"Everyone in the company would have known about the treasure in five minutes," Yeong-ho answered. "We would have taken relics to Lieutenant."

In the now quiet meeting room, Sook had his writing pen out and clicked the retractor. "I felt we should not tell anyone. We had found wealth, and it belonged to us. The North Koreans could kill us or not kill us, but we were going to be poor the rest of our lives unless we took the artifacts and ran."

Yeong-ho seemed to be thinking, tapping his foot on the bottom support of his chair. "Maybe Seong-gi should have stopped such talk, but he didn't. Why not take this crown, this jewelry, these swords, this gold, and walk out of war? Why be needy?"

Sook smacked the table top with his palm. "I told them we needed to desert. The people who built tomb abandoned the treasure a long time ago, and we should do same, leave the army."

"Seong-gi asked how we would desert, how that would work," Bin said. "We couldn't drag relics all over South Korea without calling attention to ourselves, without having someone noticing we had two bags of gold. If we continued fighting, what good would treasure do us if we got killed?"

Around the meeting-room table, the three Koreans hesitated, but then Yeong-ho continued the tale. "Seong-gi told three of us dig hole into side of crater and hide the treasure. We made plans abandon army and escape with treasure. The next night, we would return to hole and take relics with us.

"After lengthy discussion, we decided keep wealth intact or else split it up later. In the side of crater, we dug hole, concealing treasure in two canvas bags, putting bags in the hole, filling it over with dirt. We set most artifacts in bags but kept earring and chest lace.

"As we returned to the mortar position, the sky became lighter. Sang-hun lay where we had left him, comatose, an inert bloody rag."

I glanced up from writing in my notepad and tried to interpret their expressions. Fifty years later, they didn't seem happy about their decision to leave Korea. Instead, they showed somber expressions.

"Seong-gi pointed out we needed take mortar with us, so we appeared to be soldiers," Sook said. "While we walked south to leave Korea, we had to keep lookout for MPs watching for deserters. I glanced to the north and saw line of enemy soldiers returning.

"Seong-gi ordered us to leave. Before we scrambled away, we seized the mortar and all we could grab and carry. As I walked away, I racked my brain looking for a way to desert and take the relics out of South Korea."

NORTHERN VIRGINIA—17 JUNE 2000

My mobile phone *beeped.* I answered it.

"You have a problem," Roth said. "While you investigated the crime scene, Bruce discovered our Korean-American clients lied to us about their treasure. Can they overhear you?"

I glanced at Sook, Bin, and Yeong-ho, seated at the long table. "Hold on."

The three stared at me. "Have to take this call." I went out into the hallway. "Clear."

"The FBI is investigating all three of our clients."

Roth had my total attention. "Really?"

"The Korean Cultural Heritage Administration contacted the FBI about our three clients. The CHA suspects they smuggled rare national possessions out of South Korea."

I interrupted her. "Our clients just told me how they found the treasure during the Korean War."

"Did your interrogation skills discover the FBI and the CHA?" Roth asked.

Sook and I had been together all day. He had had many opportunities to confide in me. "He didn't tell me."

"You need to interrogate people more thoroughly."

I didn't answer. Roth had used her teacher's voice: "Child, go sit in the corner." Silence.

"You must determine if the FBI investigation is too hot for us to continue involving ourselves," Roth said. "Find out if the federal agents have specific knowledge our friends stole artifacts, or are the agents fishing in darkness? If the FBI knows all about the Silla crown, they can tell our state licensing board and get our licenses revoked."

Why had Sook chosen to keep information from me? Did he steal the relics this past Monday as an elaborate cover-up to hide them from the FBI? How much had I been duped?

"Bruce found nothing indicating the FBI knows about the Great Falls house," Roth continued. "Other than the CHA accusation, he did not uncover rumors about a Northern Virginia group stealing Korean artifacts. My supposition is the FBI is just nosing around."

I had stood mute while Roth fumed. Maybe I could get her thinking of something else other than criticizing me. "The FBI still considers drug dealers, gun smuggling, and money launderers as their most prominent criminals, but they now have special teams that work to recover stolen paintings, sculptures, and other museum-worthy objects."

Standing out in the hall, I waited while two office workers walked past me. "Burglars have figured out it isn't difficult to rob a museum and get away scot-free."

She interrupted me. "If the FBI is investigating our three clients, then Mr. Park's phone is probably tapped. I'll have Bruce send you a secure mobile, one not registered to you."

She seemed to be calming down. "I figure the phone companies run a line—for a court-approved tap—directly into the local FBI field office."

"We must not make calls, with operational information, to or from our client's land-based phones," Roth said.

"Agreed."

She disconnected. I remained in charge of the investigation, though with a scorched ego. I returned to the conference room, walked up to Sook, and asked, "Has the FBI or the Korean Cultural Heritage Administration accused you of theft?"

Sook was slow and forthright in his answer. "Shortly before the robbery, they contacted us. The next day the three of us went downtown to federal building in Washington, D.C. An agent from CHA attended the meeting.

"The CHA official said unnamed source alleged we took artifacts when we left South Korea. Recognizing they had no evidence, and realizing their charges vague, we denied knowledge of stolen artifacts. We told them contact our lawyer in future."

How much did the unnamed sources know? "Who told the authorities?"

Sook sucked his lower lip into his mouth. "They refused answer question about sources. I believed neither FBI nor CHA knew of Great Falls house."

Sook held his ballpoint pen in his left hand and clicked the retractor up and down. "Their search for missing artifacts is dead end. The agents probed us, hoping we blurt out we have relics in our possession."

"The agents got the scent of your Silla artifacts," I said, "I assume their source of information was in South Korea."

Sook nodded. "FBI said CHA got their information there."

Why hadn't Sook told me about this earlier? "Then the thieves may be from Korea. We should find out more from the CHA agent. Search back through your notes for his name?"

"I remember taking his business card."

"Why didn't you tell me the FBI investigated you?"

"I forgot."

I went silent and fixed him with a skeptical expression. "You don't forget the FBI."

Sook and his two colleagues exchanged glances. "It no matter. They don't have evidence."

"It does matter. I can lose my P.I. license."

Sook began clicking his ballpoint pen again. "Sorry. Won't happen again."

"What else haven't you told me?"

Sook frowned and turned to Bin and Young-ho, who said nothing. "Told you everything."

Irritated, I stroked my hair with my hand to calm myself. "You must always tell me all. Withhold information again, and I can no longer work with you."

I would accept nothing less than complete truthfulness going forward. "Ms. Roth worries the FBI will tap your phones. Mr. Yeong-ho Park, Mr. Bie, and you must avoid any mention—on your phones—of your relics or theft. We will talk to Roth Security on my cell phone, but that may change in the future."

Sook spoke in Korean with Bin and Yeong-ho and then turned to me. "You think federal agents tap our phones?" he asked.

"Probably. You have the U.S. government interacting with

another country, a state in which it is illegal to take national treasures out of their country."

# # #

Due to the steamy weather in Northern Virginia, my clothes never dried, always damp; I needed to wash and dry my garments. I walked through the outside pathway to the laundry room, next to the swimming pool at the Residence Inn. When I opened the door to the small room, with multiple washing machines and dryers stacked on the right and left walls, I found Carla Diaz doing her wash and standing in the middle of a narrow pathway between the washers and dryers.

"Hello, Donnell. Happy to see you again." She gave me that whitey-bright smile of hers. She had on short shorts and a tight, blue tee shirt. I found my eyes slipping down to stare at her shirt front, but I forced myself to jerk my chin up and focus my eyes between her eyebrows.

"Hi, Carla. How was your day? Call me Don."

"Don, it was great. To let you know, on the weekend, people jam into this laundry room."

I felt doubly lucky: finding Carla in the laundry room with no one around. "I have to clean my clothes because I am out of fresh garments."

Again, she bathed me in that whitey-bright smile. "Have you found some tasty places to eat yet? I do love a good meal. A fun place is the Sweet Sailing Tavern with fantastic beer and food."

She took red panties out of the dryer, gave them a shake in the air, and locked eyes with me. "How about you? Do you like a good meal?"

My mouth had gone dry. "So, Carla, why don't I take you out to the Sweet Sailing Tavern Monday night—for a delicious meal?" I stared at her red underwear.

She grinned back and laid her panties on top of her dry clothes. I had spoken in a croak, momentarily losing control of my voice box.

She ran her tongue across her upper lip. "Why, Don . . . so sweet of you. Meet you in our motel lobby. Six-thirty Monday night?"

"See you then, Carla. I look forward to eating a sumptuous meal."

She had finished her laundry. "I had hoped you'd call me in the evening, to find things to do. I get along well with my friends, but I think I like to party more than they."

She left with a smile and a laundry bag of clean clothes. I could only stare at her undulating shorts and think what was underneath.

Then I distinctly heard the words she sang:

Don't just tell me you love me

 Guide me out into delight

I couldn't wait to go out with Carla Monday night.

NORTHERN VIRGINIA—19 JUNE 2000

Midsummer evening—dusk— balmy—lovely nightfall. On the grassy lawn, nubile women in light-colored, floral dresses socialize in happy talk. I walk toward the group, stepping on the clipped grass. Ahead— a table covered with a white tablecloth—ice and soft drinks. The women in airy dresses and men in sports coats—on a patio—dance to slow music. A black-haired woman in a white dress—her back to me—young men in sports coats around her—stillness, silence—I stop behind her—and wait. She turns slowly. Glowing with a calm, beatific expression—it's Carla.

Hot and perspiring, I woke from my dream, darkness outside my window. I kicked off the bed covers and turned over. Tossed and turned. Couldn't sleep. Early Monday morning, I drove to Sook's office building. Sook, Bin, Yeong-ho, and I met in the fifth floor conference room.

Sook stood, observing out the windows, which stretched from floor to ceiling along one wall. "Yesterday, I talked with Yeong-ho and Bin. They alarmed Seong-gi disappeared."

I paused in the doorway. "You believe someone kidnapped him?"

"We have known Seong-gi fifty years. Believe robbers made him tell combination to the door. I fear for his safety."

"Me, too," I said.

I closed the door, set a Styrofoam cup of coffee down on the long table, and sat under the fluorescent lights. "Where we left off, you had found the gold crown and decided to desert the army. Is that right?"

Sook nodded and took a seat.

"Where were you relative to the Americans and the ROK Army?"

"The U.S. troops fought along western border of Pusan Perimeter, following the Naktong River," Bin explained. "ROK troops fought alongside the northern-most side of Pusan Perimeter, including the port city of Pohang. The four of us deserted from location south of main defense line of ROK Army."

I took out my notepad and glanced at Yeong-ho. "Would you restart your story?"

Clean shaven with white hair parted to his left, Yeong-ho revived the tale of the mortar squad's departure. "We deserted morning, leaving battlefield above Gyeongju, scrambled over countryside to dry road and followed it south. Lugging mortar, we look like four soldiers going to rejoin unit. We sweated, as temperatures high all day."

Sook set his cup of hot tea on the table and added to the story. "Clouds of dust rose ahead of us as ROK rushed convoys of troops and supplies up to defensive line. We got off the road to hide as trucks passed. We took to hills or marched along gravel roads through countryside, stopping only to eat rice at farmhouse.

"In late morning, see dead tree, as familiar a landmark as church bell tower over small village. Tree split into two blackened trunks, positioned near grove of oaks and thicket of underbrush.

"We moved into thicket and erected shelter. Soon, a small arbor, hidden from road, protected us from being seen by MPs. From the arbor, we heard ROK convoys racing up and down motorway."

I stopped writing in my notepad. "You saw no one you knew?"

"Old man and woman in farmhouse gave us rice," Yeong-ho replied. "Never saw them before or since."

"Once settled behind trees and bushes, we wondered how to get out of country," Sook resumed. "We not have money or know how to convert smaller artifacts into currency. We discussed options, like staying with our families or hiding in mountains.

"Seong-gi said we had to get jewelry out of country. Leaving meant he deserted, and looking back, I think he did not want to leave his family. But he would not leave us, his three friends, feeling he had to help us get away."

"None of us knew how to leave Korea," Yeong-ho said. "I not know but leaving had seemed like good idea night before."

I suggested we take a break, so I could refill my coffee cup in the kitchenette. When I returned to the conference room, Bin explained he had been the one to think of a way to desert their country.

"My mother had always considered my uncle to be family disgrace," Bin began. "He smuggled goods in and out of South Korea. He had centered illegal trafficking around Pohang seaport, northeast of our arbor.

"My black-sheep uncle considered me his favorite nephew. Either my uncle would help us, or we had to forget to desert and rejoin ROK Army. If our military held North Koreans back before Pohang, I had chance of finding him."

I stopped taking notes and quizzed Bin. "How did you contact your uncle?"

"I decided walk to Uncle's cove on coast," Bin said, "a trip about two hours. If I left the arbor immediately, and if Uncle worked at bay, I figured I could talk with him and return by evening."

"Bin's uncle represented our only chance, if he would help," Sook explained. "Seong-gi said give uncle a tenth of treasure, to smuggle us out of Korea. We agreed with this proportion."

"I planned to meet my three friends at arbor that night or next morning," Bin said. "Timing depended on whether I could locate Uncle. I took what little rice we had left and set out for coast."

"Seong-gi, Sook, and I searched for food," Yeong-ho said. "Later, when sun went down, we planned to return to the Silla mound, acting like stealthy cats—get treasure."

# # #

"Late that evening, Bin trudged back to our hideout," Yeong-ho said. "As he returned, he smiled broadly. His face told us he had found his uncle, and uncle had accepted him into family business— smuggling."

Bin grinned at Sook and Yeong-ho at the conference-room table. "My friends saw me and gave me big hug. Told them ROK Army waged significant battle above Pohang. Uncle did smuggling in area below combat region.

"My uncle not willing to accept tenth of the relics to smuggle us out of Korea—he wanted half. I argued with Uncle, like grim negotiator, until he agreed to one-fifth. No like paying out a fifth of treasure, but we had no other means to break away from Korea."

Yeong-ho nodded agreement with Bin and accidentally knocked his cup off the table, spilling tea on the varied-brown-colored rug. Sook ran for paper towels. Once the liquid had been mopped up, Bin resumed telling about his uncle's plan to leave the next night. "Uncle had scheduled ship to depart Korea in twenty-four hours. We were not to talk to crew or passengers about treasure. Uncle told me bring any rice and fruit we had.

"Next evening, we traveled eight miles to ship in cove. Had to be careful while we hiked as many ROK soldiers camped between us and departure point."

"I feared, once we were at sea, ship's sailors would kill us and take relics," Yeong-ho said.

"I pointed out we had no substitute plan," Bin responded. "Escape by Uncle's ship was our first, best, and only chance. We would toss mortar aside at bay, keep our small arms weapons, and not let anyone see inside our two canvas bags."

"Seong-gi said plan could work," Sook said. "He reasoned we could flee with treasure. He worried, once we left Korea, who would take care of his parents?"

I thumbed through my notepad. "Was this the point where you went back to retrieve the canvas bags?"

"With darkness, four of us sneaked back to crater in deserted battleground," Sook replied. "We saw no lights, heard no human sounds. Area had air of abandonment, with few dogs we chased off with dirt clods, scattered equipment from battle a day past, splintered tree trunks, and explosion craters everywhere.

"Crept to where we had set up mortar. Then found mound and crater. We four dropped down into pit."

"For several minutes, we poked and prodded sides of crater," Yeong-ho interrupted. "Bin's shovel hit solid object—one of the bags."

"We dug up two duffle bags with the artifacts," Bin added, "occasionally raising our heads above crater sides and peering left to right, like robbers digging in graveyard."

I held up my open hand to stop their story. "This could be important. Did anyone see you? Could you have run across the thieves there?"

All three shook their heads, evidently rejecting a connection to the burglars.

"What happened next?"

"Clutching our bundles, we headed back to our hideout," Bin continued.

I sipped the last of my cold coffee. "I suppose you slept through the morning and headed out in mid-afternoon for the coast?"

"Yes, and when we got to the departure point, it was almost dark," Sook said. "We found quiet cove had sandy beach along water, bordered by green brush and shrubs. Farther back and nearly hidden in darkness were rice fields and little hills. Bin's uncle, tall man, waited for us on sand.

"He had herded cargo and two families out to ship. Because of poor eyesight, he talked face-to-face and close. Satisfied we had valuables, he told us get in rowboat when it returned from ship."

It sounded like lots of people were at the jump-off point. Would it have been possible their path crossed with our burglar there? "Anyone on the beach who could have seen you leave with the bags?"

"Nobody," Sook answered. "Beach empty when we got there."

"Uncle yelled we had to leave," Bin said. "Seong-gi stood still with his rifle and mortar tube. When the rowboat arrived at beach to carry us, he didn't move. I shouted for him to get in boat."

Yeong-ho sipped from his new teacup, placed it on the table, and picked up the story. "Seong-gi said goodbye and told us to write him when we got to America."

"There on the beach, I explained he had to go with us," Sook said. "Told him he had agreed to leave. Said we followed him because he leads."

Sook stopped talking and seemed to be choked up, maybe out of admiration for his old squad leader. He recovered. "Seong-gi said he had to stay behind and watch after his parents. He asked us, his three friends, to keep his portion of treasure safe for him. He would rejoin the ROK Army."

"At same time, my uncle waved his arms and yelled at us to get in boat and row to ship," Bin said. "We had to leave."

"Seong-gi repeated he would stay," Sook said. "If MPs asked where three friends were, he would say he didn't know.

"As we rowed out to ship, Seong-gi gestured goodbye from the beach. Before he disappeared in the black of night, he waved at us.

He shouted 'goodbye' to us, calling out each name, in turn, his voice fading until we couldn't hear him."

# # #

I stopped writing in my notepad and faced Sook, Bin, and Yeong-ho. "What happened next? We've read our way through the first months of the war, found the gold crown, and left South Korea. The journal stops there."

"What you mean?" Sook asked.

"How did you get the crown to the Great Falls house?"

Sook leaned back in his chair at the conference-room table. "Bin's uncle got three of us into Canada. We then crossed from Canada to U.S. with two canvas bags."

I recorded this information in my notepad. "And Seong-gi?"

"He survived the Korean War and made his home in South Korea."

"Who helped you in America?"

Sook seemed to think about my question for a second. "Bin's uncle assisted us with contacts he established during his smuggling activities."

Yeong-ho had been reaching across the table trying to grab some extra cookies. Finally, he gave up and walked around the table to get a handful. When we laughed at his clowning, he gave a bow and sat back down at the table.

"What did you live on?" I asked.

"We sold smallest Silla artifacts to get started," Sook replied. "Settled in Virginia and launched careers. Began our new professions by studying first in community college and then a four-year university."

His voice trailed off as if reflecting on those days. "All three of us became U.S. citizens. Over time, we established careers. I am engineer, Bin the executive, and Yeong-ho the accountant."

Someone sold those lesser Silla pieces. Whoever marketed them knew about the treasure. "Who peddled those smaller pieces for you?"

"Isaac Hunter arranged sale for us. Bin's uncle recommended him."

My review of the squad's departure from Korea netted me two

new suspects: Isaac Hunter and Bin's uncle. "Did Hunter see all the relics?"

Sook took a sip of tea and set the cup back on the conference table. "Yes."

"Did he estimate the total value of the artifacts?"

"Five million dollars. Hunter said he could get that sum if sold secretly to private collectors."

"After you sold the smallest pieces, how did you handle the remainder of the treasure?"

"We combined our four-fifths of treasure in protected exhibit room at Great Falls home."

A timeline for the four soldiers had begun to take shape in my head: college, a job, and then marriage. "Are you three, four counting Seong-gi, married with a family?

"Yes," Sook answered.

Had they told their families? "If one of you four die, who gets their share?"

Sook paused and placed his forefinger on his lips. "When we married, we didn't tell our families about exhibit room. Wanted to keep the artifacts secret from our wives and children."

Sook turned to Bin and Yeong-ho and spoke with them in Korean. I kept hearing the Korean word *ai*—sounds like eye—which means child. Sook explained to me. "When one of us four passes away, we agree eldest son or daughter of deceased soldier entitled to one-fourth part of treasure. None of us four has died—yet."

NORTHERN VIRGINIA—19 JUNE 2000

After Bin and Yeong-ho left and returned to work, Sook and I sat in the conference room. I juggled two conflicting images of Sook Park: the warrior and treasure hunter named Sook contrasted with the immigrant engineer named Sook Park as if Indiana Jones in the *Temple of Silla* had transformed into a stolid capitalist. What would I have done in Sook's shoes? Same as he did: grabbed the gold, departed the country, and enjoyed the rest of my life.

Across the table, Sook bit his lower lip. "I think, deep down, I disappointed in myself for deserting ROK Army. Did my youth make me vulnerable—took wrong pathway?"

Sook stared out the windows. "Even now, fifty years later, I remember seeing the death, destruction, and determination of ROK soldiers. Most young people don't think of dying and killing—but I saw both as I fought for my fellow countrymen and my life.

"Summer bloodbath began when enemy invaded. I learned in short time—on battlefield, not classroom—about life and cruelty. Today, I realize I was part of something bigger, fighting to save my country and friends."

I sensed Sook spoke to himself, to some inner torment. His eyes didn't focus on me, but stared at something only he could see, in the far distance. "I stole treasure," he said. "But I look back at experience that summer as exposure no other treasure could have given me."

Sook, 67 years old in the year 2000, was second-guessing the 17-year old youth in 1950. Maybe the recent theft had caused Sook to re-examine his conduct, to question if he had been virtuous, to ask if his life's achievement had been notable. Perhaps uncertainty—brought on by a reappraisal—bothered Sook. I didn't have a cheerful answer to give him.

We both grew silent.

I looked down at the table and spoke slowly. "It is what it is. It wasn't like you killed someone to get the treasure. I would have done the same."

He looked at me with a pitiful expression, downcast eyes, and droopy mouth. I placed Seong-gi's journal on the table. "In youth, most of us forsook a true love, a lost love, and, years later, came to regret that decision. Just as an early-morning haze from the ocean drifts away with the sun, you forget it; you move on; you did what you had to."

Sook slumped in his chair and stared at the floor. "Who took the treasure?"

He had changed topics back to the investigation.

"Good question. I have a few suspects in mind to interrogate."

I brushed down my cowlick while I reflected. "In the remaining hours of daylight, you need to come with me—partner with me—to question possible perpetrators. Quizzing them will help us find the criminal."

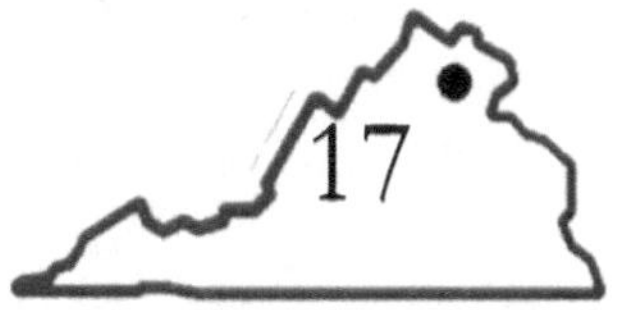

NORTHERN VIRGINIA—19 JUNE 2000

Early afternoon, I drove Sook in the Mustang with the AC blasting out relief. Both of us dressed for the tropic-like atmosphere. Sook donned a gray summer suit. I wore a blue sports jacket, a white polo shirt, and khakis. I carried no weapon other than my engaging personality.

Sook guided me through the dense traffic to Isaac Hunter's place of business. We parked and entered Hunter's building, where he worked in a suite of offices. A secretary steered us to him. Sook, Isaac, and I met in a small conference room with a row of windows overlooking a broad street, rows of eight-to-ten story buildings, and the Capitol in the distance.

Standing on his toes—as if to elongate his five- and one-half feet tall and obese frame—Isaac struck me as someone with a Napoleonic complex. Wearing a dark-gray suit of light wool, combined with a bright blue shirt, dark blue tie, dark slacks, and Oxford dress shoes with brogues, he showed a sartorial elegance. Above all, Isaac's broad grin screamed insincerity, his eyes staring without blinking, as a crocodile might do just before chomping its prey.

"A pleasure to meet you, Mr. Gannon. Not sure I can help." He leaned forward, stared at my face, and projected the impression of giving me his undivided attention, like a pillager searching for loot.

"Mr. Park told me about his theft this past Monday. Wants me to inform him if anyone is selling Silla relics." He rubbed his hand over his advanced bald spot.

"Only know a little about the house in Great Falls." He took off his wire-rim glasses, wiped them, and put them on again. This guy couldn't stay still.

I took time to think, not so much to calm an inner nervousness but to try and slow down Isaac. "I understand, back when Mr. Park and his colleagues arrived in the U.S., you helped them sell the smaller pieces. Is that right?"

"I helped him and his colleagues when they arrived fifty years ago."

Isaac stared out the window before continuing. "My clients demand confidentiality. Spoke with no one about Mr. Park's holdings."

Isaac exhibited a variety of neuroses as he dipped his forehead and tilted his chin to the side. I didn't trust this fast-talking man, but that didn't make him complicit in the burglary.

"Were you ever in the exhibit room that held the artifacts?"

"Occasionally. Always had an escort."

"Do you know the combination to get past the door?"

"I went to the house with Park to appraise the displays. He opened the door."

He stopped again to glance out the windows. "Saw the relics in the presence of Mr. Park."

"How difficult would it be to sell the stolen artifacts?" I asked.

He rubbed his bare spot for several seconds. It's why he's so bald. "Hard to set a transaction price. Challenging to keep the sale of such scarce objects secret."

"Would you know if the pieces—the crown, a Buddha statue, belts, earrings, swords—were being offered for sale now?"

"I'll alert Mr. Park the moment I detect Korean relics on the market." He paused a minute to brush lint off the sleeve of his dark gray coat. "These antiques are twelve to thirteen hundred years old. Worth millions. Their unexpected availability would ignite a market hullabaloo."

Isaac began a soliloquy. "Selling artifacts is done by either low-end or high-end dealer. Low-end artifacts sell at garage sales or a farmer's market. Artifacts can be legal or illegal and authentic or fake." Isaac glanced at Sook and me with his lizard stare.

"Dealers in the high-end trade of relics follow the law of the country where the relic originated. Each law establishes how a relic can be unearthed and legally leave its home country." He repositioned his glasses.

"Thank you, Mr. Hunter," I said. "But I wanted to ask—"

"In the past, to sell relics, the looter had to split the profits with intermediaries," Isaac continued without pause. "Using the internet cuts out the broker. Also, the robbers are shifting their focus from plundering actual historical locations to counterfeiting archeological objects."

I stood up. "We have another appointment."

Isaac ignored my signal and chattered onward. "Alongside genuine relics, forgers are now selling fake artifacts on the internet. For the sale of a national treasure, the authorities can charge a seller with breaking international law. Peddling a fake is a different matter."

He rubbed his bald spot again.

"What you saying?" Sook asked. "Silla relics could be for sale anywhere?"

"No—the opposite," Isaac replied. "Your artifacts are too valuable to offer in a flea market or to post on the internet." He turned toward the window again. "We need to watch the high-end dealers, networking with a small group of people I know well."

If he knew as much as he claimed, he would be aware of the CHA. "Did you know that the FBI and the Cultural Heritage Administration of Korea accused Mr. Park of stealing artifacts?"

"It wouldn't surprise me if the authorities picked up a rumor and went fishing. South Korea is like Egypt: both countries lost many antiquities."

Isaac paused again, fiddling with the knot in his tie. His fidgeting made me nervous.

"Chasing rumors and having proof of theft are mutually exclusive events," Isaac said. "As unalike as a pea and a lima bean in a pod. Were the FBI to contact me, I wouldn't betray Mr. Park."

I began to walk toward the door but turned back to Isaac. "Do you know Seong-gi Kim? He was Sook's squad leader in the Korean War. Has he contacted you lately?"

Isaac jerked his head up, his lizard stare changed to a wide-eyed look, and he paused before answering. "I've met him . . . one of Mr. Park's colleagues. Lives in Seoul, if I remember correctly—haven't heard from Mr. Kim in over a year."

He stopped talking and gave me an opening to pose a question. "About two years ago, a Mr. Wang Gang approached Sook. Mr.

Gang had heard rumors Sook owned a collection of Silla artifacts. Do you know this man?"

Isaac adjusted his glasses. "Several of my colleagues, who deal in antiquities, have done business with him. Mr. Gang can be quite nasty if he feels cheated."

"How might he have learned of the Silla treasures?"

He shrugged his shoulders and held both hands out to his sides. "High-end dealers in antiquities treat their clients' transactions as hush-hush. But they love to exchange scurrilous gossip about who might have extraordinary works—hitting the mark occasionally by witless luck."

"Would Mr. Gang burglarize the Great Falls house?"

"He wouldn't think twice about stealing a work of art," Isaac said. "On the other hand, he's wealthy, and he buys art."

"What does he do with his art?"

"He's fond of publicly exhibiting his pieces. Has a superb collection of Asian paintings, jewelry, and statues in the basement of his Leesburg home. Were Gang to steal Asian artifacts, he might hide them in his private collection."

Acting like we had become close friends, Isaac stood up and walked us out of the suite of offices. Sook had sworn Isaac was trustworthy, but I wanted Bruce to do a background check and confirm Isaac's honesty.

Back in the car, Sook asked, "Did you pick up any clues from Isaac?"

"No. And at the rate we are gathering valuable clues, we should be able to solve the case in twice the time," I said ironically.

"Don't despair. An old saying goes, 'You can't get blood from a hermit.'"

"Sook, that's a *turnip*."

He gave me a blank stare.

"Let's go talk with the uncle," I said.

# # #

Partway to the warehouse in Baltimore, I told Sook, "The South Koreans, the Coast Guard, confiscated a smuggling ship, one used by Bin's uncle."

Sook turned to me but didn't speak.

I reached behind me in the backseat area, snagged a small package, and gave it to him.

He turned it over in his hands. "What is this?"

"A mobile phone. Maybe the FBI tapped your land-based phones. Use it when you call us."

Out of the corner of my eye, I noticed he shrugged. "Is this necessary?"

His resistance aggravated me. "Don't ask. Just do it."

He seemed to consider whether he would use the phone or not. "Okay. I will use it when I contact Roth Security."

The vehicles on I-95 moved at high speed in the late morning traffic. As our client relaxed in the passenger seat, he remarked on how he'd enjoyed his visit to the mountains of North Carolina to see Roth. I assured him he would see more when we split the salvage in Asheville.

I pulled into the parking lot around the warehouse. The dock area behind the building swarmed with Korean workers like a mob of kids at a birthday party in a fast-food restaurant.

Sook grinned and pointed to the swarm unloading cargo. "You said Bin's uncle had economic trouble. He must be well on his way back to wealth."

We sat in the Mustang for a few minutes, observing the activity, and then climbed out and walked to the front of the building, the side facing away from the Patapsco River.

This mass of workers—unloading and transporting cargo from the ship—reminded me of a beehive, but I didn't see the queen bee, the uncle. Sook stopped one of the dock workers and spoke in Korean. The worker hunted down the uncle while we waited outside the warehouse, cooled by a breeze coming off the river.

Shortly, Seong-woo ambled to us through the entrance. "Hello, S-s-sook . . . and Mr. Gannon. Had m-m-messy morning, running here and there. We talk inside." As before, we sat with him at the pitted-wood table near the front entrance.

The building shielded me from the sun, making the interior dim with bearable temperature. I decided to ask the uncle about the bustle of his warehouse, giving me a way to ask about his confiscated boat. "Your men are unloading a large cargo. Business is good?"

He shook his head up and down. "Very good."

I pointed in the direction of the cargo ship at the dock. "This ship came from South Korea?"

More shaking his head backward and forward.

"You lost a ship off the coast of South Korea," I said. "The Coast Guard said the ship smuggled goods."

The uncle leaned over the table to position his face closer to me. "Coast Guard say I hide cargo, but I not. S-s-someone transported phony $100 bills in my cargo hold. I-I-I not know counterfeit bills there." As the uncle talked in his raspy voice, I thought of a rewording of that beautiful line from the movie *Casablanca*: 'I am shocked . . . SHOCKED . . . to discover the smuggling of hundred-dollar bills is going on here.'

"Occasionally Coast Guard seize one of my ships. Seizure has happened for many years, but not often. I consider loss of one ship as expense of doing business."

His workers continued to scurry past us, unloading his vessel as he spoke.

"I have m-m-many ships in transit any time. With limited number of inspectors and police agents to s-s-search millions of shipments arriving at U.S. ports, I have good chance of not being caught."

In other words, the uncle treated his lost vessel as an operational cost he deducted from his profit on the undetected smuggled goods. "What kind of . . . hmm . . . shipping do you do?"

The uncle again moved his face close. "No drugs. Those in drug trade known to use weapons to settle their differences."

"Has Seong-gi contacted you recently?"

The uncle looked quizzically and stuck his face even closer. "Have not talked with him for long time. Why you ask?"

"He missing," Sook said. "May have been kidnapped. The police can't find my old friend."

"I am s-s-superstitious," the uncle said in his scratchy voice. "I believe unfortunate happenings come in threes. The first is theft and second is kidnapping. Not good."

Was he trying to act as a mystic, or did he have a hunch?

I used a different approach to find out how much the seized ship hurt his business. "I notice your warehouse needs a little work. Does that mean money is tight for you?"

"S-s-saving money more important than having beautiful building. Extra money lets me make investments."

Seong-woo's answers seemed to imply he managed his financial empire well and didn't need to burglarize houses. Maybe he did have money, but he remained a suspect.

As Sook and I drove back to Northern Virginia, my mind viewed the investigation as a labyrinth. Not every tunnel would lead to a solution, but we searched in every passageway. If the thieves took the Silla treasure out of the country, our task would get more difficult.

#

Sook and I drove to a suburban house near Great Falls to meet Sook's gardener, who had just finished his afternoon chores for a client. Parked alongside the road ahead of us, I saw a white Ford F-150 pickup with Garcia Landscape emblazoned on the side. Santino Garcia, a smiling man about five feet four inches tall and maybe 140 pounds, stood next to his truck.

Sook shook hands with him. "Santino, thank you for making time see me on short notice. This man, Mr. Gannon, works to upgrade my building security."

"Mr. Park, you've been good to me for many years. How can I help?"

"Have you noticed anything unusual around my house?"

Garcia smiled and rubbed his hand over his short, black hair. "I arrive every Monday morning. I am outside, but I see your house securely locked up—no doors or windows open. Sometimes, Manny sees me and waves to me from the house."

"Did you see anything unusual this past Monday?"

"I came in the morning as usual. Everything appeared normal around the neighborhood."

Garcia stopped and smiled, showing beautiful teeth under a full mustache. He had a genial and quick-witted personality, an advantage for a successful landscape gardener.

Sook turned the questioning over to me.

"Mr. Garcia, has anything looked different? Anything out of the ordinary?"

The gardener paused as if trying to remember anything to reinforce his value to his client. "Well, one time the dog—belonging to the house near Georgetown Pike—got loose and ran through Mr.

Park's yard. I told the lady her dog had been dashing through the neighborhood. She thanked me."

"Anything else?"

"Another time I saw two men coming through the woods behind the house, but they turned around and went back toward the river." Seeing our startled expressions, the gardener stopped talking.

Maybe this was what Roth meant by searching through endless dead ends. I drew in a deep breath. "Start at the beginning and tell us about those two men."

"Two Mondays ago, I had to finish a landscaping job in Sterling, Virginia, and I arrived at your house in late afternoon. As I finished in your yard, I saw two men walking through the woods. They saw me and turned around to go back the way they had come—as if they didn't want me to see them."

"Had you seen them before or since?" Sook asked.

"Just the one time."

Sook glanced at me and then faced Garcia again. "Describe them."

Garcia turned to put a rake in the back of his pickup and seemed to be forming his words. "I wasn't that near them. One moved like a young person, but the other had a white goatee and walked rigid, like an older man. I think they were Asian."

"Why Asian?"

"The eyes."

"If I brought a sketch artist to you, could you describe their faces to make drawings?"

"Too far away. I didn't pay much attention to them."

I took out the photographs I had of Seong-gi. "Mr. Garcia, these are pictures of a man who is missing in South Korea. Could this person have been one of the two you saw in the woods?"

He took his time studying each of the photographs of Seong-gi.

"I don't think this is the older man I saw that day."

Sook's mouth turned down in disappointment. Perhaps he had grown frustrated when Garcia couldn't remember more about the two men. "Santino, thank you for your help. If we have any further questions, could we call you again?"

"I'm always willing to help you, Mr. Park."

As I drove away, Sook said, "I fear for my friend, Seong-gi. Could these two men have taken my old squad leader?"

"Maybe, but we can't be sure."

I dropped Sook at his office and drove to my suite at the Residence Inn. I updated my notepad and read back through my observations on inspecting the crime scene and interviewing suspects. I had made progress going through the paths of the maze. To reward myself, I took a Dogfish Head stout out of the refrigerator.

I drank a second stout and called Carla.

The phone rang five times until she answered. "Carla, this is Don. How are you?"

"Donnell! I'd been hoping you'd call."

She sounded happy to hear from me. "Been working on a case. Can't get to sleep. W-want to go for a drink?"

She hesitated a second. "A red-blooded woman can't say no. Trouble is I'm giving a presentation early tomorrow—you'd have to get me back in an hour."

"Done! Where do we go?"

"IHOP! I'm hungry. Treat me to an omelet and decaf coffee."

I drove the Mustang around to Carla's building. Tonight, she had on tight jeans and her college sweatshirt. She jumped in the car, flipped her ponytail as she turned her head, and gave me a peck on my cheek. Fifteen minutes later, we sat at IHOP drinking decaffeinated coffee, waiting for our omelets.

She seemed somber as if busy turning over serious thoughts. "Uh, you're a private investigator, aren't you?"

"Yeah."

She watched me for a moment. "Is your job confidential?"

"Like government confidential? Nope."

Carla poured decaf coffee from a thermos into her cup. "Uh, I've watched P.I.s on TV. What type are you? You shoot people?"

Funny question. Did she think I looked menacing? "Not as a P.I. Traded fire in Desert Storm in 1990 as a military policeman."

"Do you go undercover? Observe and get information on a suspect?"

Where did she plan to go with this? "Yeah."

Her brown eyes sparkled. "How do you follow someone without them knowing?"

"At the start, get all the information possible about the target's routines."

Our omelets arrived. At first, she ate in silence, but then she kept enquiring. "What are your rules of thumb—for tailing?"

She showed me a thoughtful side I hadn't seen earlier. "Be careful. If you see the person you follow, they can see you. If you know where the target's going, don't follow too close."

Carla opened her mouth to ask another question, but I interrupted. "Why all this interest?"

She finished the last of her omelet and appeared to compose a response. "Just think what you do is cool." Then she fired more queries at me. "Are you a noble P.I.? Do you right wrong?"

I want to be a noble guy. I try to do the right thing. "Yeah, I am. I do."

"I'm glad you're noble. I wouldn't want it any other way. Now, you better get me back."

I paid the bill and began walking her to the car. "I didn't think females had an interest in detective work."

Carla hooked her arms around my left arm. "Women are naturally curious. Why do you think the Nancy Drew books keep selling year after year?"

When I dropped her off in front of her building, she leaned over the console and kissed me. "Next time, don't wait so long to call."

Back in my suite, I went to bed, with thoughts of Carla dancing in my head. Tomorrow, Sook and I needed to check on Seong-gi. Where had he gone?

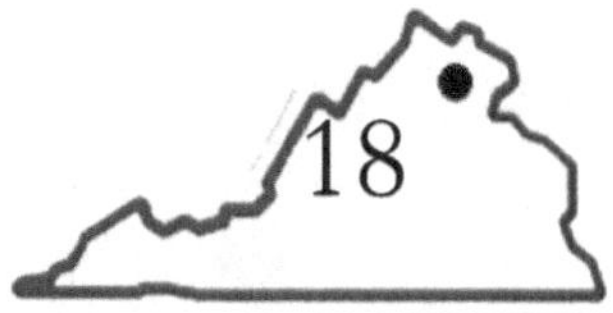

NORTHERN VIRGINIA—19 JUNE 2000

Late Monday evening, I returned to my suite in Herndon, grabbed a beer out of the refrigerator, and crumpled on the couch. Following an interval spent staring at the ceiling and growing impatient, I took a taxi to a car-rental facility at the Dulles Airport and leased an Everyman-looking car.

I bought a dark outfit—shirt, pants, and shoes—at K-Mart and drove to Leesburg around midnight, parking the rental among other vehicles and at a distance from the Gang house. My approach had always been to do fixed surveillance as far away from my target as my binoculars and camera would allow me. I fiddled with the interior lights until they remained unlit when the door opened.

The Gang house lights had been turned off except for illumination in two upstairs rooms. I guessed one chamber belonged to Gang and his wife, and the other to the bodyguard. Outdoor lights remained on throughout the night, shining next to the building. A portable generator stood at the rear of the house. Once the indoor lights went off, I saw no regular police patrols, private security, or dogs. Power lines brought electricity to the dwelling. A single police car patrolled through the neighborhood and left.

Part of my subconscious told me I needed to stop my wild scheme. I hadn't asked Roth to approve my plan. She'd have criticized me for childish behavior. Doing it without asking her had a dangerous side: she might need to get me out of jail if I got caught. Getting caught would result in my demotion as her top investigator. On the other hand, finding the crown and treasure at Gang's home would break open the case. I couldn't resist starting a break and enter.

I waited, nestled down in the long row of vehicles. My brain jumped around, pondering what I had accomplished today: discovering Sook's gardener saw two Asian men in the woods behind the Great Falls house. Finding those two unidentified Asian men in the greater metropolitan area—even if they remained in the U.S.— would be a dull slog.

Three youths walked down the street. I slumped further down in my driver's seat until they passed.

Going over everything I'd accomplished since arriving in Virginia, a fog of confusion clouded my mind. Since I hadn't been sleepy in my suite, I had had an urge to stay up. Now, as I waited and watched, I began to catnap.

Gang's back door opened and closed. My body flipped from a doze to alert in a blink. A large man—I recognized Big Guy— appeared. He walked around the property periphery as if seeking trespassers. Then he walked along the vehicle row, shining his flashlight inside the parked cars near the Gang abode.

Darn, he was sure to catch me if I stayed put in the car or cranked the engine and drove away. *What do I do?*

I opened the driver's side door, stooped down, slipped out onto the pavement, and pushed the door shut.

I lurched, crab-like, down the row of parked cars, moving away from him, putting the cars between me and any video cameras located outside the house.

I saw my chance and moved across the road to the grounds of a church.

Behind me, Big Guy shouted, "Hey you!"

I kept dashing and then hid among the cars in the church parking lot. I had blundered but hadn't yet crashed in flames. He had to catch me. I needed to be sneaky and deceptive. Across the street behind me, a dog began a loud barking. How big a group looked for me? I peeked around an SUV.

Big Guy remained across the street from the church and quarreled with a man about two heads shorter. A small terrier barked at Gang's bodyguard and pulled on a leash held by the short man. "What are you doing?" Big Guy shouted. "Why are you sneaking around the house?"

The small man stood his ground. "Get that damn light out of my face. I'm walking my dog."

"No, you aren't. You're lurking between cars."

"I live here. Go away."

Big Guy moved closer to the man. The man, his head rotated back apparently to see his assailant's face, cursed at him. The dog barked. I thought the small guy had to be thick in the brain or fearless.

They yelled a while longer and then broke off their argument. The small man walked away, his dog trailing along at the end of the leash. Big Guy rotated his body as if searching for someone and then walked back to the house.

My heart slowed its thumping. I felt childish but had to learn more about Gang. During my meeting with him last Friday, his face had been a mask, revealing nothing about any missing relics. To find if he hid the Silla artifacts in his basement, I'd have to go into his underground rooms. When subtlety and interrogation failed, my approach consisted of slam, bang, and run away afterwards.

When Big Guy returned to the house, I snuck back into my car and left Leesburg.

I returned to my suite at the Residence Inn, where my brain stopped racing. I went to bed and read a history book, *Guns, Germs, and Steel* by Jared Diamond. My reading that night was two pages when my eyelids drooped and crashed together. I barely got the book shut and the lights out before blackness settled in on me.

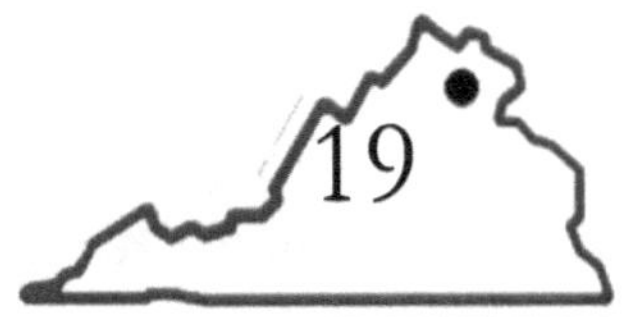

NORTHERN VIRGINIA—20 JUNE 2000

Someone banged on my suite door. I submerged my head in a pillow. The banging continued, joined by shouting. Dressed in long pajama pants and a tee shirt, I climbed out of bed and padded barefoot to the door, with light from the emerging sun edging around the drapes in the living room to light my way. An agitated, red-eyed Sook confronted me. "Seong-gi is dead," his voice quivered.

Pushing myself to wake up, I rubbed my eyes and then gawked at Sook. "What'd you say?"

"Old friend dead."

Sook paced around my small living room until I made him sit on the couch. "How do you know?"

Grimaces formed on Sook's face and tears generated trails over their folds. "Son told me. Police took son to identify his father's body."

"When?"

"Son called me hour ago."

"Where did the police find the body?"

"Washed up . . . on Han-River bank."

"How long was he in the water?"

Sook bit his lip and seemed deep in thought. "Police told son . . . about two weeks."

"What else?"

Sook stood up and paced the room again, loosening his tie. "Killer shot Seong-gi in head. Body wrapped in plastic sheath."

The burglary had become a kidnapping, which had become a homicide. "Clues?"

"I don't know."

His body kept shaking, telling me he had fallen into some deep turmoil. I had to get him calm. I wanted coffee to shake off my sleep grogginess. After getting Sook to sit again and offering him tea, I slipped into the kitchen. "What do the police know?"

"They told son they have no suspect."

I started the stove to boil water. "The family never got a call from the kidnappers, do I have that right? Captors just murdered Seong-gi?"

"Killers didn't contact anyone."

I sat on the couch beside Sook. "What did the son tell the police about you? Do they know you called?"

"Son told investigators I phoned. Said I old friend who had stayed in touch with his father. Detectives do not want talk to me."

"What do you think happened?" I asked.

He continued to weep. "Kidnappers killed my old squad leader when he told them combination to open door. Because we took gold from Korea. We got him killed."

I felt embarrassed and helpless. I gave him paper towels from the kitchen to dry his eyes. "What did you tell the son? You didn't say the kidnappers took his father because of what happened fifty years ago, did you?"

Sook dried his eyes with the paper towel. "Didn't know what to say. Son seemed hysterical about father's death. I said nothing about tomb."

"Is he the oldest son?"

Sook's face took on an aggrieved expression. "Yes. He gets one-fourth of Silla artifacts."

He sobbed again and wiped his eyes. "Just now, that is one-fourth of nothing."

I rotated my university ring on my finger and considered the situation. "Hold off telling anyone in Seong-gi's family about the treasure. Keep in contact with the son. In case it turns out the thieves took the stolen relics to Korea, we will need his help."

The ante had just gone up in our quest for the stolen gold. Our antagonist had acted with malice. I needed to get hold of my weapon, to meet the malice.

#

Sook left to console Bin and Yeong-ho. I absorbed the news about the killing and picked up breakfast at IHOP. Back in my room, eating pancakes and drinking coffee, I phoned Roth, reporting the murder. I also gave her a detailed account of my interview with Isaac Hunter and the uncle, Seong-woo.

When I finished, Roth said, "Our case is changing—from painful to ugly. You have been responding to the murderer's schemes and not initiating the action. You are acting like the killer sealed you in a coffin."

I shouted back at her without thinking. "How was I to know? The Seoul police just found the old corporal."

I could hear her fingers tapping on her desk. "I pay you to know. Your progress does not gratify me."

I waited before replying. "What do you want out of me?"

"That's the thing about anticipating," Roth said. "If you don't, you can't understand it. If you do, I don't need to explain."

I seethed with fury. "Maybe I should have connected the missing man in Korea with the burglary in Virginia, but I didn't. I focused on interviewing a dead man."

Roth could be aggravating. She waited a full minute before continuing. "How do you break out of your coffin?"

"The death occurred in Korea. Our clients took the relics from there. Likely the burglars picked up the door combination there."

"And?"

"We need to expand our investigation into Korea."

I waited to hear what Roth believed.

"I surmise that an individual or individuals killed the old squad leader," she began. "Then they left South Korea and entered this country to pilfer the relics."

She had a point. "I'll ask Sook Park who recently arrived from South Korea. If he doesn't know, then he can ask people in the Korean-American community."

"Instruct Mr. Park to stay in touch with the son," Roth ordered. "If the Korean authorities ever prove that the three Koreans stole national treasures, then we need to do a bunk—as the British say—and disengage from this case."

I took a sip of coffee and thought through Roth's words. "You want me to stay in the Virginia area?"

She waited several moments before responding. "These villains have stymied us in Northern Virginia, but we need to keep investigating there—where the thieves stole the treasure. We don't know if the burglars have removed the gold from the U.S. or not."

"I'm not going to Korea?"

"I hesitate to investigate a murder in a country where we don't know the culture and don't speak the language," she said. "However, we need to find out about the person in South Korea who planned the theft."

I knew what kind of person would execute an old man and dump his body in a river. "This killer is vicious."

"The thieves murdered Seong-gi," Roth replied. "We have to assume they might kill again."

"My pistol is back in my room in Asheville. If I understand the Virginia laws, it will take more than a day to get a handgun legally."

Roth didn't speak again until at least a minute had elapsed. This call involved a lot of silence. She had to be thinking through possibilities. "I've changed my mind. I'm sending you to South Korea to team up with a Korean P.I."

Had to find my passport. Get a ticket. Tell Sook I would be away. "What about Virginia?"

"After Korea, you will go back to Northern Virginia. Mickey will join you there with your pistol."

"One day," I interjected, "we will look back and remember this time as—just when things were gloomiest—a gunfight broke out."

Roth ignored my grand humor and continued to organize. "As soon as it is daylight in Korea, I will contact private-investigation agencies there. You and a Korean operative will search for background information on the mortar squad—find out who planned the theft."

"I will not probe the murder, is that right?"

"Avoid interfering with the police. You and our agent will not directly investigate the murder. After I hire somebody, I'll call you."

She cut off the call.

I finished my pancakes and drank the last of my coffee. I wondered what kind of breakfast I would eat in Korea.

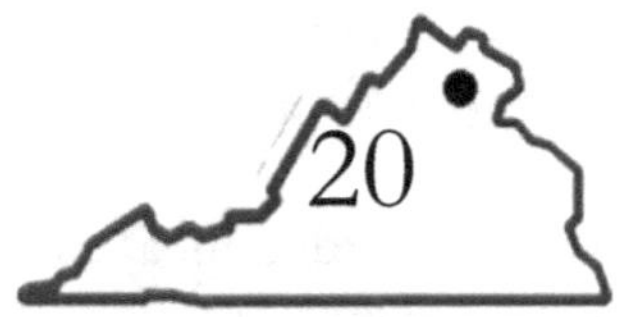

NORTHERN VIRGINIA – 20 JUNE 2000

Early Tuesday afternoon, I drove to meet Sook. I found him leaning over his office desk, pounding on its surface with the open palm of his left hand, and talking on his phone. He slammed down the receiver. "Wife says FBI at my Reston home. Have warrant to search house. You come, I drive!"

We took the elevator down five floors and rushed to his BMW parked in front of his building. I sat in the passenger seat. "What about the Great Falls house? Are the authorities also there, where you kept the Silla relics?"

Sook shook his head. "Manny would have called me if FBI banged on door."

"What do you suppose the FBI can find at your home?"

"Not a thing."

"Are you sure?"

Sook sped around a slowpoke car. "Don't annoy me. Don't want people in my house."

We arrived at his home in Reston at the same time as his lawyer. The FBI had stretched black-and-white barricade tape along the street and parked two black SUVs in front of Sook's house. Walking to the front door, I noted his lawn spread out over an acre with well-maintained flowering bushes and trees.

We were stopped at the front door by a man in white overalls with FBI stenciled across the back. "You can't enter. This building is closed off for a search warrant."

"I live here," Sook said. "This is my house."

I held up my P.I. license. "My name is Gannon. I provide security for Mr. Park."

The agent stood aside and waved us past him. Inside the house, investigators in white overalls went through the rooms, rolling hand trolleys, stacked with empty boxes, intended for sealing collected evidence. The agents had opened drawers and cabinets throughout the house.

Two individuals, who went together like beer and ice cream, stood in the living room. Beer—a shorter, white man, wearing a pressed blue suit, white dress shirt, and a tie not too tight, not too loose— seemed to be the agent in charge. Beer might as well have had "I Am a Cop" written in black lettering on his forehead. Ice Cream appeared to be a Korean male, tall and sinewy, wearing a well-tailored black suit with white shirt and black tie. Viewing the sartorial splendor of the investigators, I wondered if I'd strayed into a Sunday church service.

Using his outdoor voice, Beer introduced himself as an FBI agent and then presented Ice Cream. "This is Mr. Ji-hun Cho. He is an investigator with the Cultural Heritage Administration of Korea, the CHA."

Bingo! I had identified Ji-hun as the Korean leading the search for the Silla artifacts.

Ji-hun spoke to us in bureaucratic English with a slow, deliberate, speech pattern. "I am representative of South Korean government. I safeguard the integrity of our national tradition."

Sook's lawyer argued with the FBI man about the basis for the warrant. Beer explained—based on confidential sources—the FBI suspected Sook of stealing Korean relics.

While they bickered, I watched the CHA agent out of the corner of my eye. He talked like a bureaucrat, but appeared limber, sinewy, and more a man of action than a desk-bound administrator.

Agent Cho stood aside from the group, a mysterious person staying above the information exchange. "Where did Agent Cho get his information," I asked, "alleging Mr. Park stole ancient relics?"

All conversation ceased. The FBI man confronted me. "I'm sorry. I didn't get your name. Who are you?"

To talk to Cho, I had to get past a gatekeeper, Beer. "I'm a licensed private investigator, providing security for Mr. Park's company. My name is Donnell Gannon."

Beer frowned and then pressed his face close to Sook's face. "Is that correct, Mr. Park? He works for you?"

"Yes. I too like know informer who claims I stole."

Beer appeared to puff out his chest and reply in a loud voice. "Agent Cho is investigating a possible crime, and his sources are confidential."

I edged past the FBI man and stood closer to the Korean. "I asked Agent Cho. Could we let him answer the question?"

The FBI man shrugged and turned to Ji-hun Cho, who gave me a slight bow and smiled. "I am investigating a possible crime, and my sources are confidential."

"Are the allegations Korean-based or U.S.-based?" I asked.

Ji-hun paused, staring at me. "Our sources are in South Korea. Their identity is not to be disclosed, to protect them."

"Hmm, your English is excellent. Are you based here or in South Korea?"

His brown eyes regarded me calmly. "Thank you for kind remark. I work mostly in Korea where I do field exploration for CHA."

Standing beside me, Beer seemed unhappy, but he let me continue to question Ji-hun.

"How long have you been in the U.S.?"

"I am here on one-month assignment."

Ji-hun stopped talking and dropped his gaze to the floor. "I don't want to bully you, but I am sent to search for missing Korean artifacts. My duties require me to suspect people."

The entire time I talked with Beer and Ice Cream, my peripheral vision registered the white-overall men crisscrossing through Sook's house. Now, I spotted several agents leaving the home, pulling evidence boxes, still empty, behind them, and climbing into their vans; furthermore, they looked glum. One FBI agent approached Beer and spoke quietly into his ear. "We have concluded our search," Beer said. "We are removing no articles from your house." The FBI man and Ji-hun turned, joined the men in the vans, and departed.

Sook's lawyer watched them leave. "Well, so much for that. Why would they suspect Mr. Park kept relics here? I think they're casting nets at random."

After the lawyer had departed, I continued speaking with my client. "An item of interest."

Park stopped closing drawers in a cabinet. "What item?"

"You're being investigated based on allegations by people in South Korea. Someone in South Korea murdered your old mortar-team leader there. I wonder . . . was the burglary planned there?"

Sook nodded. "Is possible."

Sook drove us back to his office building. On the way, I thought about Beer and Ji-hun Cho.

"The Korean agent, Ji-hun," I said.

"What about him?"

"He struck me as an entrepreneur, not a government employee. How could he afford his clothes?"

"Tailors in Korea do excellent work at reasonable price."

"You noticed nothing odd about the Korean agent?"

Sook glanced sideways at me. "He guesses we took relics. He can't prove it. He probably what we think he is: CHA agent following gossip."

We rode in silence, until Sook asked, "What about you? How you become detective?"

"Me? I was born and educated in Asheville. I attended a large high school in that city and a nurturing redbrick university in Raleigh."

"Did you study criminal investigation in school?"

"I did not."

"How you learn be detective?"

"After college, I became a Military Policeman (MP) in the army and served in Desert Storm. When I got out of the military, I became the head sleuth at a private firm. Subsequently, I worked on a case for Roth Security and Harriett Roth scooped me up as her devoted gumshoe."

I stopped talking as we had arrived at Sook's office building.

# # #

Roth called. "I've hired a Korean investigator."

"What's his name?"

"Lee Do-won. He is a former police officer."

I brushed back my cowlick, feeling a little anxious about going to South Korea, a country where I didn't speak the language. "How'd you find him?"

"I called private-investigative groups in Seoul. The laws and protocols in our country differ from those in South Korea. In that country, the authorities can arrest an investigator doing what we call detective work, saying the investigator is stalking an individual."

"If a detective in Korea is not a P.I., what are they called?"

"A *security manager.*"

"How do they differ?"

She answered with an amused lilt to her voice. "Our security manager will ensure safety for Seong-gi's son, to prevent another murder. A security manager and a private investigator both explore a crime scene—future and past respectively."

"What do we want Lee Do-won to do for us?"

"Search if someone recently showed interest in the members of the old mortar squad. Had anyone appeared—after the lapse of fifty years—exploring for the mortar team? The criminals have stymied us in the U. S., and I want to find a Korean link to the theft of the Silla relics."

She stopped speaking. "Hmm. I just had a thought. Determine what ROK Army records exist for the fifth soldier, the one who died at the battle near Gyeongju. Locate any relatives."

I thought back to the discussion about the Gyeongju battlefield. What had our clients told me about the fifth-soldier's wounds?

"Maybe the assumption—the fifth soldier died—is right," Roth said. "But it's always in doubt. Ask Sook if he saw a corpse—felt the dead man for a pulse?"

"What else do we know about Lee Do-won?" I asked.

"He's read all the American and British mystery novels."

I grinned. "Wow, he is going to be valuable."

"Fly to Seoul. Help Lee search for a promising lead."

I remembered I had packed my passport when I had come up to Virginia. "Yes, ma'am. I've never completely unpacked my bags. I'll leave as soon as I get a plane ticket."

"I'll tell Lee you're on your way." She terminated the call.

I got on the phone to arrange my travel and tell Sook I would be going to Korea.

# # #

That night, Sook and I phoned the murdered man's son, alerting him to expect visitors. Our Korean security manager and I would be knocking on his mother's door. I told the son I planned to watch for ways to boost his family security.

"Tell me again. Why are you coming?" the son asked.

"We want study ways keep your family safe," Sook said. "You tell police we safeguard your family?"

The call went silent while the son may have considered Sook's words. "Okay. If detectives ask, I say you here—give security."

"Korean security manager named Lee Do-won," Sook said. "The large-size American with him will be Don Gannon."

"You pay them?"

"Yes."

"Two men study security?"

"Try stop another killing," Sook said.

"All right. I tell Mother you try help our family."

When the call had ended, I told Sook, "I'll say nothing about the Silla tomb."

"Can't. If the news slipped out, we'd have to explain to Korean police and Cultural Heritage Association."

Sook held his ballpoint pen and clicked its retractor. "When you be back?"

"Back in a few days. Before I forget, Roth had a question. Why were you positive Sang-hun Lee died back in 1950, on the battlefield?"

Sook paused, seeming to consider the question.

"Night of last attack around Gyeongju, our other ammo carrier covered in blood, as if he wore red robe. He still like stone."

He pressed his forefinger against his lips as if thinking. I waited. "But we . . . rest of squad . . . too busy figuring what we do with relics to pay attention to Sang-hun. Our ammo carrier dead or in coma-like state."

"If he somehow lived, could he have become crazy and resentful because you abandoned him?"

Sook seemed to ponder. "I remember he got upset and became violent from time to time. Hmm, he had temper that would snap like mousetrap."

I delayed speaking, but Sook added nothing. "The night you went back for the two buried bags, did you look at Sang-hun's body? Had his corpse lain there for a day without moving?"

Sook shook his head. "We focused on getting bags and leaving without anyone seeing us. Unless we shined a light on an object, we couldn't see it in darkness. Didn't look at his body."

I went back to the motel to get my bags and left for Korea that night.

SOUTH KOREA—22 JUNE 2000

I leaned back in my seat as the Boeing 747 lurched rearward in its final stop at Inchon Airport. Standing before the customs window after disembarking, I presented my passport and explained I planned to be in South Korea a few days for a business reason: to study how to be a security manager.

The terminal was open and spacious, with light pouring down from the many windows along the sides of the structure. I strolled through the airport. Preferring to walk to take in my surroundings, I sidestepped the moving conveyor belts on my way to the local transportation area; at the same time, I glanced up at the overhead signs in Korean and English.

Our Korean operative, Lee Do-won, held up a cardboard placard with the words, "American Detective." Interesting. Getting closer, I judged Lee stood about five feet ten inches tall and maybe weighed 170 pounds. He had short black stubble on his face, with straight, black hair rising on top of his head until falling to the sides. Heavy eyelids gave Lee a sleepy guise, and his face projected a saturnine appearance until he smiled.

"Welcome to South Korea." The Korean detective slightly tilted his head toward me and studied my face with his black-brown eyes.

"I'm Don, your American detective."

He gave me a big grin. "I'm Lee, your Korean guide."

Lee, a person busy observing his surroundings, strolled to the luggage carousel for my suitcase. Likewise, he paused before speaking in his leisurely English, "Let me get you to Seoul and into your room in tourist-class hotel. Room has a bed and not a mat on the floor."

Leading me out to an older, white Hyundai car, Lee carried his personal belongings in a handbag with a strap over his shoulder. He wore a white dress shirt with open collar, lightweight tan jacket, beige slacks, and black sneakers. Once we departed the parking lot, Lee put on a cap with a San Diego Chargers logo and lit a filter-less cigarette. As we drove to Seoul, Lee said, "You like my hat? My wife and I are fond of vacationing in San Diego. I enjoy the San Diego Chargers."

Lee rushed into a well-rehearsed litany about Korea. "This your first trip to Korea? I give you my tourist guide. Don't tip people unless someone gives exceptional service. Don't drink water out of tap. Restaurants usually boil or filter water. Many men smoke. Toilets be squat-style or Western-style. Toilets not guaranteed have paper, pay money for little packets of toilet paper. Use ATMs get cash. This Lee's short travel guide."

I liked this talkative individual, finding the slow cadence of his voice relaxing, reassuring. "Please go on."

"You just got off plane, and you likely have jetlag. Don't lie down until you go to bed later tonight; get used to local time and space."

My guide possessed a keen mind and had decided to give me openings to lead. "I'm not tired from the flight. Before you take me to my hotel, I'd like to see the dead man's wife."

Lee turned to me. "Okay, I call. See if we can drop by Seong-gi's home—talk with wife."

Lee drove from the Incheon Airport to Seoul on a state-of-the-art highway, about twenty-five miles in length, varying from six to eight lanes. Road signage, in both English and Korean, stood along the road. While driving and talking, the Korean detective sucked on his cigarette and frequently glanced to his right, maybe trying to read my face.

He pulled into a motorway rest area, with wooden tables and hard plastic chairs set into the floor and positioned before a row of vendors selling different foods over a counter. Each food stall listed a menu in Korean along with a picture of the meal. As I studied the food images, Lee called Seong-gi's son. After a minute, he ended the call and told me, "Son at his father's home. We go next to see wife." I pointed to a figure of chicken on a skewer with red sauce and an image of grilled buttered potatoes.

We both got a plate of food and sat at a table. "At my company office," Lee said, "several of my colleagues are studying our national databases, including old ROK Army records. Tomorrow, I introduce you and see if they've found anything."

At one of the tables, a Korean man and woman argued, speaking in a low voice, agreeing to let each talk in turn. I thought this a well-mannered way to quarrel.

"Lee, is it normal for arguments to be low-key—like that couple?"

Lee smirked. "You in Korea, not Italy."

# # #

Lee slowed as we entered Seoul's traffic. Torrents of vehicles clogged the roads, creating more jams than anything in my home city of Asheville. He turned his head toward me. "Korean cars smaller than in your country. Maneuver well on our narrow streets."

Most of the vehicles were compact sedans with hardly any pickups or SUVs. "I'm not familiar with these models."

"Majority cars my country built by South Korean companies. Lots made by Hyundai and Kia."

As we snaked our way to the murdered man's home, Lee told about Korean customs and pointed out landmarks. He seemed to have a story about everything.

We passed a crowd with placards displaying the name of South Korean President Kim Dae-jung. In a park, speakers amplified martial music, men with bullhorns shouted slogans and released balloons, older men in suits and younger people in jeans and tee shirts shouted in unison, and a long file of police with clear body shields stood stiff as stone statues and watched.

"What's that?" I asked Lee.

"In Seoul, farmers demonstrate and political parties rally. This group's happy because President Kim Dae-jung awarded the Peace Prize."

I considered the placards in the cheering crowd. "Award for what?"

"He pushed healing with North Korea. Urged democracy and human rights in South Korea. My country endured past intervals of captivity, abduction, and banishment."

Lee passed the demonstrations, and I leaned my head on the headrest to catnap. Maybe my system sensed a little fatigue.

The Korean detective drove into an older, densely-packed section of Seoul, jumping out of the Hyundai at one point to tilt the side mirrors inward before driving through a narrow alley. Lee eventually emerged from the passageway into a section of residential housing.

As he entered Seong-gi's neighborhood, Lee searched for street signs. The murdered man's house was among several traditional Korean homes with sliding panels instead of windows and ski-slope roofs of tile. Behind the old-style houses, rows of western-style dwellings unrolled up a gradual hill.

Lee parked and paused to pick his nails. "You see the murdered man had traditional tastes."

I studied a one-story, wood house, with the old-style sloped roof. A wooden walkway wrapped around the building. "Was he wealthy?"

"He was manager of a life insurance office. Did okay. Here is a photograph of Seong-gi, to show anyone you want to interview." Lee led the way to the traditional Korean dwelling and knocked on a wood panel beside the front door.

"Do you live in a house like this?"

"Nope. Western-type house."

Footsteps approached the door.

Lee put out his cigarette on the ground. "When enter house, remove your shoes—is customary."

A young Korean opened the door. I saw similarities to the photograph of Seong-gi: a long face, a slight protruding of ears to the sides, a small mouth with thin lips set in a straight line. For a long second, we didn't speak, and then Lee began in English. "I'm Lee Do-won." He gestured toward me. "This American detective, Don Gannon. Is okay to speak English?"

"Cool. I'm Seong-gi's son."

As we entered the room, I removed my shoes. The home was furnished western-style, with tall chairs, a high table, and a TV.

"Police found anything new?" Lee asked.

"No," the son said, and pointed at a table and accompanying chairs. "Please sit."

Once seated, I asked, "Are you in contact with the police? Can you get us in to see them?"

The son gazed at me for a moment. "The head detective is easygoing with me. I'll ask him for a meeting."

Lee had his elbows on the table and picked at his nails. "Your family is law-abiding. Undeserving of what happened."

"My family never embezzled or robbed. My father always did good job in everything. I aced school and qualified for American college."

"Where do you work?" I asked.

"Samsung. Started after college."

I brushed down my cowlick. "Sook Park and your father fought together. Back in 1950. Did your dad talk about the fighting?"

The son shook his head. "Didn't like speak about it."

I kept pushing. "Did he mention the battle at Gyeongju? August? The Pusan Perimeter?"

The son paused a moment, perhaps thinking back to conversations with his father. "I remember him say most his company wiped out. He separated from his squad."

"That's all he told you?"

The son nodded.

Due diligence decreed we had to check the kid for a link to his father's death. We needed to probe for a family link, but an unknown person could have discovered Seong-gi's association with the stolen treasure. However, who? The son didn't know about finding a tomb. If he didn't know, he couldn't have told anyone about the connection between his father and the Silla grave.

Before the son left the room to call the detective, he fetched his mother, who spoke only Korean, to talk with us. Lee began interviewing the dead man's wife and listened to her words. She cried and wailed, pausing to dry her eyes, her body shaking as she tried to talk.

The wife became too hysterical to speak, and Lee summarized her words. "She says husband delighted in his work. They had no worries, and then her man seized and murdered."

Seong-gi's wife wiped her tears and said, "*Naneun nae nampyeon-eul geuliwo.*"

Lee turned to me and translated, "She misses her husband."

I began to suffer from the time difference between Seoul and America. My head slipped down toward my chest until aroused by Lee's hand on my arm. "She says her husband received no unusual visitors or strange messages. He met with an agent from the Cultural Heritage Association. Police investigated that person and cleared him of wrongdoing."

I tried to concentrate, but fatigue darkened my senses. Finally, I said, "Ask her what Seong-gi told about the battle of Gyeongju in August 1950."

Lee spoke with the wife for a few minutes. "She says it was horrible fight. Enemy killed many and separated her husband from his mortar squad."

"Seong-gi told her nothing else about the Gyeongju battle?" I asked.

Lee shook his head. "Apparently not."

I felt drained. What hadn't we asked the wife? "Ask if her husband dealt with a man named Wang Gang."

Lee spoke with her some more, but it was a struggle: she had reached the point of near collapse. "She says no."

The son returned and shouted at me, "What did you do? Heard mom crying." He had turned scarlet. "She sick with worry. Don't upset her."

He hugged his mother. I said nothing. Lee said we would ask no further questions. Slowly, calmness resumed, and the son took his mother to her room. When he returned to us, he said, "Mother is sleeping."

Lee and I sat at the table with the son. He appeared calmer. "Detective will see us tomorrow noon."

"Thank you," I said. "Would you do one more thing for us? Set up a meeting with your father's staff, at the place where he worked?"

The son phoned and set up a meeting in an hour. "I'll go with you to insurance office. Wait in your car. I tell Mom I'll be gone a short while."

Lee and I got in his car. Lee adjusted his San Diego Chargers cap and rubbed his stubble. "Don't close your eyes. You won't wake up until your regular morning time in America."

Seated in the Hyundai, I had a moment of contemplation. "What is your opinion? See anything in what they said? Is the son involved in his father's murder?"

"My guess no," Lee answered. "I figure police investigated the kid."

The son didn't know about the treasure. If that's true, he had no motive. If he knew about the wealth, then he would inherit the relics if he just waited.

"You want me have an agent investigate him?" Lee asked.

I bit my lip, using the pain to stay awake. "No. We'll assume the police investigated him."

Then the son came out of the house, and we left to interview Seong-gi's staff at his life-insurance office.

The life insurance office was on the eighth floor of a fourteen-story building of gray stone. Men and women, a busy workforce, sat in cubicles spread throughout the office like a labyrinth. A short man with a wrinkled face and bushy white hair hastened over to us. "I assistant manager. My name Chul Park. He"—Chul pointed at Seong-gi's son—"asked me talk with you."

The short man twitched in small jerks. He appeared to stare at the floor and mutter to himself, "What they want?"

Lee asked the first question. "Ever see an unfamiliar man show up, ask about Seong-gi?"

The assistant manager stared at the floor and said something unintelligible to himself. Then he gazed up and said, "No. Seong-gi served many years as senior manager." He stopped speaking and bent his head. "He always talked about retiring."

Lee glanced at me with a blank expression, turned back to Chul. "Did Seong-gi have difficulties at work?"

Chul raised his head, blinking his eyes at Lee. "Why you here? Police spend long time with me. I tell them."

He lowered his head such that I saw only his frizzy white hair. The son spoke to him in Korean. The old man appeared to carry on a lengthy dialogue with himself. The son nodded at Lee.

"Were there difficulties at work?" Lee asked again.

Chul, his head down, answered Lee. "Settled few disagreements. Gave payout, in fair arbitration."

"Did the police go over his office?" I asked.

The old man stared at me, scrunching his face so that his wrinkles shifted to different locations. He mumbled in a faint voice, "Why you here? What you want?"

We lingered in quiet until Seong-gi's son restated my question. Chul glanced down at the floor. "Yes. They took printout. Got names of clients he had contacted."

The son shook his head at me and turned to the old man. "Chul, we're going to look in my father's office."

The son led Lee and me to the dead man's office, where Lee spent fruitless hours searching for a clue among the documents, written in Korean. My body whimpered for sleep. I couldn't continue. We left the insurance company. I catnapped in the front passenger's seat, and Lee drove the son home and me to my hotel.

The check-in desk stood in a bright hall with marble floors, leafy green plants, and a high ceiling. My Western-style room had two single beds, a chair and a table, a large window, and a TV mounted on the wall. I fell asleep immediately, waking up at three o'clock in the morning. I couldn't get back to sleep.

SOUTH KOREA—23 JUNE 2000

Early the following morning, I sat in my hotel room, watching time tick away on my wristwatch. My stomach cried out for breakfast; my brain idled in jetlag lethargy, my neurons in shock.

Just before six, I took the elevator down to the second floor and stood before the restaurant door as it opened. I sat, with my stomach snarling. A server placed dishes before me; I beheld cups and plates of kimchi, rice, soup, pickles, and noodles. Where would I find bacon, eggs, and toast? My stomach cramped with disappointment, as when I was a child and failed to get a present, a Daisy BB gun—one I had begged my parents for—on my birthday.

My server evidently saw the shock on my face. He rushed to my table. "Sir, what wrong?"

"I need bacon, eggs, and toast."

He bowed slightly and answered calmly. "This our breakfast meal. We no serve American-style breakfast."

I picked up the bowl of kimchi. "I saw people eating this for lunch."

"Korean breakfast like any other meal served during day." My server stood silently. When I didn't respond, he left the table.

I pulled the bowl of kimchi to me and ate breakfast.

Feeling clammy in the high humidity, I waited in front of the hotel as Lee drove the white Hyundai to the curb. "Hop in. Big day ahead of us." He wore his Chargers cap and dashed into the dense flow of vehicles. As Lee maneuvered from side to side across the Seoul traffic, he asked, "How you feel about yesterday?"

"I sense I'm depressed. The Korean police have been over everything. What'll we find that the cops didn't already discover?"

Lee bobbed his head and continued changing lanes. "I read mystery novels. Learn first rule about sleuthing is it's annoying. Second rule is sleuth can't change the first rule."

I chuckled. "Another day of sleuthing with no new suspect and I'm going to start screaming. How're your support people doing? They found anything?"

"Wizard called late last night. Found something. Wants us to drop by the office."

"Did he tell you what it was?"

"No—he is computer obsessive. Always wants to show his Eureka on monitor. If it not on the screen, it not real."

"If you don't know what your computer guy found, at least tell me what he had been investigating."

"Wizard probed everything about mortar squad in Gyeongju battle."

As Lee drove, I glanced out the window at a coal-black sky, the distant heavens hurling intense clashes announcing an approaching torrent of rain. The air was scorching and thick with water, like a steam bath. We parked at the police station. When the son arrived, we entered and waited to meet the detective, who worked for the Korean National Police.

Dressed in a brown jacket, white shirt with collar, brown slacks, and no tie, the policeman came toward us down a hallway, its walls and ceiling a drab white color. Detective Choi greeted us in broken English and a scowl. He led the way to his desk, which sat in an open room with a separate workstation for each police officer, a haze of cigarette smoke thickened at ceiling level.

I listened carefully as the detective described his murder investigation. "Coroner says body in Han about two weeks. Had started to decompose."

Choi switched to Korean, which Lee translated. "They identified dead man through DNA analysis and dental records."

Choi had seated us in chairs facing his desk. He continued to scan through a thick file but didn't let us view it. Judging by its thickness, the police had invested considerable effort in studying Seong-gi's death.

"Any lead from organized crime?" Lee asked.

Detective Choi frowned at Lee as if he didn't want to be interrupted by answering his question. "In old police files, no similar kidnappings. Our—how Americans say it—confidential informants say organized crime not involved. Murder not common in Korea."

"Any clue in the life insurance files?" I asked. "The files you took from Seong-gi's office."

Frowning now at me, Detective Choi lit a cigarette and took a drag. "None. Mr. Kim managed his business well. Clients happy."

Getting knowledge from the detective was as tedious as teaching a newbie to drive a car.

"What you explore now?" Lee asked.

"Still going through life insurance files. But our sense is threat didn't originate there. We hoping for break."

Choi had passed us little information. Based on his pained expressions, I figured he spoke with us as a courtesy to the son but probably wanted us to leave so that he could return to his assigned duties.

"May we see the coroner's report?" I asked.

Choi appeared puzzled as if he didn't understand. Lee translated my question into Korean.

The detective scowled. "No can see. Official police file."

Lee rotated sideways to me, turned his face away from Choi, and said, "We need to see more. Disagree with him, but don't raise voice. Be polite."

The detective smoked and waited.

Lee lit a cigarette. "You search for Seong-gi's killer?"

"Yes," Choi replied.

"Family not under suspicion?" Lee continued.

The detective waited, maybe trying to figure why Lee asked this question. "They not suspects."

Lee spread his arms to encompass everyone around the desk. "This investigator came from America to help ensure security for family. My company evaluates family safety. We all on same team, to protect Seong-gi's household."

The detective smoked and said nothing.

Lee shrugged. "Can't help Seong-gi's wife and son if don't know anything."

Choi hesitated before responding to Lee. "Coroner's report is official. Police document. No can see."

The son added his voice to Lee's plea. "Creep who murdered my father may return to harm Mom. Please help us."

"We want to read the report, not take it away," I said.

Choi, the corners of his mouth drooping, turned sideways in his chair, staring out distant windows at the rain beginning to cascade down the glass. "I allow you to see coroner's report and physical evidence gathered by our team." He spread the thick file out on his desk facing us. "I stay here."

We glanced over the written report and photographs. The description and photos implied the dead man might have lost weight during his captivity. Perhaps because the body had been in the Han River, the investigators found no trace elements on the skin.

"Did coroner identify marks on the body?" Lee asked.

"No," the detective said. He started to speak but paused. He switched to Korean.

"After death, his body changed from being in water," Lee translated. "Bones exposed and skin separated from body. Coroner's examination not able identify if there were abrasions on skin at wrists and ankles."

"We don't know if Seong-gi had been bound—before being cast into the Han?" I whispered to Lee.

"That's right."

"Upriver from spot where found body, police officers showed pictures of Mr. Seong-gi Kim to civilians," the detective said. "No one recognized him."

A diagram lay among the papers in the physical evidence folder, a map displaying the Han River and showing where the police found the body. An X marked a spot on the river's bank where the police suspected the kidnappers had dumped the body. An investigator had drawn an ellipse encompassing both banks of the Han around the upstream X.

"Does the ellipse indicate the region where you think body entered the Han?" I asked Choi.

"It does. Mostly buildings for storage and light manufacturing inside marked area. Few houses."

Lee locked eyes with me. "I know area. We obtain a clue."

Lee and I departed the police station, said goodbye to the son and drove to meet the Wizard at Lee's workplace.

#

The heavy showers and clamminess had faded away, leaving a clear sky and a pleasant afternoon. Lee parked in an underground garage within an urban setting of multistory buildings. The office building in which Lee worked stood among similar glass-fronted structures.

"Is your computer guy called Wizard because he's first-rate?" I asked.

"My colleague is magician at querying databases," Lee said.

We went past office cubicles, each housing an agent. I beheld the wizard in his dormant state, sprawled in a chair at his hutch, wearing a black blindfold, snoozing quietly, like a kitten. He had hung his black coat over a corner of his cubicle and finished his color-coordinated ensemble by wearing black trousers. Three computer monitors sat on his desk.

Lee smiled. "He task-oriented. Wizard searched entire night, seeking information on old mortar crew." Lee patted his colleague's shoulder. "Wake up, Wizard, Mr. Gannon here to see you."

The man in black opened his eyes wide and sprung up with a broad grin. "Mr. Gannon, pleasure meet you. I have lots to tell you."

Our computer sleuth, awake and animated, energized his monitors. He turned toward me, his face full of pride. "I queried ROK Army database, keying in fifth crewmember, named Sang-hun Lee. He assigned to squad as ammo carrier. He got to a hospital—back in August 1950—and recovered from his trauma."

Startled, I stared at Wizard. Lee had told me this guy had talent, but he had turned out to be the Big Kahuna. "The fifth soldier didn't die?"—I gaped at Wizard—"Is he alive and breathing now?"

Wizard grinned like he'd received the gold medal. "He alive."

"Holy mackerel!" I blurted.

Wizard pulled up a file on one of his monitors and read to us. "After discharge from hospital and ROK Army, Sang-hun Lee got occasional work as laborer. He never married. He lives in small village east of Seoul."

"Any living relatives?" I asked.

Wizard printed out a sheet of paper with a name and address. "I identified family member—a niece—who lives in same village."

An important clue had lain in the background story. Sang-hun Lee had stayed alive and possibly knew who had taken the treasure. I hadn't deduced the connection, but Roth had pulled it out of the air. "Roth nailed it. The fifth soldier survived the battle at Gyeongju."

"Good work, Wizard," Lee said. "You found key suspect."

He beamed with pride. "I'll continue searching through records relating to old mortar-squad members."

"Find out everything you can about recent whereabouts and present location Sang-hun Lee," Lee said. "We need talk with him."

"I do that," Wizard said. "Send information as soon as I have it."

Our young magician had found the fifth soldier alive, but I had a curiosity about another suspect. "Did you search for a man named Wang Gang?"

"I found no connection between man named Wang Gang with any member of mortar squad. I keep examining."

"Try harder," I said.

Wizard pointed to his monitors. "I will keep searching for Gang association, but already been through a mass of data."

I answered him with an aphorism Roth had taught me. "If you hear voices in your head telling you to stop, inform each voice you have to go on."

I left the office with Lee.

"Get me back to my hotel. Try to contact the niece. Let's start the investigation with her tomorrow."

I followed Lee down to his Hyundai. "I'll phone Roth with the news. Somehow, she had deduced the fifth soldier survived the last battle. She can trigger a grand agony in my head with her pigheadedness, but she is sharp."

SOUTH KOREA—23 JUNE 2000

From my hotel room in Seoul, I called Roth at the Asheville mansion. I summarized my progress since arriving in Korea two days previous. When I finished, Roth began launching questions at me. "So where's this fifth soldier now?"

"Determining that now. Wizard is searching for information about relatives of Sang-hun. Once he recovered from his wounds, the fifth soldier worked as a manual laborer for years, living alone in a hut and looked after by his relatives."

"Go on," Roth said.

I reached for the Hite beer, for which I had been developing a taste, on the desk beside me and took a swallow. "Wizard found Sang-hun applied for a tourist visa to the U.S. and purchased a round-trip ticket between America and Korea. I'll fax his passport picture to you. He left Korea and hasn't returned."

"Remember to send Sang-hun's picture to Sook Park."

I jotted her request in my notepad in case I forgot. "Will do."

"As best you can tell," Roth asked, "could our fifth soldier have kidnapped and murdered Seong-gi?"

"At the time someone kidnapped Seong-gi, Sang-hun hadn't departed Korea," I answered.

Before Roth closed our discussion, I interrupted her. "Ask Mickey to bring six feet of detonation cord when he comes to help me. We may want to trim a tree."

After we terminated the call, I caught the lift down to the hotel business office to send the picture of Sang-hun to Roth and Sook. As the staff transmitted the image, I glanced at the fifth soldier's appearance. He had a grim face, like those pictures of farmers who had lived in the Dust Bowl of the 1930s in the Southern Plains of America. He came across as someone who had worked all his life and grown tired of constant labor. The fifth soldier had blank eyes and white hair, eyebrows, and goatee. Sook had described him as massive in 1950; in comparison, he appeared thin today, with sunken cheeks over a small neck.

Back in my hotel room, I lay with my head on the pillow, as visions of Carla Diaz darted around my head and wouldn't go away. I turned over, the images in my mind rolling with me, a visualization of her cleverness and good looks, an enthralling combination. I thought back to the times when I'd run into her around the Residence Inn; indeed, she always possessed a constant smile, a pixie-like spirit, and perkiness. I recalled Carla enjoying dinner at the Sweet Sailing Tavern, stealing French fries off my plate.

Sitting up in bed, I couldn't get her out of my mind. Darn! I lay back down, closed my eyes, followed by thoughts of magnificently-snug blue slacks and a button-down blouse with the top buttons undone. My glands generated sweat, cooling my overheated body.

I figured day had broken an hour ago in Virginia. I called her.

At her greeting, I said, "Hi, Carla. Don calling."

She waited several moments before speaking. "Who?"

My heart froze. "Don Gannon. We had dinner—"

"Donnell! I'm kidding you."

My heart jumped from icy to lickety-split. "Yeah, well I was thinking of you—"

"Please tell me they were dirty thoughts."

My tongue froze up.

After a moment, when I didn't pick up the conversation, Carla continued. "How is Korea? When do I see you again?"

I tried to sound glib, even though I ached to see her. "Oh, Korea's outstanding. And I've solved some of the world's problems."

"Good on you. What's it like?"

"Hustle and bustle. The Koreans are energetic and polite."

"Did you see the DMZ?"

"Not yet. Been interviewing suspects and talking to—"

"Your job is so interesting. Virginia today. Foreign lands the next day."

"Not that exciting. I spent lots of time sitting in my car—"

"Are you packing your pistol?"

"No. Don't need one—"

"That's nice. When do I get my dinner? Recall I hold your raincheck?"

"Sorry I had to break away from our dinner. I enjoyed your company. We'll do the makeup shortly—when I return."

"I'll hold you to that. Keep thinking sexy thoughts. Bye."

She had disconnected my call. I slumped back on my bed and tried to block lecherous thoughts. *You are so in over your head.*

SOUTH KOREA—24 JUNE 2000

My third morning in South Korea, I woke at three. My focus, vigilance, raced at a high intensity, like a gerbil running on an exercise wheel. A residual jet lag persevered in keeping me wide-awake, and we were making headway in Korea. The case had begun to break my way. How did I know? Because every time a mystery started to unravel toward a solution, I lost my desire to sleep. It was time to ram forward with the hunt. I arrived at the hotel curb fifteen minutes before Lee had arranged to meet me.

He picked me up on time. "Wizard found house of Sang-hun's niece. She lives near her uncle, in village about two hours outside Seoul."

Lee pulled away from the hotel, puffing on his cigarette, and I cracked open my window. "She knows we're coming?"

Lee frowned at me, maybe miffed I felt the need to check on him. "I call. She talks to us about Sang-hun. I no slacker."

Lee took off, driving through traffic breaks with the steering wheel in one hand and a cigarette in the other. I lowered my window further and glanced outside, eyeing a darkening sky.

"I told niece," Lee continued, "we study security of old mortar-squad members. No say we search for her uncle."

Once Lee maneuvered his car farther to the east beyond Seoul, we rode on four-lane divided highways and then two-lane paved roads. I studied the countryside, green and surrounded by mountains. "So mountains cover how much of Korea?" He twisted sideways to glance at me and then turned his eyes back on the road. "Seventy percent my country is mountainous. My nation beautiful, but we must use other thirty percent of land grow crops and erect homes and businesses."

"Mountains surround your capital city."

Lee put out his cigarette and threw the stub out his window. "Mountains to sides. Han River flows through Seoul. Empties at Incheon, where you landed."

Lee located the village where Sang-hun's niece lived and drove to her isolated house. He stopped the car. I stepped out and glanced up at a sky with a dark gray hue and clouds heavy with water. My stomach tightened; this interview would likely solve the case or leave us rudderless. I wanted to lead the interrogation—just my nature. Deep down, I knew I should let Lee lead. My partner knew the culture and the language. He had a quick wit. My smart approach would be to let him lead the interview, to squash my need to control. "Torrential showers coming," I said.

Lee glanced at me and then started toward the niece's home. "Is okay. We have all morning to talk."

We walked to a one-story house with a thatched roof and light-brown adobe brick siding. An outer wall curved around the building and stood about five feet high with a covering of straw on top. The family farmed; a cultivated field rose to the right with rows of green plants, like the fields back home.

Lee glanced at the countless plants. "Strawberries."

A woman, surrounded by flowers in pots, hoed weeds in the yard, her hair pulled back in a bun. She turned to us, gave a small bow, and said, "*annyeonghaseyo.*"

I returned her bow and said "Hello."

She ignored me and spoke directly to my partner. Although she had studied English in school, the niece preferred to converse with Lee in Korean. He chatted with the woman and then translated for me. "Her uncle lives close by, in hut. He lives on chance of unskilled jobs and food from her garden. She says her uncle got well from severe wound suffered in defense of Pusan."

The woman began to frown and glance back at her house as if she had started to grow suspicious of us. I knew I should have taken the lead. *Sweet talk her, Lee. She's growing skittish.* I felt a surge of apprehension. If we could keep her talking, maybe we stood on the cusp of solving the case. "Is her uncle here?" I asked. "Will she take us to him?"

They continued talking. She frowned and appeared to hesitate in answering Lee.

Finally, he turned from the niece. "Her uncle left Korea last month."

"Will she show us his shack?"

Lee started talking to the niece again. Dressed in a white blouse with half sleeves and blue jean overalls, she looked away from him and began to water her garden. He conversed with her for a little longer and then spoke to me. "She will take us to hut, so we'll know where to find him when he returns. She won't let us go inside shed."

"Where is her uncle?" I asked.

After conferring with the niece, Lee said, "He flew to U.S., but didn't say when he gets back. Her uncle bought new clothes, and maybe the mysterious man paid for them. She's worried—he never travels outside Korea."

"Hold on—what mysterious man?" I asked.

The niece and Lee continued talking, and then Lee said, "Sometime in April, after the last snow, she saw her uncle speaking with tall man. Her uncle wouldn't tell her man's identity. The person was Asian and well dressed."

"Did her uncle work for him?"

"Must be," Lee said. "Her uncle had money. Man would pick up Sang-hun Lee in morning, and they would be gone entire day."

"Was the mystery man young or old?"

The niece knelt and begun to weed a plot in her garden. I figured she had just delivered an unspoken message for us to leave. Regardless, Lee spoke with the niece before turning back to me. "Maybe thirty years old."

"How did the tall man employ her uncle?" I inquired. "Did his job have anything to do with his old mortar squad?"

Lee glanced again at the sky, now coal black. "She doesn't know. Uncle was cautious."

The niece again conversed with Lee and after they had finished speaking, she went inside her house. Lee lit another cigarette. "Her uncle rented a house. A realtor came by and spoke with her. She searches for agent's business card."

She returned, holding a white card.

Lee thanked her and jotted down information after reading the agent's card.

She led them down a narrow road through her village and off into a hilly field of scrubs and bushes. A stream ran through the area. Beside the creek, a shack of old wood panels and plastic tarp stood, topped by a flat roof, possessing a few small windows to admit light. On the opposite side of the stream, I saw a thick tangle of bushes and small trees.

Lee paused, gazing from the hut to the woodland tangle across the creek. "She says this uncle's shed. She won't let us inside."

Small drops of rain began to fall, changing to large globs. As the niece ran to her house and we rushed to the car, Lee shouted after her, "Thank you. You big help."

Lee started the engine and drove through the village, exploring the local roads. "Before we leave, I want to examine area on the other side of hut." Afterwards, he took me back to Seoul. "I will call the realtor," Lee said. "Find if the uncle rented a house."

The windshield wipers stroked back and forth. Lee wanted to smoke. I asked him to wait until the rain stopped and we could lower the windows. I wrote on my notepad, getting my case notes up to date. Lee did well to get as much information as he did. I sensed the niece wouldn't talk with us again. She wouldn't allow us in the hut. I had come halfway across the globe. Had to see what Sang-hun had in his shack. Lee seemed to be reflecting as he drove.

He turned his head toward me. "Shack is isolated."

"Yeah," I said.

Lee drove for another minute before speaking. "I'm going back tonight."

"Yeah. I'm going with you."

Lee seemed to think before he answered. "We can't take anything property from the hut. That's theft and would carry maybe jail term for you, a foreigner."

"See but don't steal."

He grinned. "See but don't steal. Get some rest in your hotel room. Pick you up at dusk."

Back at my hotel, I talked to a friendly porter in the lobby about Korean law and then settled down for a nap. My mind raced like NASCAR vehicles doing laps around the track. We needed to identify the mysterious Asian man. Was he the CHA agent or Wang

Gang or had we found another suspect? I slipped into a welcome sleep.

# # #

As dusk started, Lee picked me up from my hotel and drove east. We arrived at Sang-hun's village and parked in darkness on the shoulder of a dirt road.

Lee put out his cigarette and tossed the butt out the window. "Don't leave the car. I want make sure no villagers, no dogs, wander this road."

As we waited, I considered the seriousness of my action. If you break the laws of another country, you are subject to the judicial system of that country. When I had asked Lee about South Korea, he told me the authorities usually kept foreigners locked up throughout the investigative and trial process. Courts did not commonly grant bail. The Korean procedure is the law could hold me at first without formally arraigning me for up to 48 hours. If found guilty of an offense, South Korea would likely deport me after I had served my sentence. To justify the risk of burglarizing Sang-hun's hut, I had to find a clue. "Sure is dark," I noted. "No house lights."

Lee shifted around in his seat. "We in rural area. The crop in field to our left is cabbage. What the farmers grow around here." I peered through my side window to the right. The rain had stopped. The hut lay on the other side of thick vegetation, including shrubs and trees. Sang-hun lived on a lot with an irregularly shaped contour, unsuited for farming. Earlier, the niece had shown us her uncle's hut by taking us there from the side opposite from where Lee now parked. I couldn't see Sang-hun's shelter, but the woods would hide us once we started through the thick vegetation.

Fifteen minutes passed. Lee opened his door and stepped out into the darkness. "All I hear are crickets. Let's go. If anyone sees us, we nature lovers enjoying outdoors."

Feeling nervous, I brushed my cowlick. I remembered an unpleasant memory from a summer in childhood. Four of us entered a deserted house. We broke in through a rear porch, and I felt frightened, going into a blackness about which I knew nothing. That night in Korea, my fear of going into darkness returned. Wearing dark clothes and carrying wood poles, we picked our way through the woods and wet shrubbery, occasionally flicking on a flashlight, with some black tape over the lens to reduce the light intensity. Both of us wore goggles that shielded our eyes from limbs and branches. Lee moved slowly, occasionally stopping to listen. I heard faint rustling in the brush, some small nocturnal animal. Lee got us to the hut, visible in the light of the moon occasionally emerging through an overcast sky.

It loomed before us: rectangular, topped by a flat roof, with small windows, surrounded by boxes, plastic sheets, and poles on the ground. To enter, Lee pulled sideways on the door until it jerked away from its asymmetrical frame. The single room was austere, with rough-hewn boards on the sides and floor. It contained a jumble of clothes and boxes, smelling like a portable toilet. Searching the inside of the hut with our shielded flashlights, we found few papers, no books, and no journals.

"He not keep records," Lee whispered. "I can't find anything about his job or mysterious man."

"I found nothing," I replied.

A rectangular shape, the size of a postcard, stood out on the back wall. Except for a calendar, Sang-hun had left the other walls bare. I moved closer and flashed the reduced flashlight beam on the shape. He had pinned a wrinkled photograph to the wood.

Lee slid to my right side. He peered at the photo and then whispered to himself. "The old mortar crew—from the past."

"Yeah."

Lee moved his face closer to the photo. "I bet large man to the right is Sang-hun, our fifth soldier."

I realized someone had crossed out the face—of one of the soldiers—with an *X*. "I expect that's Seong-gi, the old squad leader."

Lee gave a low whistle. "Crossed out old squad leader's face to show he dead. How Sang-hun know?"

I didn't answer him. The apparent response would be our fifth soldier had been at the old man's death. In the dim light of the shielded flashlights, I detected Lee staring at me and then turn back to the photograph. "Isn't that odd?" I said. "The fifth soldier hasn't seen his former crew for ages, but this photograph is the sole memorabilia in his entire hut. Why?"

"Not sure," Lee said. "Maybe he had been obsessing for long time."

I considered Lee's thought. "Love or hate?"

Lee shook his head and photographed the old picture with his digital camera. "Leave it."

Lee and I took up a board from the floor, determining the flooring lay directly over dirt. He used a knife he had brought to pry for loose boards. We found nothing under the flooring planks. Putting the loose floorboards back and pulling the front door back into its frame, we left the hut and started back through the thick brush. The moon broke through the clouds and lit the bushes and shrubs in shades of gray. We began walking back to the Hyundai.

Lee said, "*Ugh!*" and jumped back toward me.

A streak, an animal, black against the gray background, flashed past. Low to the ground.

Lee ran through the thicket. I tore after him.

He fell, yelling in pain. I saw a massive black shape with short, thin legs leaning over him.

I hit the animal with my hiking staff. The thing had a solid mass.

Lee rose and ran. A second black form overtook me. I struck out with the staff, missing, striking nothing but air.

I ran, hearing no sound but the swish of shrubs and bushes.

Lee reached the road first.

I stood, filling my lungs with air. "What hit us? It was big. Moved like a blur."

Lee bent down, rolling up his pants legs and searching for a wound. "Wild boar."

"I saw it, and then it was gone," I said. "Low down."

Lee inspected his calves. "I think there were two. We lost them."

"Lucky to get away."

"Boars breed fast. Their predators—tigers, leopards, and wolves—no longer here."

I listened for any sounds in the woods but heard naught. "They didn't follow us."

Lee discovered deep scratches on his left leg. "We escaped. It smells and hears okay, but doesn't see so good."

Lee could drive okay. We left the village, returning to Seoul.

I relaxed in the passenger seat. Not going to serve time in a Korean prison. Had the venture been worth the risk? Our search of the hut unearthed no itinerary for the fifth soldier. An old photograph likely exposed the state of Sang-hun's mind, but did it mean he felt love or hate? We had many questions to ask when we caught up with him.

SOUTH KOREA—25 JUNE 2000

Early Sunday, Lee phoned my room. "Talked with realtor. He remembered locating small building for Sang-hun. Doesn't know anything about second person—no tall man."

Lee had worked quickly. Roth had done well to choose him. She had book smarts, which hid her talent to read people, to mix seemingly incompatible individuals who worked well together. She had an eccentric nature, but her ability to understand individuals made up for that drawback. "Anyone in the place now?"

"Agent said building empty. No one there."

We caught another break. The building would be as Sang-hun left it. We might find something.

"I pick up agent, then come get you," Lee continued. "He will lead us to the building. He remembered it in undeveloped section of Han River. I told him we interested in renting such a place—play along."

"When we get inside the house," I replied, "we need to split up. One of us keeps the agent busy while the other snoops around."

"Okay and bring raincoat. It's raining—what is English expression? Small animals fall out of the sky."

Once the three of us were in the Hyundai, Lee followed the realtor's directions and traveled east out of Seoul on a two-lane highway. He maneuvered through traffic reflecting a city packed with roughly ten million inhabitants. As Lee steered his car alongside the Han River, the scenery changed from urban to rural. Like yesterday, I saw a sky gray with dark clouds and constant rain. At times, trees and brush extended along both sides along the road. Toward the end of our trip, the Han flowed on the one hand and full fields of crops sprouted on the opposite flank. I rated the area as partially rural and partially small-scale industrial. We finally reached the house. Lee parked just off the road, and we sloshed through rainfall and muck to get to the structure. Past the building and down a slope, I spotted an extensive body of water, the Han River. Following the realtor and Lee, I scanned the outside walls of rough adobe, deteriorating in spots, in need of repair.

As the realtor stopped to get a door key from his briefcase, I whispered to Lee. "Are we near where the killers tossed the body in the Han?"

"We are."

I stood before a grimy structure, surrounded by shabby trees, dingy grounds, and an overgrown pathway. If this house had a personality trait, it was repulsive. I stared at the hovel in disbelief. The agent appeared sheepish and said, "This isolated location what Sang-hun Lee wanted."

The realtor unlocked the door and led us into the front room, which had a desk, a few chairs, cardboard boxes, and debris—trash, newspapers, and magazines—pushed up along the walls. A small bathroom stood off to a side of the front room. "The larger space is at rear of house," our guide said. The realtor and I wandered toward the rear, leaving Lee behind lingering close to the desk cluttered with paper.

The agent and I entered the back room, halting abruptly, our way blocked by a roughhewn bench in the middle of a dark, dank area. A pale light floated down—from the windows high on one wall—in shimmering waves through the dust motes. Through the stagnant air, I sniffed the odor of mold and old, wet cardboard. I paused to let my eyes adjust. The agent found the light switch and turned on a single overhead bulb. "I don't know what that thing is," the agent said. "Was not here before." I recognized the bench as a torture rack, like the one I had seen in a museum in the U.K.

The realtor stood on his tiptoes to see above the rack. "What is metal funnel over table?"

I spied a wooden packing box in a corner. "Help me move this box so I can stand on it. We can get up close to the cone." I moved the box beside the table, stepped up, and glanced down into the cone-shaped device. "There's liquid in here. Looks like water." I turned the knob at the bottom of the funnel. The liquid slowly dripped onto the rack. I stepped down to the floor and stuck my finger first on a liquid drop and then on my tongue. "Yeah. Think its water." I glanced at the sides of the rack and saw ropes hanging down.

The agent fingered the next drop and sampled it. He nodded. "Water. What is dark stain on bench under funnel?" A giant bloodstain discolored the bench. Lee and I had found the link between Sang-hun, the fifth soldier, and the murder of Seong-gi, the old squad leader.

"Can't stand smell," the realtor said. "We need clean-up. Maybe you've lost your interest in this place."

To keep our realtor occupied, I had him help me examine the walls in the back room while Lee continued going through the documents in the desk in the front office. Presently, I glanced toward the front to see Lee giving me the okay sign and saying, "If you have seen enough, let's start back to Seoul."

On our return trip through the rain, I realized I was hungry and suggested we stop for barbeque chicken. As we ate at a restaurant, I peeked at Lee and, when the realtor glanced away, mouthed, "Find anything?" Lee grinned and nodded. Seeing his grinning face with his San Diego Chargers hat on top of his head, I felt euphoric. After eating, Lee dropped the agent at his office. On the way to my hotel, I asked, "What'd you find?"

"Interesting paper in waste basket. Lists Sang-hun's flight number and hotel where he planned to stay when he got to America."

I cocked an eyebrow at Lee. "Wizard has already provided us with a copy of his passport, including his photograph?"

Lee switched to a slower lane. "He did." He reached into the back seat for his satchel and removed the papers he had found in the trash, which he handed to me.

I studied the itinerary. "These past two days have been productive. The fifth soldier is still in the U.S., and we can search for him there. Lee, keep watch in Korea and alert us should he return."

"Won't be a problem," Lee replied.

I pressed my cowlick down and faced Lee with a grin. "We found the murder scene. We did well together."

Lee grinned back. "Part of our method was dumb luck and Wizard."

I laughed at Lee's comment. "There's nothing like a little luck to give you a pleasant chuckle."

I thought it peculiar Sang-hun hadn't come back to Korea immediately after the theft. Because the fifth soldier hadn't returned to his hut, I guessed he might have the relics with him in America. Roth had worked out a prudent approach for us: searching for the Silla gold in Northern Virginia and using our investigator, Lee, in Korea to help us with our probe.

Lee smoked; I cracked my window; I was quiet in the car. The criminals were smart, planned well. The house on the Han gave us our first real clue. Finally, I asked, "Did the killers do a clumsy job cleaning the house on the Han? Or, did they plant misinformation to deceive us?"

Lee drew on his cigarette and seemed to be considering the question. "I heard the person doing the planning is smart. Sang-hun is simple laborer, not brains of the team. I assume the smart one is the mysterious man." Lee broke off to take another puff. "I believe Sang-hun did the cleanup—did a sloppy job. Maybe he thought we wouldn't find shack on the Han. Maybe he just stupid."

I moved my head closer to my open side window to escape Lee's exhaled smoke. "You're suggesting we caught a break when Sang-hun, the fifth soldier, got the job of cleaning up any evidence they left behind."

Lee looked at me but didn't answer.

We stopped talking, and I lost myself in thought. Two opportunities existed: find Sang-hun in America and identify the mystery man in Korea, the brains. I couldn't be in Northern Virginia and Korea at once. I wanted to team with Lee to determine Sang-hun's accomplice, but my partner could handle the search by himself. I could better assist the investigation by returning to America and locating the fifth soldier. "I've made notes on Sang-hun's itinerary," I said. "I'll call from my hotel and pass along his schedule to Roth. I'm going to suggest I return to Virginia."

# # #

Before dropping me off at my hotel, Lee said, "Fellow workers in Korean company eat together, the tradition of *hoesik*, denotes harmony and camaraderie. Tonight, you and I must eat and drink together—for companionship."

"Thanks, Lee, but I'll pass. Need to get up early tomorrow and go to the airport."

"Cannot let you leave without farewell gathering."

I thought that was thoughtful of Lee. "Can't do it. Have to pack and get to bed early."

Lee frowned at my response. "In America, you spend little time with few friends at lunch. In my country, we believe essential eat and drink with co-workers, at least once a week."

He had achieved a lot for our case. I didn't feel right ignoring him. "Okay. I may not stay the whole time."

He beamed a big smile at me. "See you at your hotel tonight. Six o'clock."

Lee and three of his fellow operatives—including Wizard—picked me up for *hoesik*. Lee wore his San Diego Chargers hat. Wizard—in black clothing, including a vest and sunglasses—had a stoic expression. We walked to a restaurant, where we had dinner and drank *soju* and Hite beers. My Korean colleagues sat comfortably on a mat with their knees under a low table, but I couldn't get my legs entirely under it. "Eating together once a week puts us at ease with each other," Lee explained.

Leaving the first restaurant, Lee led us to a bar where we drank whiskey. As soon as I had an empty glass, one of my new friends refilled my container. My Korean P.I. explained, "If I see you have empty glass, I fill to be polite. Keep eye on your neighbor's drink container and be ready to fill it."

After exiting the second place, Lee led the way to a karaoke bar. While the karaoke speakers reverberated, we ate *galbi*, or Korean barbeque, grilled on a single communal grill, located in the center of our table amid many drinks.

In a shared approach, like eating fondue, everyone took his food from the grill. Between drinks, we wrapped the roasted pork in greens. Lee covered the meat on the heated surface with garlic, kimchi, and rice. I watched my friends stuff the whole wrap in their mouths in one fell swoop. No small nibble but one giant gulp.

Following the act of stuffing the meal into their mouths, they chewed and swallowed. Wizard kept his passive expression but downed food rapidly. I felt tipsy with so much alcohol. My new friends kept ordering more whiskey and *soju*.

At the fourth venue, I ate more food and drank Hite beers. I saw my Korean friends summon the waiter by the convenient doorbell on the tabletop. I sat at the table, blotto from drink, gawking at the waiter-call button, thrusting the button repeatedly. Waiters surrounded me, pleading with me in Korean to cease pushing the button. I sensed deep intoxication.

Lee stopped the evening's entertainment and led my joyful group back to my hotel. As I walked, my surroundings wouldn't stay still, swirling around me. I sensed myself bob first one way and then lurch the opposite. To keep me upright, my new friends walked beside me and held on to my torso. My colleagues dumped my body face up on my bed. I remembered Lee firmly shook my hand, wished me a safe flight back to America, and left the room, turning out the light just before he shut the door.

The next morning—I thought it was the following morning, but days could have gone by—I struggled through a hangover to pack my bag. Then I took a shuttle bus to the Inchon Airport and somehow boarded the correct plane back to Virginia.

NORTHERN VIRGINIA—26 JUNE 2000

I returned to Dulles Airport Monday morning and got to my Residence Inn suite early afternoon, dropping my bags on the floor. My body slowly moved when I willed it to go; my brain felt numb. I dozed irregularly on the flight from Inchon to Dulles. I fell flat on my bed and snoozed. Shortly after my slumber began, a knock sounded, followed by further thumping, and then banging. I remembered Mickey Ploughman had been scheduled to drive up from Asheville today.

When I opened the door, he faced me. "Heard you cracked the case?"

I rubbed my eyes. "No, Roth and Wizard did."

Mickey, a muscular, hefty man with short brown hair, pushed past me into the suite. "Wizard, like pointy hat and wand?"

"No. Wizard, like a computer geek."

"Roth told me to drive up."

I smiled at him. "Got too much for one person to do. You're a lifesaver."

He handed me a box. "Your cherished gun."

"How do you feel? Ready to hunt a suspect?"

"Need a short lie-down first."

He had driven straight up from Asheville, taking two quick stops for gas, and now planned to do a catnap. I got him settled into his room in a loft above the central part of the suite. He had brought my Wilson Combat M1911, a semi-automatic pistol. While he napped, I cleaned my gun. I felt secure now, with my pistol and Mickey present.

He would protect my back while I searched for a violent killer. When I finished wiping down my weapon, I sat on the couch and phoned Sook. "I'm back. Where are you?"

"In my office with Bin Bie. Ms. Roth told me Sang-hun, our dead ammo carrier, lived."

I brushed down my cowlick. "I think he's still in Virginia with the relics. We need to find him. I'm on my way over to see you."

We hung up. I stood up and shouted for Mickey to wake up.

I introduced Mickey when we arrived at Sook's office. He recalled Mickey from his visit to Asheville. "You married Ms. Roth's cook? She served me tea."

I nodded at Sook. For everyday tranquility at Roth mansion, I do not bellyache—in front of Mickey—about Taylor's mania for Appalachian cuisine. "Yeah, Taylor is our chef."

Sook studied us. "Ms. Roth must believe crown still in Virginia. She sends two operatives here."

We—Sook, Mickey, Bin Bie, and I—walked to the fifth-floor conference room and sat, beginning activities to locate the fifth soldier. We might get lucky and pick up Sang-hun's trail at the motel where he stayed when he arrived at Dulles. Too easy. I figured the planner—the mysterious man—would have hidden him away so we couldn't find him. If we couldn't trace Sang-hun from his motel, we would be stuck dragging the city to locate him. I wouldn't enjoy looking for a single Korean in a vast metropolis like Washington, D.C. - Baltimore. We had one thing going for us—Sook had the staff and the resources to search the city.

Sook picked up his ballpoint pen and clicked its mechanism. "How we find Sang-hun?"

I looked at my case notepad to find the hotel where Sang-hun arranged to stay when he got to Virginia. "He planned to stay at the Marriott hotel at Dulles Airport. We know because we found his itinerary."

Bin Bie slammed his open palm on the conference-room table. "We have done it. We are going to catch Seong-gi's killer."

Sook's eyes bugged out and his jaw dropped. "You nitwit. Nothing solved yet. Keep your outlook small."

Sook and Bin scowled at each other. Mickey and I gazed out the windows along one wall. Koreans are polite, but these two occasionally flew into a rage between themselves.

Monday evening, Mickey, Sook, Bin, and I went to the Marriott. After we tipped the assistant manager, he explained Sang-hun had checked out of his room long ago and left no forwarding address. Sang-hun didn't use a credit card to reserve the room but paid a hefty upfront cash amount and paid cash upon checkout. The hotel security no longer had video records from his stay. We had struck out, but I had expected the criminals would cover their trail well.

Standing outside the hotel, Sook kept studying the passport picture of Sang-hun. "Hard to believe old comrade lived on after his trauma and came back to steal Silla relics."

Bin took the picture and studied it. "It's Sang-hun. We deserted him on battlefield. How horrible must have been for him."

I stood beside the front passenger door to Sook's BMW. "If he's still in Northern Virginia, we need to find him. He likely kidnapped and murdered Seong-gi, your old squad leader, and stole the artifacts."

Bin Bie hung down his head. "Sang-hun murdered. We must punish him. Our fault—we deserted him."

Sook ignored Bin and seemed calm, maybe sensing we were making progress, however slow. "Did Sang-hun ever travel outside of Korea?"

"We checked. He never left Korea until this trip," I replied.

Sook got into his car and seemed to be thinking what to do next. "Maybe—after he checked out of hotel—he took room within the Korean-American people."

I slid into the passenger seat. "Why?"

Sook frowned at me as if I had asked a silly question. "Hide among people look like him."

"Exploring for lone Korean in his ethnic group tough, like search for fur on a snake," Bin observed from the rear of the car. "Hard find single individual among many Korean-American inhabitants in Washington, D.C."

Sook turned his head to stare at Bin. "Difficult or not, we must find Sang-hun."

Mickey cleared his throat while seated in the rear. "Next moves?"

I closed the car door. "Let's get back to Sook's conference room and figure it out."

Sook, Bin, Mickey, and I got together—in the conference room on the top floor of Sook's office building next to the Dulles Toll Road—to hunt down the fifth soldier. As I sat, the skin on my arms felt a lovely jolt of cold air. Outside, I had suffered a muggy day: no cloud cover, temperatures in the mid-90s Fahrenheit, and 95 percent humidity. In the summer air, my shirt stuck to my back like a suction cup.

"How do we find Sang-hun Lee?" I asked. "The thieves meticulously planned the burglary. I bet he's using an alias. We search using his passport picture, not his name."

Bin snorted. "Good luck with that. His passport picture looks like every fourth Korean man."

He voiced the truth, but I needed useful ideas, not moaning. I glared at him. "We have two realities to work with: we have this picture, and we know he recently arrived in Virginia. Got a better idea, let us have it. Otherwise, help pull the load and shut up."

We sat around the conference-room table, overhead fluorescent bulbs illuminating the room as the sun went down. In the open floor area outside the conference room, eager-appearing Korean-American employees sat in cubicles ready to do Sook's bidding.

"A second Asian took part in the murder and robbery," I continued. "We have little information about this additional person, a tall man."

Sook, who had slouched in his chair, now leaned forward, spread his arms on the table, and cleared his throat for attention. "We start our search for Sang-hun now. Remember, a rolling stone gathers no boss."

Mickey, seated across the table from me, glanced at me with a quizzical expression.

"Moss," I said, "that's *moss*. Gathers no moss."

"Oh," Sook replied, before continuing. "Seven to eight million people live in greater Baltimore–Washington region. We can't search everywhere at once. Suggest we begin hunt Sang-hun in smaller area, maybe Fairfax County."

"About thirteen percent of county's population is Asian," Bin recalled. "Thirteen percent might be higher—illegal immigrants."

"Where in Fairfax County do we begin?" I asked. "To show his passport picture?"

Bin brushed his eyebrow with his right finger, perhaps taking time to consider. "Start off in areas like Centreville, Annandale, Herndon, McLean, and neighborhoods near them. What do we need get started?"

I realized we had little to use in a search. Were our fifth soldier to return to South Korea, Lee would alert us; we would break off here and catch up with Sang-hun in his native country. If he returned, I wondered if he would continue to be of use to the second man, the planner. There was always the Han River. Also, maybe Lee, working at his end, would find a new lead to Sang-hun? I doubted the niece would help Lee. She seemed to have grown weary of him. Anyway, we had the passport picture of the fifth soldier and we could start. "We'll work out how to ask people if they saw Sang-hun. As we hunt, we'll get better at asking." *And hopefully we'll catch our man.*

Mickey had brought donuts into the conference room from the kitchenette. He stopped eating. "Hand out the missing guy's picture. Offer a reward for information. Set up a hotline for phone calls." He went back to eating.

Sook and Bin glanced at each other. Sook spread his arms out to his sides with his palms up. Bin responded by raising his eyebrows. Thinking, Sook stood up and walked to the side windows, glancing down at the ducks in the pond at the building's rear. "Fat ducks. Everybody feeds them." He returned to his seat at the long table. "We offer one-thousand-dollar reward."

Bin nodded in agreement. "Our company ID card is plastic and size of credit card. Put Sang-hun's picture on side of card. Opposite side, print message in English and Korean, offering thousand dollars for his location."

Pausing again, Sook continued to peer out the conference room windows at the pond in the dying light, studying the Canadian geese, who's honking cut through the double-pane glass windows. "Make plastic handouts on ID-card machine. List hotline number. Hand out many cards; make snow blizzard."

I estimated we had a small likelihood of success in finding Sang-hun; nevertheless, using a plastic identity card along with a generous reward could work. We would hire students—home on summer break—to augment Sook's staff. They'd hand out the plastic articles, like Girl Scouts selling cookies. We spent the next half hour finalizing our game plan and then turned Sook's team loose on making the cards and organizing teams to hand them out to the public.

That evening, the first teams deployed with cards. Sook and Bin saturated Centreville, Annandale, Herndon, McLean, and Vienna with the picture of Sang-hun. By late evening, we had begun to receive phone calls. Bin frowned at a sheaf of papers on the table. "Nothing useful in notes about calls to hotline. Some are funny."

"Funny? Like what?" I asked.

He turned through his papers. "Woman reported her Ford Focus stolen. Maybe Sang-hun took it. Two guys we sent found weeds had covered her car."

I nodded and smiled. "What else?"

Bin continued flipping the papers. "Another woman heard strange noise in her house. Intruder might be man we search for. Turned out to be her noisy cat."

We had to be patient and keep our spirits high while searching for Sang-hun—like waiting for a tax-refund check to arrive in the mailbox.

Mickey and I stayed in the conference room, eating the sandwiches Sook had ordered for a casual dinner. My partner had moved little during the planning meeting. He had cat traits: he could sit back motionless for extended periods, escaping notice, or jump into action in an instant.

Sook walked past the conference room, and then stopped and turned in to join us. He took out his ballpoint pen and repeatedly clicked its retractor.

"Something bothers you?" I asked.

He stopped clacking his pen and sat down. "Sang-hun kept picture of our old mortar crew pinned to wall in his hut?"

I nodded. "It's a wrinkled photograph, timeworn. He crossed out the face of Seong-gi, your old squad leader."

He clicked the retractor again and then stopped. "We deserted our comrade. Ran away with the relics, ditching him on battlefield. He must hate us?"

I lowered my half-eaten sandwich. "Don't know," I replied.

"What if he put up picture to hate us, to plan revenge on us?"

Mickey and I remained quiet.

Sook bobbed his head up and down as if agreeing with himself. "One day I turn around, and he is there to kill me." Sook seemed moribund, his head drooping, almost down between his legs.

I changed the subject. "We don't have proof that Sang-hun stole the artifacts. However, I don't think it's a fluke he flew to Northern Virginia just before the theft occurred. Maybe your gardener could tell us if Sang-hun's picture reminds him of either of the two men in the woods behind the Great Falls house."

Finally, he raised his shoulders and stood. "You right. Worth trip." He called Garcia, who agreed to meet us at a nearby Starbucks.

At the Starbucks, we parked beside the gardener's Ford F-150 pickup. Inside the shop, Sook and I ordered tea and coffee respectively and sat down across from Garcia. Based on my previous meeting with Garcia, I judged him as overeager to please Sook. I worried he might fabricate his story to satisfy the man who paid him.

Sook sat down with his tea. "Thank you—meet us again."

"Anytime, Mr. Park. Have you found the two men who were in the woods behind your house?"

"We think they wanted rob house," Sook said, "We have picture of man we suspect, the older one. Would you examine and tell us if this was person who came through woods?"

Sook handed Sang-hun's passport picture to the gardener, who studied it carefully. I sipped my twenty-ounce coffee and waited, trying to fight off the sudden return of jetlag.

"Could be the man," Garcia concluded. "His goatee and the way his eyes peek out from under his eyebrows . . . reminds me of the face I saw in the woods. He was the slower-moving guy of the two."

I set down my drink. "Are you sure?"

Garcia studied the photo again. "Not sure."

As Sook and I left Starbucks, I went over our investigative strategy in my mind. I didn't think it smart to concentrate only on Sang-hun and ignore Wang Gang. I wanted to do more to investigate him. What if he had the crown and gold jewelry and in my rush to find the fifth soldier, I didn't catch Gang? Bruce would never miss an opportunity to rub my nose in the grime of that shortcoming. Friends are like that—hubris checkers. Sitting in the passenger seat, I pondered what to do about Gang. I had been casing his residence and had an idea how I could learn more about him. Now that Mickey had arrived, I would ask him to help me.

NORTHERN VIRGINIA—27 JUNE 2000

I took Carla Diaz out for a date at the Sweet Sailing Tavern, finishing beers and a meal at a rectangular bar, sitting and joking with a visiting real-estate group well on their way to inebriation. She had the day off, and I had taken her out to lunch. Carla appeared magnificent, wearing black dress pants, an oyster-white, button-down, silk top, a string of white pearls, and high heels. She talked about people she knew at her job and made them funny and alive for me. When I described my experience with Roth and Taylor and Mickey, Carla laughed and empathized with my encounters. At times, I sensed she knew what I thought before I spoke the thought. Carla understood people. Ever so slightly, she made me uncomfortable. After I'd downed a few beers, Carla's appearance grew naughtier in my eyes, my libido swelling with lust. Sure, beauty is only skin deep, but with beer, it goes deeper.

I had just ordered a growler of the Barking Frog Ale to take back to the Residence Inn—along with Carla. My mobile phone rang. I answered. Sook.

The Sweet Sailing Tavern maintained a high noise level, forcing patrons to lean close to converse. Because of the merriment around me, I could not understand what Sook said. I sensed grief in his voice, stumbling through phrases with a squeaky voice. Excusing myself to take the call, I stepped outside onto the patio, moving into a hush like after the conclusion of a Fourth of July fireworks display.

"Sook, slow down. What happened?"

"He's dead."

"Who?"

"They killed him."

"Killed who?"

Sook moaned. "Someone killed Yeong-ho, shot him in his backyard. First Seong-gi—now Yeong-ho."

Young-ho is gone? But why? The burglars had already taken the crown. What danger did he pose to them? Maybe Sook had figured it out. It could be Sang-hun had begun payback because his old mortar crew deserted him? "Yeong-ho? Our comedian? When?"

"Last night."

My brain slowly grasped Sook's news. "Why shoot Yeong-ho? Who told you?"

"His wife called me. She in house when Yeong-ho killed."

What had happened? I had to get to the site. "Has the crime scene been cordoned off?"

"Fairfax County police taped off backyard area."

"Tell me everything she said."

"Yeong-ho prepared barbeque behind house."

"Then, what?" I asked.

"She went outside, onto deck," Sook said. "Tall man . . . in black . . . shot her husband. Killer left, police arrived."

I needed to get there, to move swiftly. What would I do with Carla? She was too classy to dump. Couldn't take her to a murder. "Stay with the wife. We need to know what police tell her."

"Wife frantic. Wanted me come to house—help her."

"Did you tell her about the Silla relics?"

"I did not."

I heard Sook's muffled snuffles through my mobile phone, a traumatized man. "Listen, Sook, don't talk to the police without me present."

"Okay."

"Say I'm security guarding you, and you want your bodyguard there. How soon can I talk to the wife?"

"Come now. I am at Yeong-ho's house."

After terminating the call, I sat on a concrete bench outside the Sweet Sailing Tavern. Was this slaying revenge by Sang-hun or a red herring by the thieves to get us off the trail, divert us from tracking down the stolen relics? The robbers didn't need a red herring because our investigation had slowed, while we searched for Sang-hun. Had I investigated one way when I should have gone another? Instead of chasing the artifacts, should I have been guarding the soldiers who stole the objects back in 1950? Did the killers intend to continue slaying until Sook and Bin were dead? I considered my investigation might have just capsized like an overloaded ferry in a rough sea.

I stood up and went back into the restaurant, walking into the room chill, leaving the extreme mugginess behind. First, I had to apologize to Carla, explaining something drastic had happened at work.

She watched me as I sat down on the stool beside her at the inside bar. "Was it bad news?"

"Terrible," I said.

She stuck out her lower lip. "You're going to drop me back at the Residence Inn, aren't you?"

"Sorry about that."

She stood up from the barstool and leaned against me, pressing her blouse front against my arm. In response to her touch, adrenalin poured into my bloodstream. "Don't apologize. Tell me what happened."

"Someone murdered."

"You're investigating?"

"Yeah."

She pulled back and stared into my eyes. "Your job's fascinating. Can I go with you?"

"No."

"I want to learn."

Learn what? Did this have to do with that time she had asked about how a detective operates? "No."

Carla watched me intently as if planning. "If you take me along, you can start finding the killer sooner." She pushed against me again. I couldn't think straight. I was a puppet to her strings. I didn't answer her.

Her big brown eyes fixed on my face. "If I'm in the way, I'll stay in the car."

Silence. I felt my face sweltering. I wanted to talk with Yeong-ho's wife as soon as possible. To drop Carla off at her room would cost time. "Promise me you'll stay in the car if I ask you," I said.

She immersed me in her mega-bright smile. "I promise you."

"Yeah, you can come."

She stood on her tiptoes to pull my head down and kissed me. Then she brushed a strand of her ponytail out of her face and said to the waiter, "Check."

Our relationship had taken an unusual twist, based on her curiosity and my rush to get to a crime scene. "Carla, I'm not sure this is a good idea. There's been a killing."

She grasped my hand and pulled me toward the door. "I'll keep out of the way. Let's go."

"Yeah, you said that." As we departed the tavern, I pulled out my cell phone to call Sook back and tell him I would have my assistant with me.

# # #

I drove to the home where Yeong-ho had been gunned down. White, billowy cumulus clouds gathered above me, followed by black clouds further out where the sky met the horizon. A summer rain headed my way. The ever-present humidity grew. I put up the Mustang's windows and switched on the AC. In a tree, a murder of crows with glossy black plumage shouted out their calls. Wearing a white blouse and skirt, and blowing her nose into tissues, Yeong-ho's wife waited with Sook.

Sook led Lilly, the wife, into the kitchen, where she cried for a few moments.

He stood beside her. "I talked with a detective named Powell," he said. "Medical examiner took the body away. Police examined backyard crime scene."

Lilly stared at the kitchen walls and sobbed. She would be difficult to interview. I hoped Sook had already talked with her and learned all that took place. "How did this happen?"

He began telling Lilly's story. "She spoke in spurts and sobs. Difficult to understand her."

I had my notepad out and began jotting. "Tell me what you've got."

"She told me Yeong-ho arrived home—yesterday evening—hot and exhausted," Sook said. "He had soaked and wrinkled his suit and shirt during the day."

Carla heated water on the stove and poked in a drawer beside the stove, evidently searching for tea bags.

Sook fiddled with his ballpoint pen as he talked. "He shed his suit and tie; showered to cool off."

He paused. Carla found tea bags and put them in cups to brew.

Lilly wiped her nose and stood straight. "I tell now. Last night, my husband came home depressed."

"Why was that?" I asked.

"He had learned his old squad leader, Seong-gi, no longer lived," Lilly said. "Grieved he never again drinks *soju* with old friend. Husband kept saying no way his dear friend deserved to die violent death. Yeong-ho declared killing because of a treasure brought from Korea."

Sook and I listened carefully to hear what Lilly said next. In his grief, had Yeong-ho told her about the Silla tomb and relics brought to America?

"I asked husband what *treasure*, but he no tell me. He repeated word *if . . . if . . . if*, like stuck phonograph record. Said he'd missed opportunity give back something and save Seong-gi." Lilly bawled again.

Yeong-ho had thought the Silla treasure brought a curse like a ransacked Egyptian tomb would bring forth a mummy in an old black-and-white movie.

The doorbell rang. Carla put her arm around the wife to comfort her. Sook went to the front door and came back with a casserole, from a neighbor expressing condolence. Lilly had stopped crying and could continue. "Yeong-ho looked at backyard as sun went down. He headed to gas barbeque with platter of chicken and vegetables. He wanted cook evening meal."

Carla gave Lilly a cup of tea. "I made salad," Lilly said. "Joined Yeong-ho on patio—kept his spirits up. He sprayed vegetable oil on grill, with his back to woods behind our yard." Lilly stopped to sob and talk to herself in a mumble.

Then she resumed describing what had happened. "Man, in black, appeared behind us—no sound, no warning. In Korean, he said, 'Long time, Yeong-ho.'"

Lilly put her face down. "Husband jumped as if large dog had barked. He turned, holding can of vegetable oil in one hand and hot mitt in other. Man's face covered with dark mask, and he had object in his hand, a pistol."

Carla gave Lilly a tissue, and she blew her nose and restarted her story. "Yeong-ho stared at gun and said, 'What you want?'"

Lilly broke down again, sobbing and struggling to get her breath. Sook had begun fidgeting and busying himself clearing plates off the kitchen table.

At this point, Sook related what Lilly had told him. "'Revenge,' the dark man said, 'Revenge for awful thing you did.' He shot Yeong-ho—*Pop! Pop! Pop!*—in chest."

Just then, Lilly regained her composure. "My husband screamed as if in terrible agony, and his legs collapsed, dropping him onto patio deck. With my Yeong-ho flat on his back, the dark figure shot him twice—*Pop! Pop!*—in head."

Lilly's arm jerked and swatted across the kitchen table, knocking over a box of cereal. "Husband lay still. Dark-cloaked man dropped card on Yeong-ho's chest."

No one moved. She kept talking. "Masked man says, 'This my vengeance.' I screamed."

When Lilly shook with tremors and stopped speaking, Sook picked up her account as she had told him earlier. "Neighbors opened windows and called offers of help. One friend saw large figure in black—pants, shirt, gloves, and balaclava—leave patio and walk into darkness of trees behind house. Assassin walked with stiff gait, like old man."

"Must lie down," Lilly said and left the kitchen.

I watched her leave. "Why didn't the killer shoot her?"

Carla answered. "Didn't need to. A black mask covered his face."

I rinsed my cup and saucer and placed them beside the sink. It was growing dark. "Turn on the patio lights. Let's examine the murder scene."

Carla rotated to me with a questioning glance. "What about the yellow tape? Says 'Police Line Do Not Cross.'"

"Don't see an officer," I replied. "Let's peek."

As Sook, Carla, and I walked under the yellow tape into the backyard, the overhead clouds turned dark, and rain seemed in the cards. I studied the far corners of the yard. A thick border of deciduous trees—red maple, sweetgum, and red oak—surrounded their backyard. Yesterday, as the sun had just set and the area had faded into blackness, Yeong-ho's neighbors had likely settled down to dinner or cocktails. I observed Yeong-ho had mounted floodlights to illuminate his wooden patio upon which stood a barbeque grill.

"He had a nice set up to enjoy suburbia."

Sook nodded. "That he did. The police found the gas grill still ignited."

Based on what Sook and Lilly had told me, I visualized the progression of the assassin: emerging from the tree line, coming up behind Yeong-ho spraying vegetable oil on the cooking grate, and firing his pistol at Yeong-ho point blank. "Can I see a copy of the card the dark man dropped on his victim?"

Sook handed me a paper copy of the assassin's note. The card—written originally in Korean but translated into English—had the message, "Let the revenge begin."

"The original note's in Korean," I said. "Makes sense the killer spoke to Yeong-ho in Korean."

"Yes," Sook agreed.

The police, to show the location of the homicide, had drawn—in white chalk—an outline of a dead human on the patio. Carla took off her shoes and knelt at the edge of the wood deck, poking in the grass next to the wood frame. "I saw the patio light reflect off a shiny object."

She bent her head closer to the grass. "Mr. Park, would you hand me the fork on the grill?" Carla stabbed in the lawn with the fork and pulled it back with a spent shell casing resting in a tine.

I took the fork from Carla, found a transparent plastic envelope for food, and put the shell casing in the container. "You did good, Carla. We'll get this to the Fairfax County police."

I studied the spent casing. "It's a .22, same as the caliber used to kill Seong-gi."

Sook pointed at the casing. "The same gun that killed my old friend in Korea?"

"Doubt it. Easier to buy a .22 pistol here than carry one into the U.S. But it's someone's weapon of choice."

Sook kept staring at the chalk outline of where Yeong-ho had fallen. Sook's mouth hung open, and he didn't move. Small raindrops began falling, reminiscent of tears.

# # #

I departed Yeong-ho's home and drove Carla to the Residence Inn. She hadn't gotten in the way.

She grinned at me from the passenger's seat of the Mustang. "You owe me a raincheck. You cut short our outing today."

"You did well calming Lilly—got her to talk," I said. "Good on you for spotting the shell. Sook is getting it to the police."

Carla smiled again, kissed me on the lips, and jumped out of the car. "You have a grim job. But it's stimulating. See you soon—right?" She glared at me.

I grinned back. "Right."

After opening a beer, I called Roth from my suite at the Residence Inn and filled her in on the death of Yeong-ho.

"We have a problem," she said when I had finished.

"It's like Brer Rabbit driving his fist into the Tar-Baby," I suggested. "The more we delve into the theft, the more we sink into a bog."

Nervous about the next step in the case, I settled back on the couch and brushed down my cowlick. "Sook may be wondering if he's safe. He appears shaken by these two killings."

"Tell me again," my boss asked. "Do the Fairfax County police have a suspect? Does the wife know about the theft from the Great Falls house?"

"No and no, not that we are aware. The police haven't talked with Sook or me about suspects." How did I let Yeong-ho's death happen? I should have seen it coming.

"You think Sang-hun left the message?" she asked.

"I do."

"Considering the two deaths," she asked, "will Sook Park disclose information to the police about the artifacts?"

"He's determined to say nothing to the officers about the relics."

Outside, the rain continued to beat against the window of my suite.

Silence descended on each end of the line. After a minute, Roth said, "So we speculate one of the thieves shot Seong-gi in South Korea, traveling immediately afterward to the U. S.? If the person, or persons, is still in the U.S., then the artifacts may be here, waiting to be smuggled out?"

Roth couldn't see me, but I nodded. "Yeah."

I carried the phone into the small kitchen area and tossed my empty beer bottle in the trash. "I'll keep checking with Lee to see if

Sang-hun returns to Korea." I opened another bottle of beer and settled back on the couch.

"Bin's uncle has many workers coming and going from Korea," Roth said. "I'll have Bruce fire up his computer to find out what he can about those Korean workers at the uncle's warehouse in Baltimore."

"We need to scrutinize Wang Gang more carefully and either drop him or find something connecting him to the theft," I said. "He is the one person who declared he wanted the relics." The line fell silent again. I didn't want to discuss my plan to check out Gang.

"Be there when the Fairfax County police question the widow or Sook Park," Roth continued. "Inform me immediately if the officers learn of the artifacts."

Having given me my instructions, Roth disconnected.

As I hung up, I thought I needed to be careful tomorrow. I had to seal my lips concerning the theft of the Silla treasure and, at the same time, pump the cops for information about a murder. How would I do that?

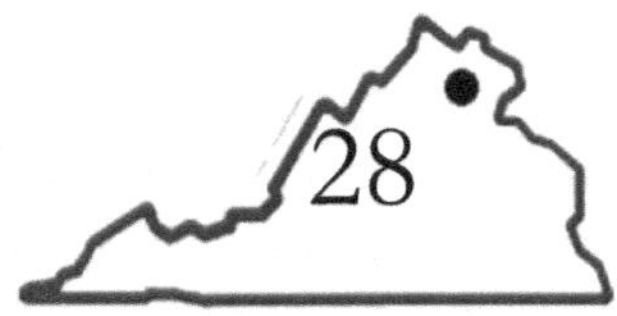

NORTHERN VIRGINIA—28 JUNE 2000

The Fairfax County police arranged to interview Lilly, Yeong-ho's wife, at her home. She called Sook and asked him to assist her at the meeting. After agreeing to join them, I drove to her house in McLean, again expressed my condolences, and waited with Sook for the authorities to arrive.

The police came around ten o'clock and quietly gathered around a couch at one end of the living room. Sook, sitting close beside me, whispered this police department had a solid reputation in the community for professionalism. Lilly said nothing but sat beside Sook with her head down, avoiding eye contact. If the size of the police contingent were an indicator, the county had thrown enormous resources into finding the killer. Sook continued leaning toward me and pointed out the man in charge of the homicide investigation, Detective Russell Powell.

"Met him yesterday," Sook said softly. "Asked about him. He is leading expert in criminal investigations. Considers all possibilities in a case."

"You're saying the county assigned their best man?"

"Yes. Well-known for tracking down criminals."

I leaned back in my chair and studied the detective and his troop. A single Fairfax County patrol officer stood behind him. Among the officers, Beer and Ice Cream, from the FBI and CHA respectively, sat noiselessly. The Fairfax County police had linked Yeong-ho's death with the FBI investigation into missing Silla relics.

Powell stood and began the interview, dominating the room with his bulbous nose, broad face, and fixed, predatory gaze. He dressed to be dapper: azure-blue shirt, matching tie, and tan suit. In asking each person present to identify themselves, he used a loud, jarring voice resembling a fog horn. I took an instant dislike to him; to evade his attention, I needed to control my sarcasm, comparable to holding back an escaping hiccup.

Sook introduced me as a private investigator in charge of security for his business. Powell glared down at me and declared his investigation had priority over a private enquiry. He asked to see my P.I. license, subsequently examining my North Carolina license cautiously, making notations in his notebook. I sensed he didn't trust me—even though I have a virtuous face. The homicide detective wrote down the address of the motel where I was staying and pursed his lips.

Detective Powell turned away from me and began to question Lilly. He asked if her late husband had adversaries. The wife knew of no one seeking revenge. With Sook's aid, she reiterated the events in the backyard. She had little knowledge of her husband's job but knew he worked closely with Sook Park. Seeking an explanation of the murdered man's work before his death, Powell asked questions of Sook. In answer, our client reviewed Yeong-ho's business projects. The detective asked for permission to search the dead man's office for clues. Sook agreed.

Detective Powell told us not to share any info, which we would learn in the meeting, with reporters. He admitted he had no likely suspect or leads. Someone had shot Yeong-ho with a small-caliber weapon, a .22 pistol. As the neighbors had not heard the shots, perhaps the shells were subsonic rounds. The crime-scene technicians found no shell casings on the ground and no fingerprints on the card left near the dead man's body, but Sook Park had found one shell casing in the backyard. The police laboratory had gotten a forefinger copy and a thumbprint off the shell and had begun analyzing them. Searching for sightings of the assassin or his getaway car, officers had been ringing doorbells in the neighborhood and hunting for home-surveillance footage.

Powell flipped through his notepad and then closed it, evidently satisfied he had asked his questions and gotten answers. He glanced at the FBI agent. Turning back to Sook, Powell said, "I understand the FBI talked to the late Mr. Yeong-ho Park about artifacts taken from South Korea during the Korean War. The FBI has follow-up questions to ask you. They suspect Mr. Park's death and their investigation are linked."

I figured the detective had left Sook with a quandary: he would want to assist in catching Yeong-ho's killer, but should he insist on having his lawyer present? I leaned near his ear. "Want your lawyer?"

Sook stared ahead and sucked his lower lip into his mouth. "I help detective catch person who killed Yeong-ho. No lawyer."

At this point in the questioning, the FBI agent, the man I termed Beer, took over interrogating Sook. "Mr. Park, we meet again. You knew Yeong-ho Park from your army days in the Korean War. Is that right?"

"Yes."

"In August 1950, you two were together near Gyeongju in South Korea, is that correct?"

"Yes."

"Then the two of you left Korea and journeyed to the U.S.?"

Sook appeared unruffled so far. "You know that."

"Did you carry stolen Korean artifacts to the U.S.?" Beer asked.

Sook leaned back in his chair and nonchalantly picked at his left ear before answering. "I have no artifacts. You asked that question before."

"Mr. Park, you want to catch the murderer of Mr. Yeong-ho Park, don't you?"

Sook stared at him for a long while and then gradually nodded.

The FBI agent spread his left arm out toward the CHA investigator. "My colleague from Korea, Mr. Cho, has evidence suggesting you stole artifacts from the area where you last fought in Korea. We need to know if you took objects. Could this murder be connected to those purportedly stolen artifacts?"

"I have no artifacts. Told you before."

"Think deeply about what you are saying, Mr. Park," Beer responded. "Detective Powell needs to know all the facts to solve this murder."

"I have no artifacts."

During the questioning, Beer did the talking. The CHA agent, Ji-hun, listened and gave a slight node of an agreement after each Beer question. Ji-hun didn't ask questions himself. I had a hunch the two of them had arranged to let the FBI agent lead the cross-examination.

Why was that? Maybe Beer was a *bad cop,* and Ji-hun was a *good cop.* Or maybe Ji-hun just didn't feel comfortable with his English.

All during the interrogation, Sook took on an inscrutable guise. He did not let slip any information about the recent theft or the death of Seong-gi in Korea. Eventually, Beer gave up questioning Sook and turned the lead back to Powell. The detective thanked Lilly for answering questions and closed the interview. I felt thankful Sook had maintained his composure during the interrogation. The detective's issues had not been difficult, but he had just begun his case investigation. I expected Powell's queries would become more challenging going forward.

As the police left, the detective, a fireplug of a man about six feet tall and two hundred and twenty pounds, asked to speak with me outside. On the lawn of the home, he turned to face me. His body language projected a no-nonsense stance: crossing his arms over his chest and standing with his face about a foot from mine. "Gannon, I expect you to stay out of my investigation."

He didn't scare me—Roth scares me. "I understand, Detective, and I will accept your direction." I flashed my most obsequious smile at the police officer.

Lee and I had taken fingerprints in Sang-hun's hut in Korea. If those fingerprints matched the prints on the .22 spent casing, we would have connected the fourth soldier to Yeong-ho's murder. I doubted the detective would share his copy of the fingerprints. He seemed hardnosed. "Could I get a copy of the fingerprints on the .22 shell?" I asked.

He pulled on his chin, a frequent twitch of his, and tried to terrify me with his glacier stare. "We'll see. I intend to check you out with the Asheville Police. Will they tell me you are trustworthy, or that you are a smart-aleck *know-it-all?*"

By his tone, he emphasized know-it-all. How could he categorize me so quickly? Was I so transparent? Anyway, I sensed I wasn't getting anything from him. "I have had my misunderstandings with the Asheville Police, and I have helped them in the past."

Powell paused several seconds. "Let's see if you'll help me. I gather that you were in Fairfax Country when the slaying took place. Is that right?"

"Yeah."

"What were you doing here?"

"I worked on general security upgrades for Mr. Park's business."

Powell smirked. "You flew up to Virginia to do general security upgrades?"

"Yeah. We're conscientious." I smirked.

He emitted a snort. "You expect me to believe that? There must have been more than general security. What are you not telling me?"

"My business with Mr. Park is confidential."

"So much for your helping the police when you can. What are you keeping from me? I'd better not find you are holding something back regarding my case."

"Detective, I am just a plodding private eye. Good luck with your case."

Powell moved such that his face was inches from mine. "A consequence always happens in response to our actions. You will come to rue your attitude toward me."

I stared back at the detective like we were two kids on a playground. "Detective, unless you plan to kiss me. Back off."

He backed away. "I don't like you, Gannon. You're big, overdressed, and you're loud. Stay out of my way." He turned and strode to his car.

I felt shattered since I had dressed well—khaki moleskin slacks, white polo shirt, a dark-blue blazer, brown derby shoes, and sunglasses—and I had been on my best behavior. As he got into his vehicle, it came to me—why hadn't I spoken the old cliché, "takes one to know one"? *Darn, too late.*

After Sook and I had watched the detective drive off, I asked, "What happens if Detective Powell finds out about the Great Falls house and gets a search warrant? He'll find a vault-like room with nothing in it. How would you explain an empty high-security room?"

Sook bit his lower lip. "What you think I should do?"

"If Bin and you've got some oil or watercolor paintings, you might carry them to the Great Falls house and hang them in the exhibit room. You'd establish the place is secure to protect your pictures, and you'd eliminate any suspicion about empty walls."

Sook considered me and nodded. "Anything else?"

"Tell Manny you are continuing to keep him on as a caretaker at the house. He seems concerned about losing his job. Get him to relax and treat the burglary as confidential."

"Okay," he said. "Paintings and watercolors to Great Falls home and talk to Manny."

"Great," I said.

#

I left Sook with Lilly and, on my way back to my motel, stopped at the Lakeside Inn in Reston. I ordered a cheeseburger with an ESB beer and relaxed in a glass-enclosed patio. Diners ate and, viewing through the plate-glass sides of the dining area, watched small rectangular boats—like floating docks—motor across a lake. A few individuals in kayaks paddled over the water. When the lunch-time crowd had thinned out, I phoned Roth and reported verbatim on the police interrogation of Yeong-ho's widow and Sook.

"The FBI presence at the questioning means they're trying to locate the relics," Roth said. "I presume they've tapped our client's phones."

"Yeah. But the authorities haven't learned our clients own the Great Falls house, or they would have said something," I added.

"Plus, they don't know thieves stole the crown," Roth replied.

As I talked to Roth, my subconscious had been working on an idea. "Oddly, I got the feeling the CHA agent, Ji-hun Cho, had things on his mind other than questioning Sook about the Korean relics."

After a few seconds of silence, Roth responded, "Well, he may figure Sook Park isn't going to talk in front of the FBI. Ji-hun might want to speak alone with Sook."

The line went silent, except I could hear Roth tapping on her desk. "Hmm, it might be valuable to discuss the theft and the shooting deaths of Seong-gi in Korea and Yeong-ho in Virginia—a discussion with our clients. Arrange a talk for me with Sook Park and Bin Bie."

I said I would do so.

"We need to plan our next action and not wait for Lady Luck to rescue us," my boss said. "The trouble with Lady Luck is she doesn't care who wins."

NORTHERN VIRGINIA—28 JUNE 2000

I drove to Sook's office building in the early afternoon, parked, and rode the elevator up to the top floor. Heading to the conference room, I passed a sizeable work area filled with gray cubicles and a youthful workforce. Ahead of me a man, his back to me, stood in the doorway to our meeting space.

Approaching closer, I heard him speak, "I shoot first."

He's dressed in black. It's Sang-hun.

I rushed toward the man as I tried to pull the M1911 pistol from my belt holster. I reached him before I could grasp my gun. He must have heard me because he began to turn his head.

I rammed my shoulder into his back.

His head smashed into the door frame—*Thack!*—his body collapsed to the floor.

I grabbed the intruder's right arm above the elbow and drove my left knee into his back. I rotated his right arm behind his back, turned my head slightly, and called out, "I have him."

Sook stood above me with his mouth open. "Gun-woo."

I realized Sook's workers stood back from me, some uttering the Gun-woo name and others shouting for medical aid. The man under me had the limpness of a bag of laundry and bled on the variegated-brown rug. He had the face of a youth, the early twenties. A semiautomatic pistol lay on the carpet. "You know him?" I asked Sook.

"Wants to safeguard me. Works for me."

An EMS team arrived with a gurney and took a conscious Gun-woo to Reston Hospital. When I had first seen him, he had held a Ruger 9 mm semiautomatic pistol in his hand to explain how he would protect his boss. The medical team put Gun-woo in a hospital bed for observation, and Sook agreed to cover the costs for his employee.

Mickey, Bin, Sook, and I had assembled around the long table in Sook's conference room.

"Not your fault," Mickey whispered. "Kid had a weapon. Your MP training kicked in."

I grunted at him. "Jeezus, what if I had gotten my pistol out first?"

Our two Korean-American clients began by discussing a link between the burglary and the assassination in Virginia.

"Stealing treasure shows high intellect and planning. Killing without reason shows great stupidity," Bin said. "Work of two different people."

"Hold on," I said. "If not great stupidity, it could show vindictive anger. A single person with two different aims."

"But why would anyone kill Yeong-ho if he already had the treasure?" Bin asked. "It draws police attention and risks death penalty or life imprisonment."

"Hate," I said.

There was no financial benefit in killing the humorous Korean, but Sang-hun had stuck the photograph of his old mortar team on the wall of his hut in Korea. "The note the killer left tells us who did it," I said. "Sang-hun is stalking and killing the members of his old mortar squad."

Sitting at the head of the table, Sook clicked his ballpoint pen. "We argue for and against a theft-murder link. The link exists, and it is Sang-hun's settling of a score for our deserting him on the battlefield."

"We'll inform Roth when we call her," I said. "We're searching for a crown and for a murderer who's going to try to kill again."

Sook continued clicking the retractor on his pen. "What our next topic?"

I brushed my cowlick. "Sang-woo, Bin's uncle, had a ship confiscated by the South Korean Coast Guard. They put financial pressure on the uncle—by impounding his property. If he needed funds, then the uncle had motive and knowledge of the treasure's location."

Bin shook his head. "No, not crucial. My uncle didn't know the combination, and he is always up and down. Somehow, he always evades being a poor man. Losing a ship now and then part of smuggling business."

"What if your uncle's monetary needs were severe enough for him to kill?" I asked.

Bin pursed his lips and closed his eyelids. "No. Uncle always been trustworthy. Leave him out of this."

"Is he a killer?" Mickey asked.

"No. He is smuggler," Bin answered with a red face. "Drop it."

I waited for Bin's breathing to slow and his face to lose its flush. "I understand your loyalty to your uncle. Now understand me. Talking to your uncle is what I will be doing because I don't know who took the relics."

Bin jumped up, hurling his chair rearward, slamming into the conference room wall. He cursed at me. "Damn you." Bin stomped for the door.

Sook stood up. "PRIVATE BIE!"

Bin, his face a beet red, stopped and faced Sook.

Sook spoke calmly. "We going to locate who took our treasure and who killed our corporal . . . Seong-gi Kim. Mr. Gannon helps us. Sit down."

The room went noiseless while Bin's color returned to normal. He rolled his chair back to the table and sat. I waited for my breathing to slow and then phoned Roth on my mobile phone. I explained Sang-hun likely stalked Sook and Bin.

"Increase security," she told me. "Use Mickey to protect our clients. Arm yourselves."

"We have," I said.

Speaking over the phone to our two clients in Virginia, Roth continued, "Mickey Ploughman is an able member of my staff, highly dependable, and an excellent bodyguard. During the evening hours, we'll put armed security guards at your residences. Don will arrange for four operatives to defend you."

At that point, Roth broached the shadowy topic of ethics. "If we keep the existence of the artifacts secret, are we obstructing a police investigation and helping a murderer escape? Is our situation like the well-known example in which one can harm by deliberately drowning a child in a tub of water, but one can also harm by doing nothing to rescue a child drowning in a tub?"

At our end of the call in Virginia, Sook raised his right eyebrow. "What is your point, Ms. Roth?"

"We must weigh all risks and choose the best path to stop evil. If we tell the Fairfax County police about the theft, the Korean government will charge Messrs. Park and Bie with stealing the treasure from South Korea—they'll be deported. Revealing the burglary harms our clients and doesn't catch the murderer."

I rotated the college ring on my left hand. "I agree. Keep knowledge of the theft to ourselves."

Roth knew the theft and Korean deaths were linked just as a pair of socks; at the same time, I felt sure she had rapacious eyes connected to half the treasure. If we told the authorities about the burglary, she would lose her half of the wealth; her thinking was as simple as that. I agreed with my boss. I considered myself a moral person, but I had altered my ethics to match our circumstances.

Silence settled over the phone call as the ethics examination died.

"Bruce found information on Wang Gang," Roth said. "His companies handle imports and exports—generate a significant amount of revenue. Mr. Gang hasn't served jail time."

I wanted to know more about Gang. "He associates with known criminals, is that right?"

"He does," my boss replied. "Many of his confederates have criminal records. Federal prosecutors have indicted Mr. Gang for smuggling."

"Why does our gangster buy works of art?" I asked. "For his enjoyment or investment?"

"He's purchased many valuable paintings and sculptures. Bruce found he had occasional showings at his Leesburg home."

"In which room did he show his art?" I asked.

"He had public viewings in his basement," Roth replied. "It has air conditioning units to protect against sudden fluctuations in temperature and humidity. I gather he's a private collector who wants others to see his collected works."

Gang had power and connections to take the Silla artifacts, i.e., he had the means. He also had the motive, and he could have found out about the Great Falls house. Isaac Hunter, the fence Sook had used to sell the smaller relics, had summarized the situation: Gang might or might not be our burglar.

Roth closed further discussion. "Bruce will continue to collect information on our suspects. I'll have him suck out every shred of information about Gang.

"Mr. Park, continue to call Seong-gi's son to gather updates on the police investigation in South Korea. As you interact with Detective Powell in Virginia, take Don with you and share new developments with us."

Sitting beside me in the conference room, Sook nodded his head and said, "Will do."

Silence.

Sook glanced at me and then spoke to Roth. "I nervous. Dangerous man always ahead of you. When will you catch him?"

"We face a vicious murderer. Don't panic, but remain patient and calm," Roth said. "Remember we solve cases with persistence and infinitesimal steps, interspersed with occasional strides forward."

# # #

In late afternoon as everyone searched for a trace of Sang-hun, Sook burst into the conference room where I sat in his office building. "Have new problem. Always difficulty!" Sook was agitated, his eyes darting all around the chamber and his skin covered in a sheen of sweat.

"Manny, our caretaker, in my office. You need to hear what he say."

"What?" I asked.

"Manny wants guarantee we not dismiss him, else he tells police about theft of artifacts."

We locked eyes while I considered what Sook had just said. "Let me talk with Manny—hear him first-hand."

We walked through the open, chaotic area on the fifth floor on our way to Sook's private office. Wearing a tee shirt and jeans, Manny sat in a chair before Sook's desk. To me, he appeared forlorn and a little desperate, like a student waiting for the teacher to pass out the final, make-or-break exam. Maybe I could work with him. I sat next to Manny. "Mr. Park tells me you are thinking about going to the police, is that right?"

"I don't want to, but I be afraid the police might arrest me over the relics. Cuz I can't get a pharmacy license if I got a criminal record. I'm going to lose my job anyway, aren't I?"

At first, no one answered Manny's question. I brushed my cowlick down. "Mr. Park and Mr. Bie believe you're innocent of any complicity in the theft. Talk to them, but I understand they'll continue to employ you to take care of the Great Falls house."

Beside me, Sook nodded vigorously at Manny.

"As to the police arresting you, I assume you are referring to the allegation of taking items from Korea," I said. "No such articles are at the Great Falls house. Neither Mr. Park nor Mr. Bie has illegal items in their possession, and you certainly don't have stolen goods—no one will arrest anyone."

Sook had taken a seat behind his desk. "I not know who took items from Great Falls house night you slept, but I believe you innocent. We continue employ you as caretaker at Great Falls home."

"But why you need me? Someone took them relics. What I do at house to get paid?"

"We place oil and watercolor paintings at house. You watch over everything, including the pictures. Work for us just as before theft and forget about going to police."

"What if the police come to the house and ask me about the artifacts?" Manny asked.

"What artifacts?" Sook replied. "You no see articles. We have receipts for paintings in secure room, and those artworks are all you remember or know."

Manny sat up straight, the corners of his mouth curving upwards in a slight grin. "Okay, Mr. Park. I be a loyal employee. I didn't steal anything. I need this job to complete my schoolin'."

Sook smiled at Manny. "Good—and if asked—reply we only keep paintings in house. You don't know about other art because it not in the house."

"Got you, Mr. Park. If the police come, I know nothing."

"That's right," Sook replied.

Manny, with "Howard Pharmacy" on the front of his tee shirt, studied Sook. "Before the theft upset everything, I intended to ask you for a raise. It's been a long time since I got an increase."

Sook's eyes and mouth opened wide. "You already paid well for sleeping, eating, and studying in our house."

Manny smiled. "But getting a degree in pharmacy means a lot to me. I could lose everything by lying to the police."

Sook grimaced. "How much raise you want?"

"Because my responsibilities now include talking to the authorities, I think you should double my pay."

Sook glared. "Too much. Fifty percent increase."

"Lots more responsibility. More risk. Increase salary by 100 percent."

Sook didn't respond at first but stared angrily at Manny.

"I could get in deep trouble by fibbing to the police," Manny stressed.

Sook lowered his head. "Okay. We double your salary."

Manny and Sook shook hands. After Manny had left, I stayed at Sook's desk to talk with him. "I don't know how to evaluate Ji-hun's offer for you to call him for help," I said.

"What about him?" Sook replied.

I tapped on his desk with my college ring. "At the police station, was he willing to work with you?"

"Don't know," Sook replied. "We can't work with CHA agent if wanted to. Don't know where Silla treasure is."

I nodded. My mind returned to the hunt for the fifth soldier. I thought we might never find Sang-hun if he had already fled northern Virginia. If he had shot Yeong-ho, then maybe he remained nearby. Where was he? I wished for something, anything, to happen.

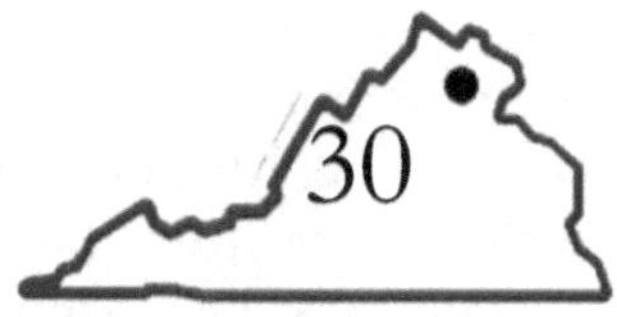

NORTHERN VIRGINIA—29 JUNE 2000

I grab a tennis racket. I stand at one end of a tennis court—a court longer and broader than regulation. From a fence behind me, people speak in low tones. An instructor—he must be the tennis pro—is on the other side of the net and hits a ball toward me, a ball bouncing far in front of me and dropping to the court—lifeless—before I can get my racket on it. The pro frowns. I hit a ball that lands in the net. Another frown. The pro hits a tennis ball that speeds past me on my left. He frowns again. I fail—no matter how hard I try—I fail repeatedly.

I woke from my nightmare. Over the years, sad dreams tormented me as I worked a case. A case gave me an opportunity to cast out my horror by solving the mystery. I couldn't run away from the investigation or my bad dreams. As soon as I succeeded, my unpleasant visions would vanish, go away, turning into a happy nightmare. I arose and prepared for another day of searching for the missing soldier, the elusive fifth.

Thursday morning, Mickey and I continued the search for Sang-hun. Sook's staff put out our query in the Korean-American community, circulating the missing man's picture in the Northern Virginia area. Once our search team identified a look-alike, a suspect, Mickey and I would investigate to determine if we had netted the fifth soldier.

Our approach was sound; the team organized and motivated. I worked through the morning. There was little for me to do but watch and wait. Occasionally, I went out and investigated a possible Sang-hun sighting. My mind grew stale like coffee simmering too long in a warming pot. My eyes stared vacantly out the conference-room windows.

Afternoon arrived and turned into evening. Mickey approached me. "The guard teams are here—waiting in the parking lot."

I spoke to Bin, who sat in the conference room with me. "When Sook and you are ready to go home, Mickey and I will hand you off to your bodyguards." Our client rose from the table and headed for the door. "I am ready. I round up Sook." My partner and I walked our two clients down to the parking lot. The security teams took over; they would guard Sook and Bin at their respective homes overnight and bring them back tomorrow.

# # #

After Mickey and I returned to our suite, our phone rang. The desirable Miss Diaz had called me. "I finished work early today. Have nothing to do. Are you working?"

My heart rate sped up. How did she do that? "Nope. Already loaded my sixteen tons."

"You're funny. I cash in my rain check for our shortened evening at the Sweet Sailing Tavern. Show me a fun time tonight at a friendly tavern in Herndon."

My throat and stomach contracted. I wanted to see more of her. However, I couldn't just abandon Mickey. "Carla, I would be delighted to check out a friendly pub with you tonight, but my colleague who just recently arrived—"

Mickey, who had his head stuck in the refrigerator, searching for food, called to me. "I'm sleepy from my drive up here." Mickey rolled his head to rest on his shoulder and closed his eyes as if sleeping. "You go ahead and wine and dine this lady."

A surge of adrenaline flushed the all-day lethargy from my system. I craved Carla, wanted to get away and be a foolish man. "Miss Diaz, I'd like nothing better than to hop over to this tavern with you."

"Marvelous. Come around to my building. We'll take my car."

Sitting in an older part of Herndon, Billy's Tavern had features like the tavern in the TV series *Cheers* but with a slight Southern accent in place of Boston enunciation. My date parked in a public lot near the pub. Upon entering and passing through the merrymakers in the first room of the bar, a smiling server called out Carla's name and instructed us to take a table in the back of a second chamber. The two large rooms had battered wooden floors, tables, and chairs; beer signs covered most walls. We started with Yuengling draft beer and a Philadelphia cheesesteak sandwich.

Over the top of my beer glass, I admired her petite shape in tight white jeans and a dark-green shirt, with the top two buttons undone, baring the onset of cleavage. I switched from leering to scanning the construction of the room, which carpenters obviously had built in a previous century. "How old is this tavern?"

"I visited the tavern's website," she said. "The town of Herndon named itself after a captain who went down with his ship in a hurricane off the coast of North Carolina. This building dates to 1897."

As she chatted, Carla gave me a full grin, making me feel warm and want to hug her. We had another round of drinks. Then she switched topics. "Do you have a nickname?"

I scooted closer to her and slid an arm around her shoulder. "Bruce and Mickey call me *Rooster* because my hair sticks up like a rooster's comb."

She placed her left hand on my thigh and flashed a wicked smile. "Oh, I bet I know why they call you rooster—and it isn't your hair."

"So, Carla, do you have a nickname?"

She leaned against me. "I do. I don't want you to hear it."

"Tell me."

"Think back to when you were growing up. It's impossible to live down a frank nickname."

"What's your nickname?"

She grimaced and raised her eyes toward the ceiling. "*Heartbreaker.*"

"I bet you are."

The corners of her mouth turned up and her eyes beamed. A lively crowd around us continued to be loud, having a grand old time. We had another round of drafts. She drank as much beer as I did. As our beers flowed, she and I began to giggle and snuggle against each other. "I'm gettin' woozy," Carla said. "Let have one last beer . . . and pay our bill." We left the bar and lurched across Elden Street to the public parking lot. Maybe I should have called a taxi. However, the

Residence Inn stood nearby, and I decided to let her drive. Once in her car, she suggested she show me her apartment; that seemed like a fantastic idea.

We were glued together as I walked to her building, bending over slightly to rest my right hand against her hip. Going in through a door to her building, she held her right index finger to her lips. "We need be . . . quiet," Carla said dully. "My fellow workers kid me about . . . bein' a party girl. Don't want a bad reputation."

"I know why . . . they think that," I said. "You . . . people person."

"Don't hear any . . . sounds. I think my colleagues asleep."

Quietly, we entered a dimly-lit living room with a small kitchen. I kissed her, and she kissed me back. I held her, and she guided me to a couch, where she sat me down and started toward the kitchen. "I've had . . . lot of beers," Carla said as if in a fog. "Thirsty for a glass of water." I watched Carla—and her snug white jeans—walk into the kitchen, drink from a glass of water, and return to the couch.

Carla snuggled close to me. I leaned on her and circled her with my arm. She moved with me, like plastic wrap sticking to a bowl.

"Take me to . . . bedroom," she whispered.

The next I remembered, we were in her bedroom in the dark. She might be drunk, but she appeared sexy to me. I slipped off my shoes. I clumsily began undoing the buttons along the front of her blouse. Everything was quiet. I inhaled and exhaled. My heart rate increased.

Dee! . . . Dee! . . . Woo! . . . Woo!

What had I done? Had her blouse been linked to an alarm?

This sound was loud; it didn't come from her. My brain couldn't focus—like just before I would fall asleep.

Carla gave out a little groan and slurred, "Oh no . . . fire alarm. They make us . . . troop out of building."

Bam! . . . Bam!

Someone banged on her front door. "Fire alarm . . . everyone out," a woman's voice announced.

"Can't move," Carla declared. "Need to evac . . . evacuate. Everybody . . . group together in the parking lot."

I tried to button up the front of her blouse but failed. The buttons had become small and my fingers fat.

"Firefighters checkin' if there a fire," she continued inarticulately. "Don't let my colleagues . . . see me drunk."

She sat up in bed, staring about as if she had lost something.

"Help me go out the window . . . on the side of the buildin' . . . no one will see me there." She abruptly laid her head back on her bed and didn't move.

I found my shoes and arranged my disheveled clothes. I wrapped the bed cover around Carla, hoisted her up over my shoulder, and walked out of the bedroom, across the living room, through the door of her unit, and out through the open front door of her residence building.

Residents were standing under the overhead lights outside the building; fire trucks, with sirens blaring, were pulling into the parking lot. The people grouped and chatted. The hotel fire alarms had gone silent.

My burden appeared sound asleep. I sensed the chattering decrease in intensity, dying from an encircling *hum* down to complete silence.

"Is that Carla?" one woman asked.

"Is she okay?" a second woman asked.

"Oh, Carla!" a third woman tittered.

"What an exit!" the second woman exclaimed.

Her friends began clapping and whistling. My head spun. I didn't know what to do. Sit down with Carla? Drop her with her friends? The crowd of women surged toward Carla and me. I placed her on a bench, wrapped in the blanket. I left her and—as I walked away—I mumbled, "Good night, sweet princess." Her friends parted to let me pass and then swarmed toward her.

I had a pounding pain in my head, but I walked toward distant lights, hoping they came from my building. I passed people standing outside the other resident structures.

The building where Carla and the other members of her team stayed had park-like grounds with BBQ grills, volleyball courts, and basketball backboards, separating it from my building. "I think the fire drill is over," one man said. "See, the firefighters are letting those people go back to their rooms."

I tottered past Mickey, standing in front of our structure.

"Good night, Don."

"Night." I entered the suite, went to my bedroom, pulled back the covers, and crawled into bed.

The next morning, I found a note under my bedroom door. In

Mickey's handwriting, the message said,

"Ms. Roth called. Told her you were exhausted from a full day of sleuthing and sleeping soundly. Miss Diaz called to say you are 'the scum of the earth,' and all her neighbors saw you carrying her out of the building over your shoulder. She said something about your failure to sneak out a side window as she instructed."

Mickey and I drove to Sook's office building. When we got there, our client explained he had been summoned to meet with Powell, the loud, overdressed police detective, at the McLean District Police Station. Sook said the interview had the purpose of exploring the killing of Yeong-ho. Sook and I agreed to say nothing about our search for Sang-hun, the fifth soldier, or the theft of treasure. Why had the detective wanted to interview our client? Had Powell picked up a rumor of the recent robbery of the Korean artifacts? Had he discovered the Great Falls house belonged to Sook and his colleagues?

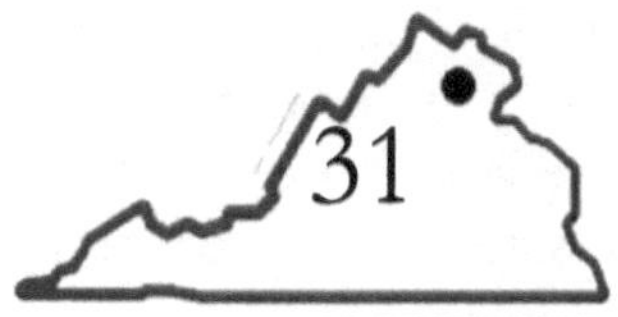

NORTHERN VIRGINIA—30 JUNE 2000

Sook and I parked the Mustang and walked toward the Fairfax County Police Station. I heard footsteps behind me and turned to see Ji-hun, the South Korean agent, hurrying after us. Sook, at medium height, and the tall Ji-hun talked in Korean for ten minutes. They spoke rapidly, and even with a Korean phrase book, I wouldn't have been able to follow them. When they finished, the Korean agent gave a small bow and hastened away.

"What was that?" I asked.

"Not sure," Sook replied. "Asked if he could talk with me. I talk."

"And?"

Sook glanced around to check if anyone could hear us. "He spoke 'off the record.' Told me call him, Ji-hun. He says he sorry for death of my two friends.

I waited while two police officers walked past us on the sidewalk. "He said 'two friends?'"

Sook stared at me. "Two dear friends."

I brushed my cowlick. "What'd he say next?"

"Needn't be adversaries. If I helped him recover relics, I am agent of Korea. No punishment."

I shook my head. "What game is he playing?"

"Told him not have relics," Sook said.

"You answered well," I said. "What else did Ji-hun say?"

Sook again glanced about and confirmed no one listened. "Ji-hun smiled and fidgeted with coin. He said, 'Call me, I help.' Then he left us and walked into the station."

I viewed Sook with raised eyebrows. "We'll wait and see. Maybe he thinks he can work a deal with you?"

Fairfax County located the District Police Station beside two critical crossroads through McLean, whose house prices are among the highest in Virginia. It was a white-collar town, with roughly ninety-seven percent of the labor force working in an office, cubicle, or another administrative setting. The community around this police station included many diplomats, members of Congress, high-ranking federal government officials, and entrepreneurs. Sook and I stood in the sun. Mickey and Bin Bie had stayed back at the office, keeping up our search for Sang-hun, the elusive fifth soldier.

Sook took out a handkerchief and wiped sweat from his temple. "Might as well go in. Hot out here."

We entered the police station, where Detective Powell waited. He sat at a desk in a room with stacks of paper files in two bookcases against a wall and paper records covering a credenza. The room had the odor of burnt coffee. He had a frown; his jet-black hair was brushed straight back with slight gray at the temple, and his prominent nose thrust forward. He dressed more like a diplomat than a policeman with a two-button blue suit tailored from worsted wool fabric, Bengal-striped dress shirt, and a black tie dotted with white circles.

The detective had his entire team with him: a patrol officer, the FBI agent, and Sook's friend, the Korean official, Ji-hun. While I waited for Powell to begin the meeting, I gazed out a window, glancing along the sides of the station that consisted of one-story red brick, with the flags of the United States, the Commonwealth of Virginia, and Fairfax County in front.

Powell began the interview by asking about Sook's early involvement with the deceased man, Yeong-ho, in Korea. Sook gave a coherent explanation of three young men leaving South Korea to start anew in the U.S. and escape a war. Since 1950, like millions of others before them, they had been poor immigrants working and making a success of themselves on the eastern seaboard of the U.S. Sook gave a convincing reiteration of the traditional rags-to-riches tale in a soft voice, omitting excessive detail. Powell pummeled Sook with queries; at the same time, he punctuated his questions by pointing his finger at Sook.

"What happened to the other soldiers in the squad?"

"Not know which soldiers survived their wounds. Not aware of their contact information," Sook said.

"So have you called anyone in South Korea recently?" Powell asked.

This question reminded me of when my mother knew the answer and quizzed me to see if I would tell the truth.

"I don't recall calling anyone," our client replied. Pointedly, the detective stared at Sook and then studied his open case notebook.

"How about the home of a Seong-gi Kim? Did you call his house in Korea on June 16 and June 20?"

Sook pursed his lips and held his chin with the thumb and forefinger of his left hand as if signaling his in-depth consideration of the detective's question. "Hmm. I did."

Powell turned and spread his arm out in a smug gesture toward the FBI and CHA agents. "Mr. Kim is deceased, shot in the head."

Sook pulled out his pen and began clicking the retractor. "I know. His son told me."

"Investigator Cho"—and here Powell pointed to the Korean agent—"talked with the authorities in Seoul. The Seoul murder investigators informed Inspector Cho you called and spoke with Seong-gi's son. Is it correct you asked the son about the death of his father?"

"Yes, I did," Sook said. "Seong-gi is an old friend, and we often talked."

"So you don't know people in Korea," Powell said, "but you and Mr. Kim often spoke. Is that what you mean?" Powell waved his finger at Sook.

I thought our client might collapse under the detective's questioning and my mind raced—without success—to think of a ploy to help our client break away from the penetrating interrogation. To Sook's credit, he retained a calm face.

Then our client pulled out the hoary No Speak English stratagem. Brilliant! "Eh . . . yes. I meant I don't know *many* people living in South Korea. Sometimes, my English not good."

Our detective gritted his teeth and continued punching his finger at Sook. "Don't you find it odd that two people from your old mortar squad were suddenly shot dead after fifty years?" He slammed his open palm down on his desk.

In response to Powell's red face and shouted questions, Sook appeared placid. "Is odd? Yes. Don't know why happened."

Powell leaned close to Sook's face and smiled. Then he settled back and spoke to the CHA agent sitting calmly in his chair. "Inspector Cho, do the Seoul investigators believe the two murders are a coincidence?"

"Seoul police believe murders connected," Ji-hun Cho responded.

Ji-hun's English was clear and succinct. His eyes were steady, seeming to catch every nuance of the exchange between Sook and Powell. The detective and his team had the same tight-lipped expression. Maybe they realized they listened to a narrative of quick evasions and smokescreens from Sook in response to their questions.

Ji-hun rolled a gold coin over and under the fingers of his left hand. "The Seoul detectives asked me to act as a liaison between them and Detective Powell. I have extended my stay in America to assist the investigators in both countries. I advised my country's detectives to question Seong-gi Kim's family about knowledge they may have of ancient Korean relics."

"Do not have Korean artifacts," our client replied.

"That may be," Ji-hun said. "I have to ask. I work with people— get national treasures returned to South Korea."

While Powell again leaned into Sook's face, Ji-hun sat back in his chair, rolling his gold coin back and forth with his left hand.

Powell leafed back through his notebook. He pointed to a page. "In our previous discussion, these agents from the FBI and CHA asked you about possibly missing artifacts. Do you remember your answer?"

"Yes. I know nothing about where to find Silla artifacts this country."

At this point, the FBI agent entered the fray and repeated his questions about Sook possibly taking objects from Korea. Overall, Sook was consistent in his answers to the FBI interrogator. Sook had taken some hits during the hail of questions, but he was still afloat. If Detective Powell suspected stolen artifacts caused the two deaths, he had no proof. He likely had checked Sook's whereabouts and concluded that he was nowhere near Yeong-ho during the shooting. The police did not ask Sook about the property in Great Falls, Virginia.

Powell finished by questioning Sook about a few of Yeong-ho's business projects. When our detective had asked all his questions, he stopped the interview. I stood to shepherd Sook out of the room.

"I'll be in touch," Powell said.

I drove from the McLean station to Sook's office building, a drive taking about fifteen minutes along the Dulles Toll Road. "The Fairfax County Police and the FBI are searching for the artifacts. They might tail you to see if you'll lead them to the relics."

"But Bin and I no longer have the pieces."

Being midday, I drove through an empty lane on the toll road; Sook explained the four lanes typically were jammed in the morning, going to Washington, D.C., and in the evening leaving the Capitol. "But the police don't know that," I said. "When we do find the artifacts, we don't want the authorities following along behind us to snatch the relics out of our hands."

"How do we know if the police are tailing us?"

"Keep your eyes open—pay attention. It may be easier to spot a tail by getting in the right lane and driving slowly. The tail would be forced to get into the right lane and drive slow as well."

"Will Powell himself be following me?" Sook asked. "I look for him?"

"It could be a two-man team but probably no greater than a six-man team," I said. "The authorities might place a small, unnoticeable transponder on your car."

I signaled to get off the toll road. "Your building has a loading bay, doesn't it?"

"Yes."

"I suggest we follow a practice of leaving our cars in your loading bay and have one of your technicians investigate for any device that doesn't belong."

As we pulled up to Sook's office building, I said, "Let's get back to finding the fifth soldier, Sang-hun."

NORTHERN VIRGINIA—1 JULY 2000

I swim upriver into logs—bobbing up in tandem, blocking me, each log following a previous wood chunk. Holding my breath, going under one log, coming up out of the water to gulp air—I face another log. Bulky cylinders of wood, always flowing at me. Logs without sound—just coming up toward me. No matter how I struggle, ducking under each blockage, I can't crawl up the river. I look for a break in the monotonous flood of logs. Now I hear a sound—Bang! Bang!

Mickey pounded on my bedroom door. He kept knocking, calling me a slacker; I shouted I had awakened, gotten up. He responded he was hungry, and I needed to get going. In addition to his knocking, the AC made sounds with its repetitive on-and-off blowing air; today was going to be another heat demon. I threw off the covers and lumbered into the shower, afterwards dressing, and following him out the door.

I talked Mickey into skipping breakfast at the Residence Inn and going out to a pancake restaurant. The sun baked the pavement. All that day, we scampered to and from AC, moving through sweltering areas like running through the rain to reach shelter.

Mickey and I got to Sook's office building with its welcome coolness, met the overnight security team, and escorted our two clients inside. The bodyguards would return in the evening. On the fifth floor, Sook's search team labored away, pursuing the fifth soldier. The searchers saturated the nearby regions—Falls Church,

Fairfax City, Herndon, McLean, and Vienna—with plastic cards featuring Sang-hun's picture. The two phones rang constantly; Sook's workers were installing another phone line to take calls. Alleged reports of a Sang-hun sighting trickled in. Many callers sought the one thousand dollars offered as a reward, but no one had seen him.

During what started as a slow and routine day, Mickey and I strolled around the fifth floor of Sook's building, staring out the windows at the horizon, a skyline composed of the Dulles Toll Road and many three- and four-story office buildings. Occasionally, a worker walked up to me with a question, and I answered as best I could. By mid-afternoon, we had made no headway. The hunt moved on to Chinatown in Washington, D.C., a small, historic neighborhood a little north of the U.S. Capitol building.

Sook stuck his head into the conference room. "Isaac Hunter, the antique dealer, left message. Has something tell us." Mickey and I followed Sook into his office.

He called Isaac back. "We all here. Go ahead."

He didn't speak right away. I imagined Isaac busy fiddling with his glasses. "I contacted my antique-dealer network. No Silla artifacts on the market. I repeat, no one is offering Silla relics for sale."

Sook sat at his desk and stared at me with a pained expression.

After a moment of silence, Isaac continued. "Either the criminals are hiding the pieces, or they moved them out of the country."

"Maybe the Silla pieces are still in this country," I said. "Lee, the operative Roth hired in South Korea, says Sang-hun hasn't returned home."

Sook grasped his ballpoint pen and began clicking the retractor mechanism. "You have nothing."

"One odd bit of information. Wang Gang—the gangster—has been asking if Silla pieces have come on the market. If he has the artifacts, he's acting like he doesn't have them."

Beside me, Sook persisted in clicking his pen. "How hard you search? Artifacts must be somewhere."

"Patience," Isaac answered. "When the crown appears, I'll tell you."

A gleam of sweat had formed on Sook's forehead. "Try harder."

Isaac hung up.

By late afternoon, we were in the watching-paint-dry phase of our investigation. The search for Sang-hun had been diligent and extensive, but we couldn't find him. Sook and Bin told their team to continue working, but the bosses were going home; when the guards arrived in the parking lot, Mickey and I escorted our two clients to their security team.

After the bodyguards had taken Sook and Bin away for the evening, I drove back to the Residence Inn.

"The weather report calls for heavy rain tonight," Mickey said from the passenger seat, "and possible thunderstorms."

I turned my head to Mickey. "Yeah."

"You plan to visit Gang?"

I stroked my cowlick. "I do."

"Tonight?"

"Tonight. You willing to help?"

"I am."

I noticed his frown. "You think we haven't done enough homework—to hit Gang's house."

Mickey didn't reply; he stared ahead. "Roth doesn't know, does she?"

"I can't sit around and pass out cards. I need to go search for the Silla relics."

He had a blank expression on his face. "Roth will kill you."

"Find the crown; she won't care."

Mickey appeared to study the dark clouds forming in the sky outside the hotel window. "Hope thunder comes with the rain."

I nodded at him. "Let's get some food, a short nap, and then head for Leesburg."

# # #

Mickey and I ate supper and then returned to our suite. Planning to be up later that night, I took a short nap. Before retiring, I phoned both security teams. They had tucked Sook and Bin into their homes. Around ten o'clock, when the phone rang, I jumped out of bed to grab my mobile.

"Yeah?"

"Gannon?"

"That's me."

"Blalock. Better get over here. Someone shot at us."

I recognized Blalock, one of the security men at Sook's home.

"Anyone hurt?"

"My partner . . . Macon . . . shot in the arm. Neighbors called the police."

Jeezus cripes, we were going to be swimming in police officers. "Mickey and I are on our way."

We dashed to Sook's house in Reston, Virginia, and parked on the side of the street. I couldn't see clearly, because clouds hovered low and not a single streetlight lit the block—Reston's home-ownership rules fostered pitch blackness at night. Rain cascaded down, along with lightning and thunder. In an ambulance in front of the house, one of the security guards lay on a gurney. A police car stood in the road, its lights flashing. Two wet officers kept a small group of neighbors away.

Mickey and I walked around to the rear of the house, meeting up with Sook and Blalock. They stood under an overhead deck. Our client seemed jumpy and spoke rapidly. The bodyguard dressed in a uniform, all blue clothing.

"Hell's bells," I said to the security guard. "What happened?"

He stared at me through glasses with thick lenses. "Ten-forty tonight, I stood at the back of the house. Turned my head slightly and suddenly glimpsed an intruder."

I felt a hot fury; I was beginning to lose my control. The security service had the responsibility for making the area safe. Because the backyard was as murky as a deep coal mine, anyone could get close to the house without being seen. "What did you do? Call for support?"

"I just saw him—a glimpse," Blalock replied. "I shouted for him to freeze—caught him in my flashlight beam. Dressed in black—head to toe."

"What happened then?" Mickey asked.

"He shot once in my direction—heard a small-caliber pistol. He ran away behind that eastern white pine."

Blalock waited a few moments before continuing. "I fired my weapon—aiming where the intruder had been. Didn't hit him. My partner, Macon, came around from the front—with his flashlight on."

An Asian woman opened the patio door behind me. "Sook. Come inside."

Sook went to the woman, explained he was okay, and told her to stay inside the house.

Our guard in blue continued his report. "The intruder probably fired at the flashlight—hit my partner in the arm."

I cringed because they'd left the front of the house unguarded. "What about our client, Mr. Park, did you shield him?"

Blalock shook his head. "I fired at the intruder's gun flash. He retreated out of sight—through the woods."

I heard another police car approaching, its siren cutting through the din of the relentless rain. "I saw the EMS team taking care of Macon. What did they tell you?"

"My partner has a shallow wound in his upper arm," Blalock said. "Need a doc to evaluate bone and muscle damage. It doesn't seem like a major blood vessel was damaged."

At least we had escaped without significant injury to the second security man. "You saw one person. Could there have been a second?"

Blalock glanced back at the dark woods behind the house. "One intruder . . . one came into the backyard."

"We're sure at least two men are in the gang," I said. "You left the front of the house unguarded. Had the second man been here, he could have walked in the house."

Our guard in blue stood with his mouth agape, anger darkening his face. "That's not fair. We attacked the intruder. Macon got shot in the arm."

He didn't understand that, but for blind luck, he could have gotten Sook killed. "A killer came through Yeong-ho's backyard to murder him. You were responsible for preventing the same thing happening here."

"But I guarded him—he's alive."

I stood close to his face and shouted, "The killer almost got into Sook's house." Blalock's eyes had become big.

Behind me, Sook held my arm and pulled me back from the guard. "It's over. I'm okay."

Sook sent Blalock around to the front of the house. "Sang-hun came to my house and tried kill me."

"Yeah."

I forced my breath slowly out through my mouth. My racing heart slowed back toward normal. Then I grinned. "One beneficial thing. Sang-hun stayed in Northern Virginia to shoot at people. We have an opportunity to find the relics."

"I don't want report this attack to Detective Powell," Sook said.

Then, attired in a black double-breasted raincoat and waterproof hat with a wide brim, the Fairfax County detective lumbered through the rain, around the corner of the house, and into Sook's backyard. He brought to my mind a cross between a male fashion model and a black bear. Two officers followed him. Powell walked up to Sook and leaned forward, positioning his nose inches from Sook's face. "What are you up to, Park?"

Sook slid behind me, using my body as a buffer to keep Powell away. I raised my arms in the air in a surrender gesture and tensed my legs to resist the detective's charge. He tried to push me aside. "Get out of my way, Gannon."

"Call your lawyer," I said to Sook.

The big detective circled my left side; accordingly, Sook circled to my right flank.

"Stand still," Powell shouted.

"Stay away from me," Sook replied.

The rain pelted down, Powell and Sook orbited me, and everyone else stood in the downpour and watched. "Answer my question," the big detective said.

Sook stopped and peered at him. "What ask me?"

Powell pushed us back into the dry area under the deck. "Who shot the guard?"

"We not sure," Sook answered.

Powell moved toward him again, causing my client to jump behind me. "Tell me what's going on. Bullets were flying through the neighborhood."

Sook sounded panicked by his violent questioning. "I don't know who shoot. I no see him."

"Why are you searching for a Korean man? Yes, I know you are passing out hundreds of cards with a man's picture."

Face to face with Powell, I couldn't view Sook behind me, and he didn't say a word at first. "Think murders tied to old mortar squad," he began. "Two members killed and two alive. We search for fifth team member."

Powell grew red in the face. "You told me the murder in Korea had no connection with Yeong-ho's homicide. You lied."

"Maybe murders linked. Not sure. We hunt for missing fifth

member of mortar squad."

"You're not telling me all. Tomorrow, I want you to explain this fifth soldier nonsense. I'm going now to talk with my CSI people."

The gruff detective walked away to see what his men had learned about the shooting.

I patted Sook's shoulder. "I think you are safe with these policemen around your home. Mickey and I are going back to our hotel."

As Mickey and I drove away from Sook's home, I believed Sang-hun had attempted to shoot him. Blalock and Mason had managed to foil an attempt to murder Sook. But was it Sang-hun who took the relics? What if Wang Gang had stolen the Silla artifacts? I had to find out what Gang had stored in his basement.

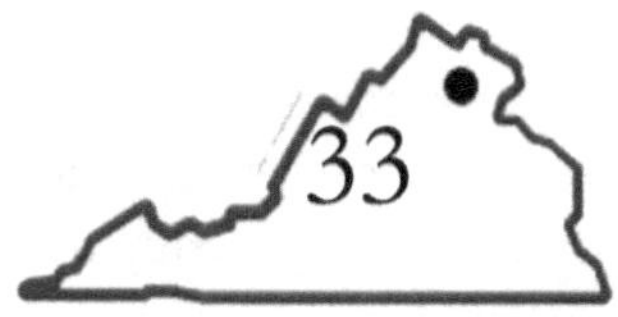

NORTHERN VIRGINIA—2 JULY 2000

Mickey and I dressed in dark clothing and soft-soled work boots. We returned to the rental-car facility, turned in our rental car, and leased a dark, nondescript minivan. Anticipating we might be igniting explosives in the dark of night, I took out full insurance on the van. Before departing, we fiddled with its overhead switches until the interior lights stayed off when the doors opened or closed; also, we spread plastic sheeting over the seats and interior surfaces. Finally, we transferred two canvas bags and a backpack to the minivan and drove to Leesburg. On our way, evening rain and a thunderstorm began and continued without let up. The overhead carpet of rain clouds made the night as dark as the paint finish on a new black car.

Parked on the street across from Gang's home, I saw his security lights illuminating the outside grounds; the interior lights in the house were off. To confirm all inhabitants slept, we waited, watching the house for any change in the inside illumination. I was fidgety, jumpy as a rabbit out in the open; Mickey seemed tranquil.

"We're alone as far as I can verify," I said.

"We are," he said.

As we sat in the minivan, I thought back to the start of this day, when the morning sky improved from dark to overcast, with a promise of more rain to come. All through the daylight hours, on the top floor of Sook's office building, his search team slogged along hunting for Sang-hun, like fishing all day on a lake without a single bite. Mickey and I visited the wounded security guard at Fairfax hospital; later in the afternoon, the doctors declared him recovered from a minor injury and released him. Summoned for an interview at the Fairfax County Police Station, Sook gave an account of the shooting the previous night. Detective Powell grilled Sook extensively, but he didn't reveal the theft or the existence of the Great Falls house where the robbery occurred. When night finally arrived, Mickey and I drove to our suite and sucked down a few beers. Then we had left for the rental agency to pick up the minivan.

I brushed my cowlick and broke out of my night dream. "His electronic surveillance system is Gang's primary defense. If that goes down, the security operators will first hunt for a system glitch. Probably ten or fifteen minutes would pass before any backup would start for his house."

Mickey pulled a donut out of a paper bag. "You've said that several times. Relax."

I started the engine. "We've waited long enough. Let's go."

My partner put his donut back into the bag. "Mischief waits for no man."

I drove to the grove of oaks beside the power lines, parking near the tall tree we had previously selected. Mickey opened the minivan door on his side and fastened tree-climbing spikes to his lower legs and boots. Working in the dark and rain, we oriented ourselves with the base of the tree and its tree limb arcing about twenty feet above us. I couldn't see the tree limb against the coal-black sky, making it awkward to throw a rope over the big branch. When I glanced up, rain fell on my face, blurring my vision. I reached into the bags and pulled out a pair of safety goggles; they kept the rain out of my eyes, but I still looked at blackness.

Mickey pointed a flashlight skyward and flicked it on and then off; at intervals, he continued to flick the light, finally pinning down the location of the tree limb. After several unsuccessful tosses, I got the first rope, the thin throw line with a small sandbag at one end, to loop around the upper branch. The throw-line had wound around the limb.

I let the sandbag come down, the rest of the throw-line following the bag. I had attached a climbing line to the end of the throw line and pulled the climbing rope around the tree limb. After looping one end of the climbing rope through a knotted loop on its other end, I next tugged on the climbing rope until one end wrapped around the branch, and the other end was on the ground, giving Mickey a single cable to climb the tree.

I moved back into the minivan, getting out of the rain. Mickey sat beside me pulling on dry gloves. "Take a Herculean effort to mount that tree in this rain," he said slowly.

"Yeah."

"You're lucky you have a talented athlete like me on our team."

Okay, he intended to make me grovel. "You're the only one I know capable of getting up that wet rope."

Mickey cupped his chin as if thinking. "Would you say I'm the best athlete in our group?"

"I'm always thrilled when we're on the same team. You're a marvelous athlete. Now, climb the damn tree."

My partner used his boot-spikes and the climbing rope to start his ascent of the tree to the branch. Because he had to grip the wet line with a large force, he moved slowly. Also, Mickey had to avoid his hands slipping as he jerked a boot-spike out of the tree and replanted it higher up the trunk.

He finally reached the branch and wrapped detonation cord around the limb six times and tapped an electronic blast cap to the end of the line. He dropped the other end of the blasting-cap cabling down to the ground. I heard the wiring smack the earth and picked it up. Using his spikes and the rope, Mickey came down the oak tree. His progress going down was as slow as going up; he had the same problem with a wet line and wet hands.

And then he stood beside me.

"You are good," I said.

"Had to grip hard," Mickey replied.

I slapped him on the shoulder. "Well done."

"If I must climb this tree again, we're coming back another night."

While he removed the spikes from his boots, I ran the loose end of the blasting-cap cabling into the minivan. My partner hooked the wiring to a battery and an open throw-switch. Wearing our safety goggles and a hard hat, we sat there in the van with the rain coming down. We waited.

"Is this going to work?" I murmured.

"As I mentioned," Mickey said, "don't want to climb that rope again. Throw the switch now?"

"Wait till you see a flash of lightning. And then ignite the cap.

With a bit of luck, the det cord going off will sound like thunder."

In the best of all possible worlds, the branch would crash on the transmission wires, the power lines would come down, and the power would go off. Far away, I saw lightning flash. "Now."

He flipped the throw-switch, completing the circuit. The blasting cap fired the det cord—*Boom!*—and the dark of the night turned to day in the white light of the flashing detonation cord.

I heard the bang of the blasting cap and cord happening together with the arrival of the thunder boom from the distant lightning.

Small branches and twigs rained down on the vehicle's roof, causing dinging sounds. Separately, the overhead tree branch crashed to the ground, missing the minivan. Total darkness and the pitter-patter of rain on the van returned.

Mickey pulled the loose ends of the blasting-cap cabling and the rope into the minivan. A small flame burned high above us because the heat from the detonation cord had started a slight fire, which soon self-extinguished. Around us, I saw no house lights or flashlights, sensing only the patter of rain against the minivan's roof. I started the engine, turned on the running lights, gradually pulled out into the street, and drove away.

"Too dark to see if the power lines came down," Mickey said.

"Wait, didn't that house have a porch light on?" I said. "I don't see the light now." As we got closer to Gang's house, we saw the outdoor lights of the security system were off. I parked on the street a distance from the home.

"No lights outside or inside the house," my partner said. "If anyone got up, I would expect to see a flashlight through the windows." The rain formed little gushers of water that flowed over the windshield and down the windows.

I pulled a navy-blue watch cap over my head, slipped my arms through the straps of a backpack, tugged on gloves, and stepped out of the minivan. "I'm on my way. Keep a lookout. Call my mobile phone—I have it set to vibrate—to tell me to get out of the house."

"Good luck," he said.

Because the space between the street and the house was vast and open all the way to the house, I crouched and ran to the electrical generator outside the home. The generator was not running. I pulled cutters out of my backpack and snipped the power cord in two, my heart pounding like a drum solo.

I made entry from the side of the house with a brick patio, covered by an overhead wooden deck. Twin doors with glass panels offered a way into the structure. To break in, I chose one of the windows to the side of the glass doors.

From my backpack, I pulled out a towel to clean the outside of the lower window pane. Extracting a flexible plastic sheet with adhesive on one side, I stuck the layer over the entire lower glass pane. Next, I removed a ball-peen hammer. The noise of the breaking glass came like the sound of a drawer closing. The adhesive sheet held the glass fragments to keep them from falling onto the floor. I reached in, unlocked the window, and stepped through the opening and onto the first-floor level.

Waiting and crouching on the floor, I urged my breathing to slow. The snare drum in my chest beat vigorously. Nothing made a noise in the house.

I took out a small flashlight and balled my fist over the lens. I opened my fist enough to allow a low-lumen beam to lead me around furniture in the room.

Working my way around a coffee table, I spotted a familiar object. Examining it in a quick beam of the flashlight, I recognized our ID card with the picture of Sang-hun, the fifth soldier. Gang knew about our effort to find him.

In the hallway, next to the stairs down to the basement, I stopped again to listen. Nothing: no voices, no floorboards creaking, and no cell phones in use.

After sliding open the door in the hall and descending a paneled stairway into the basement, I entered a room through a door labeled "Chinese Artifacts." Going counter-clockwise around the chamber, I found a jade burial suit. Next, I walked past a bronze vessel in the form of a duck. I passed a bronze wine cup, then an array of bronze bells. Wang Gang had a collection of Chinese relics, but no Silla artifacts from Korea. I disturbed nothing.

I went into the next room through a door marked "Japanese Artifacts." I found Buddhist and Shinto sculptures. I passed Samurai warrior swords and an iron helmet. The room had Japanese relics, but no Silla artifacts. I departed without touching anything.

I hurried along to another room in the basement, searching for pieces matching the Silla relics removed from South Korea back in 1950; I was no art expert, but they were not in that room either.

I entered a final room through an unmarked door, to find empty shelves lined the walls. A placard labeled "Silla Kingdom Artifacts" lay on a ledge. No historical objects—only this sign. Did this mean Gang expected Silla relics shortly? After checking the room didn't have windows, I snapped a picture of the sign with my Canon PowerShot G1.

Finding no Silla relic and having run out of time, I left everything untouched and crept up the basement stairs.

Above me on the second floor, a door shut. "The electric clock is off, and the lamp won't turn on."

Emerging on the first floor, I detected a slight glimmering of light seeping down the stairs from the second floor. My heart pounded, and my senses cried, *get out now*.

Just as I stepped away from the basement stairs, I heard voices from the second floor. "Lights are out in my room, too. The electricity isn't working."

My mobile phone vibrated. Mickey sent a text: LEAVE!

More voices from upstairs. "Can't find my flashlight. Call the electric company and ask about the blackout. Phone security—tell them to get here now."

"Okay, boss."

"Start the emergency generator."

I hurried across the first floor and out the window. Back on the patio, I determined the rain had abated, but visibility beyond a few feet remained challenging in the pitch-black night. I ran across the yard and jumped in the minivan, sitting beside Mickey. He started the engine and slowly drove away.

"Did you find the crown?"

"Not there. What happened out here? I don't see any lights."

"Lights back toward the downed power lines," he said. "I think the utility people are working to figure out what happened. One or two cars drove past me without pausing."

We got out of Leesburg and back on the highway, going east. It nagged at me Gang had one of the Sang-hun ID cards and a placard for the Silla Kingdom pieces. I worried if he knew more about my investigation than I thought. Did I get away clean or would I see more of him?

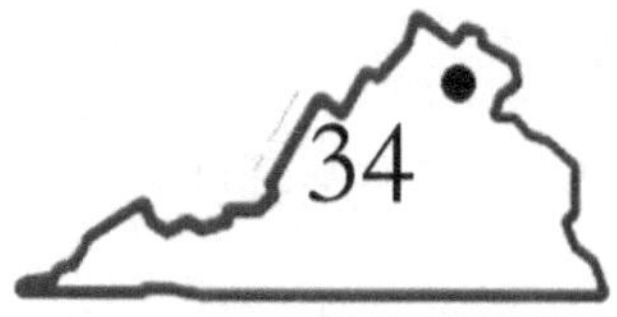

NORTHERN VIRGINIA—3 JULY 2000

"It's crazy," I whined at Roth. "Unreal. Nothing is going right."

She hurled back silence over the line. I hung on, wanting her to make things right, needing her to make sense of the stunning destruction of my investigation. "Take deep breaths," she replied. "Compose yourself."

To slow my thudding chest, I held my breath and wafted air through my nose. Roth seemed to have been following my breathing because, after a while, she said, "Describe."

I took the time to arrange my thoughts. "This morning, Detective Powell, the lead investigator on the Yeong-ho shooting, materialized at Sook's office building. He had his notebook in his left hand, rubbed his chin with his right hand, and interviewed us in the conference room."

She interrupted me. "The detective questioned Sook about the shooting at his Reston home?"

"He didn't pursue the attempt on Sook's life but dropped a new topic on us like a dump of sewage from an overhead airliner. Told us, 'Another Asian man died last night.'

"Powell pulled a sheet of paper from his notebook and handed it to Sook. It was a photograph of the deceased's face. An early morning walker found a dead man, shot with small-caliber bullets in the torso and two in the side of the head, his body left on a local jogging path."

Roth stopped me again. "Fax the photo to me."

I wrote a reminder on my notepad to send the fax. "I sensed Powell examine Sook's face for a sign Sook knew the dead man. Our client appeared to be in a fog, as ignorant of the murder as I was. Powell observed the Asian appeared to be an older Korean, like the recently deceased Yeong-ho Park and asked if we knew him, the body left on the trail."

Roth had reasoned ahead of me. "The dead man was Sang-hun Lee, the fifth soldier?"

I nodded at the mobile phone in my hand. "Sook gazed at the picture, taking his time like he was at an art museum. Then he passed the photograph to me, and I saw the fifth soldier had truly and finally died. Just when you least expect it, the unpredictable happens.

"Powell took our ID-card picture of Sang-hun out of his notebook and held it next to the photograph of the dead man. He asked Sook, 'Had you been searching for this man, murdered last night? What did you call him—the fifth soldier?'"

"How did Sook answer the question?" Roth asked.

"Sook took several seconds. Finally, he said, 'Murdered man had Korean facial structure. Could be the fifth soldier, but not sure.' The detective asked Sook if he had seen the fifth soldier recently. Sook replied he hadn't seen Sang-hun in fifty years."

Roth cut in. "Where had the dead man been staying?"

"I asked the detective what he knew about the murdered man. Did he know if the slain man had a room? The detective replied he found nothing in the pockets of the deceased, who wore a cheap jersey and baggy pants with a cheap pair of sneakers.

"I reminded Powell a killer had shot Yeong-ho Park in his backyard with a small-caliber gun. Could a .22 pistol also have been used to kill the man found on the jogging path? The detective replied attackers had shot both men with small-caliber bullets."

"What else did you learn?" Roth asked.

I had little more to disclose. "The detective wanted Sook to ask around the Korean-American community to identify the dead man. Where had this man been staying? Funny, we both wanted to know where he had been rooming."

"So, the fifth soldier had an accomplice," my boss observed, "who kicked him out of their fraternity—permanently."

My investigation had capsized and had sunk into an abyss. Two of our clients were dead, and the only nexus back to the Korean War in

1950 was gone. "We've been working this case for twenty-five days, but we got a breakthrough with the fifth soldier," I said. "What do I do now? Our chief suspect just got removed."

When Roth responded, her voice came unruffled and assured. "When we took the case, we knew we were in difficulty. The lone question was could we get control of that trouble or not?"

"But what do I do now?"

"Before Sang-hun's death, you hunted for where he stayed. Now that someone eliminated him, it's essential you find where he hid. Don't lose hope."

Don't lose hope? Our search with the ID-card had taken an enormous amount of time and accomplished nothing. Continuing with our approach to find the fifth soldier's hideout would take forever.

"Be patient," she said. "You said the police didn't find anything on the body?"

"Powell said the killer stripped the body of papers and identification."

"Hmm, what about Wang Gang, the gangster? Could he have been the one who found the fifth soldier and then murdered him once they had the crown?"

I decided to tell Roth about my break-in at Gang's home. "A-a-and . . . as to other findings, the Silla relics are not in Gang's basement."

The Asheville end of our phone connection went silent.

"Did Gang invite you into his home?"

"Not exactly."

When Roth resumed speaking, her voice had a slow, cold tempo. "Will there be fallout from establishing Silla gold is not among Mr. Gang's possessions in his cellar?"

"Maybe," I said. "I think not."

I heard nothing for a moment until the soft clank of Roth putting down a coffee cup carried over the connection. "We've discussed your tendency of going rogue. We should have talked and made a plan."

I had angered her. How could I justify what I had done? "I had a hunch, based on my experience and observation."

"You should have told me," she said.

My body grew hot, with sweat trickling down my back. "Would

you have given me the okay to case Gang's collection?"

More silence followed by a second coffee cup clink. "No."

"That's the thing about intuition," I began. "If you don't have it, you can't understand it. And if you do, no explanation is necessary."

Roth didn't respond immediately. I knew her: she had begun a slow burn. "Do not—ever again—act in open defiance of me," she said in an ice-covered voice. "You will no longer be an investigator for Roth Security."

I decided to acquiesce. "Yes, ma'am."

"Is Gang still a suspect in your eyes?" Roth asked.

I felt relief. She had finished chastising me in an ice-coated voice and changed subjects. "A suspect, yes. But I'm not sure Gang has the crown."

"Why do you still suspect Gang?" Roth asked.

I hesitated and then described what I found in Gang's house. "Gang knows we had searched for Sang-hun—he has one of the ID cards with his picture. Why is Gang interested in him? Maybe he worked for Gang?"

"Anything else?" Roth asked.

"Yes. In Gang's basement, he has a room with a placard labeled 'Silla Kingdom Artifacts.' He's expecting Silla relics."

Roth didn't say anything for a minute. And then she continued. "Find where Sang-hun stayed in northern Virginia."

"Yes, ma'am."

"I'll tell Lee, my investigator in South Korea, to stop waiting for Sang-hun to return. If our fifth soldier was a poor laborer, then who paid for his travel, room, and board? I want Lee to dig into his past like a badger."

As we disconnected, she said, "Carry out my instructions. Find where Sang-hun hid. Be patient."

I thought about what my boss had asked, who had funded Sang-hun. Then my thoughts switched to how Gang might react to the break-in at his house? Would he identify Mickey and me as his intruders? Could he have recorded us, parked on a side street, on his security tapes?

# # #

Manny Jackson, the caretaker, phoned the next morning from the

Great Falls house. Sook and I were sitting in the conference room in his office building, studying reports about the search for where Sanghun had been staying before his death.

"Hello, Manny," Sook answered. "What? Hold on. Don!"

He turned to me. "Detective Powell at door of Great Falls residence—with many policemen."

"I assume he has a court-authorized search warrant in his hands," I said. "Has he shown Manny the papers?"

Sook appeared calm, unperturbed the police had finally found the Great Falls house. "The detective showed it to him through a peephole in door."

"Tell Manny to let them in. We better go see Powell."

Sook left the rest of the search team behind to hunt for Sanghun's hideout. When we got to the Great Falls area, we saw police cruisers and vans parked along Georgetown Pike, the main road leading to the house.

Manny hurried out to us as we stopped our vehicle. "Mr. Park, the police want to get into the exhibit room. I told them you have the combination."

The detective confronted us with a scowl as we walked in the front door. "Two deaths resulted from your stealing artifacts from South Korea. I believe you have those Silla artifacts in this residence. Open the door with the combination lock, now!" Powell, Ji-hun Cho, and police officers surrounded our client in front of the door to the exhibit room. He punched in the combination and swung open the door into the exhibit area; the authorities swarmed through the doorway.

The CHA official, Ji-hun Cho, projected a calm demeanor, smiled, bowed slightly to Sook, and followed the others into the room.

"What's this?" the detective asked. He had a tomato-red face. The red clashed with his purple sports jacket. "Where are the Korean artifacts?" I followed the crowd into the room and saw that the walls—previously empty—now displayed paintings in oil and watercolor. Scenes of rivers, beaches, still-life compositions, and mountains, hung around the room with cards identifying a painter and the year of completion.

Sook beamed with pride and pointed to the paintings. "Our exhibit area holds works by local artists who deserve support. Collection is behind locked doors because its total value is high. No stolen artifacts here."

Powell commenced jabbing at him. "Why didn't you tell us about this house?"

"You didn't ask me. This residence is sanctuary. Mr. Bie, poor deceased Mr. Yeong-ho Park, and I walked in woods, contemplated serene paintings, and discussed business and family life over wine."

An officer came through the door and whispered into Powell's ear. He confronted Sook. "The neighbors report you recently had a theft. What did they take?"

"Nothing important," he replied. "Crooks took coins out of parked cars. We told the neighbors. Wanted find out if friends see suspicious people in the community."

I could almost see smoke coming out his ears and nostrils. Then he turned to the student housekeeper and asked, "How about you? Where are the artifacts?"

Manny wore blue jeans and his Howard Pharmacy tee shirt. He appeared confident as if he had practiced what he would say. "No artifacts be here. I am merely the caretaker. I know nothing."

"How long have you worked at this residence as a caretaker?"

"About three years."

"I know this is not the first time you've seen this room. Besides these paintings, what did Mr. Park display in here?"

"I don't remember. I can't tell you what art in this room represents—what they depict. This room is not part of my primary duties."

Detective Powell calmed down, his red face turning to a more placid pink.

The caretaker turned from the authorities to gaze toward our client. "Has my job description been upgraded to include duties in the exhibit room?"

Manny, with open mouth and wide eyes, continued facing Sook. "Mr. Park, I'd be happy to help with all the rooms. Bigger job, more money. What you think?"

"I will do that," he replied. "We talk later."

Given the way his house sitter handled the police questions, Sook should put him in for a bonus.

The detective glared as he scanned the room, finally focusing on me. I smiled. He pursed his lips, realizing it was pointless to ask me anything. The other officers had begun to walk out to their cruisers.

Powell stopped at the front door and turned, staring straight at me. "The most cooperative man in this world is a smart-ass in jail. If you don't start talking straight with me, you're gonna be in jail charged with conspiracy." He left.

Ji-hun hung back, walked up to Sook, and spoke in Korean. Then the South Korean agent followed his law-enforcement colleagues out the door.

I brushed my cowlick as Ji-hun walked out of sight. "What did he say?"

Sook translated for me. "If I give relics back, he gets any charges against me dropped."

I locked eyes with Sook and whistled softly. "Give back the relics you don't have? Something to think about."

I now knew the fifth soldier's present location in the morgue, but where had he been previously? Who had shot him?

NORTHERN VIRGINIA—4 JULY 2000

"Something's up," Mickey said.

Sook, sitting across the table from me in the fifth-floor conference room, listened on his phone and then asked, "He's downstairs now?" He concentrated on his call and then turned to me. "Gang, the gangster, wants to talk with us."

Oops! Gang must be here for our Leesburg break-in. Maybe he figured Sook authorized the action. Inside my head, a thought popped out: how had he tracked me? "Who's with him? His one tough or a group?"

Sook talked over the phone with the front-desk security and then said, "One man. Maybe the bodyguard we met in Leesburg."

"Have security escort them up."

Sook appeared nonplussed and studied my expression, maybe wondering if I had brought this intruder knocking at his door. "Do you want to tell me something?"

Feeling a tad to blame, I brushed my hair. "Everything's okay. Let me lead."

We gathered in Sook's office. Gang entered with a stroll, as laid-back as a golfer going into the nineteenth hole. His guppy-shaped mouth tilted up at the corners in a smile. He wore a gray suit today. The big bodyguard, who trailed him through the door, dressed in a matching gray jacket with a blue turtleneck jersey. The two men projected style. Gang shook Sook's hand. Then he turned to me and said, "Mr. Gannon." I shook his hand. The gangster, our client, and I sat down; the bodyguard and Mickey stood with their backs against a wall. I assumed the bodyguard had a weapon; nevertheless, both Mickey and I carried pistols.

Gang faced Sook. "Three Fridays ago, I was puzzled about your visit to my Leesburg home. I inquired and found Mr. Gannon is the chief operative at Roth Security. They perform many aspects of security, including recovery operations."

He had done his homework. I listened carefully to understand where he planned to take us.

"This information explained much to me," Gang continued. "Mr. Park would not employ a team of this quality to investigate a simple burglary attempt."

He had flattered me, not reprimanded. Why? Nothing keeps me alert like an intense fear of a ruthless criminal.

An Asian member of Sook's staff brought in cups of coffee and tea. I was pleased to see our gangster take his time sipping his tea. Maybe our civilized discussion would end peacefully? Both Mickey and Gang's bodyguard declined coffee, likely wanting to leave their hands free. The gangster put down his tea and resumed speaking. "You turned up at Leesburg searching for a telltale sign I burglarized your home. I concluded a burglar stole your Silla relics—no, don't bother to deny. You visited me to learn if I took your artifacts."

He stopped to sip from his teacup. I watched both Mickey and the bodyguard. Mickey stood motionless. I saw a small twitch in the right forefinger of the guard. A lot was going on in the room. Gang put down his teacup and rubbed his nose before continuing. "You considered me capable of a base burglary, and that hurt me. Then, I realized I was a natural suspect. I knew about your Silla artifacts and had offered to buy them."

Gang put his teacup down on Sook's desk. His drooping eyelids partially hid his eyes, leaving his pupils free to study stealthily those around him, giving him an uninterested appearance. His straight white hair projected an honorable look, reminiscent of a medieval knight. Villains who snarl and bare their teeth are easy to spot, but those who clothe themselves in splendid trappings are well-camouflaged. Even though he showed nobility, he was a gangster at heart. I had to evaluate him based on his actions, not his words.

The gangster viewed Sook while discussing the Silla treasure. When he finished, he turned his gaze on me. "Two nights ago, someone took down a section of Leesburg's power grid. Afterwards, a light-footed individual broke one of my windows, slipped into my basement, and viewed my art gallery. The intruder stole nothing."

He stared straight into my eyes. "My guess is you are now satisfied the Silla relics are not in my basement."

I boldly stared back at Gang. He had figured out the situation correctly, but my intuition screamed he had reached his conclusions by guessing. He hadn't used proof, but his instincts. I could always bluff instinct.

During the time Gang talked, Sook had clicked his ballpoint pen and frowned suspiciously at me. "I know nothing of break-in."

Gang smiled at Sook and turned back to me. "I prospered by that night's prank. Someone shredded my security system, but I learned its weaknesses. Based on the intrusion, I am improving my safety measures."

He waited for me to comment. I didn't speak, pretending ignorance with a vacant expression.

He continued his solo discourse. "I guessed the intruders had scouted my house. My staff reviewed the old tapes—recorded these past weeks—from the CCTV around my house."

Maybe to let his words register, he paused his speech. "Occupying a car parked on the street near my house, we identified two large men who came at night. I estimate one had your size, Mr. Gannon, and the other the size of"—he turned in his chair and glanced at Mickey—"the gentleman leaning against the wall to my right."

Mickey didn't twitch.

Gang locked eyes with me again. "Why am I here? Two reasons. First, I state again I wish to purchase the Silla artifacts—when you regain them.

"Second, I learned—by the recent antics at my home—of an imaginative operative. I like a smart burglar. I haven't told the Leesburg authorities who tore down the power lines, not yet anyway."

Our gangster finished his tea. "Anything to say, Mr. Gannon?"

It's only when the lights come on that you learn which couples were making out during the movie. The moment to show a digital record nailing me to a cross had passed. Our gangster had instinct, but he didn't have proof. Three stories existed to cover the events that night: mine, his, and the truth. Gang had started with the truth part and had subsequently slipped into his made-up story. He had begun to fib about the videos.

I relaxed and lied. "Hmm, two nights ago, I went to bed early in Herndon. In the morning on the TV, I saw Leesburg experienced a power outage while I slept."

Gang fiddled with his teacup and shook his head. "I see. Allow me to discuss an opportunity. What would you trade for my not telling the police what I know about the blackout?"

I crossed my legs and shook my head. "Not interested."

Gang stared at me with his unblinking fish eyes. "That will not do, Mr. Gannon. My security company enhanced the images of you outside my house. And we traced a vehicle—parked near my house—to a rental company at Dulles Airport."

Mickey and I had washed and vacuumed the minivan before returning it. The plastic sheeting, put down to cover the vehicle's interior, lay in trash receptacles about Herndon. The van harbored no clues to the power outage in Leesburg. I was close to a clean getaway. "I repeat I slept in my motel room two nights ago. Tell me about your *opportunity*."

Gang spilled his deal. "Either you sell me the Silla artifacts when you regain them, or I'll turn your name over to the police."

My gut feeling told me he didn't have videos with sharp images. Anyway, unless we found where Sang-hun hid the stolen treasure, we had nothing to trade.

"Do we have a deal?" Gang asked.

"Show me your video," I said.

He didn't move.

I uncrossed my legs and sat up straight in my chair. "If and when we are ready to deal—I say if—with you, I'll contact you."

The gangster got up and moved toward the door. "Good day, gentlemen. I look forward to working out a future deal." He walked out of the room, followed by his big bodyguard.

He didn't seem upset. He wanted the Silla relics. His desire for the art trumped his hurt pride at our breaching his security system.

# # #

I returned to the conference room to continue investigating where the fifth soldier hid out before his recent demise. The air smelled musty, carrying the odor of burnt coffee and stale pastry. The room grew warm due to the number of people studying printout and computer screens. Bin's uncle called him. Bin explained a man—murdered and dumped on a local path—was the fifth member of his old mortar squad. The uncle asked to see a photograph of the deceased. After all, he'd interviewed many Asian men seeking a job unloading his ships. Bie went to fax a picture to his uncle and then returned to the search slog in the conference room.

"How many ID cards have we distributed?" Sook asked.

"A little over four thousand," one of his workers replied. "We've been over Falls Church, Fairfax, Herndon, McLean, and Vienna. Tomorrow, we start on Centreville, Annandale, and Chantilly."

"How can we improve our approach?" I asked.

"We hire three more students to join the search," a second worker said. "Need to bring in another telephone line to handle the volume of hotline calls we're receiving."

"Where do we go next?" Bin asked. "I suggest Baltimore, D.C., or Leesburg." He stopped to take a call from his uncle. Bin listened for a while, his gaze gradually going from sleepy-sloth eyes to bug-out eyes.

Turning to us, he said, "My uncle knows where Sang-hun hid. He unloaded cargo and bunked at Uncle's warehouse in Baltimore."

I stood up, leaned over the table, and grabbed the phone from Bin. "We need to explore your building. Now! How many people in there?"

"E-e-empty now," the uncle replied.

"We're coming, as fast as we can. Don't let anyone in at the gate. No one removes packages or crates."

I handed the phone back to Bin and turned to Sook. "Mickey and I are going with Bin and you to Baltimore. Only we four."

As we left the conference room, I turned to the staff working around the table. "We located where Sang-hun stayed. You are geniuses. It takes a genius to be as lucky as we are."

We hustled down to my Mustang. I checked my pistol had a full load. I knew our flashlights were in the trunk.

"Powell might have a tail on us," I said. "We need to get to the warehouse in Baltimore, but we don't want to attract the police to the artifacts, bring them like barracudas seeking prey."

I drove out of the garage and started toward Baltimore. From the rear seat, Bin asked, "How you shake a tail?"

I drove in the slowest lane of the toll road. "First, drive along slowly, like this. Most of the cars behind us are passing, not following us. A dark sedan is behind us."

I took an exit and drove to the next down ramp going back onto the toll road. "That dark sedan followed us off the exit and back onto the main road. If a car follows you off and back on the road, the car's tailing you."

Bin locked eyes with me in the rearview mirror. "You spotted follower?"

"We identified him," I said. "Losing him will be more difficult."

Next, I pulled off the toll road into a large shopping area, making only right turns, going in circles. "No vehicle stuck to me through our final maneuvers."

I drove back onto the toll road and preceded toward Baltimore. "No car followed us through those last twists. Hope for the best. We head to the warehouse."

Waiting had been boring. To go down to the wire brought life. That was the excitement. Adrenaline flooded my body, forcing my heart to throb. *Get to the warehouse. Faster. Thrust the accelerator down.*

NORTHERN VIRGINIA—4 JULY 2000

Behind me, in the rear seat, Sook said, "Distance from my office to warehouse . . . fifty-miles. Time is Tuesday evening. We in rush-hour traffic."

Bin added, "You think we be lucky? Will treasure be there?"

Traffic in the lane to my left moved. I clicked on my turn signal and forced my way into that row of cars. "Why did Sang-hun stay at that storage facility? A good reason would have been to smuggle the treasure to South Korea in the hold of a ship. I think he hid the loot near his bunk."

Sang-hun Lee, the fifth soldier, had found a job and a bunk bed at the uncle's warehouse in Baltimore. We needed to get to the unloading facility quickly before the assassin arrived; indeed, we could not, must not, allow the killer to snatch the artifacts from us. Because the traffic crawled, keeping me from the uncle's building, I seethed with frustration and a sense of powerlessness. The beltway circling Washington had four lanes in both directions. Around my car, many vehicles traveled, tightly packed together, moving briefly at five miles per hour, increasing to thirty miles per hour for no apparent reason, and then dropping back to five. Off to the right side of the roadway, concrete sound barriers loomed with deciduous trees rising above their tops. To the front and back of me, vehicles stretched into the distance.

The lane to my right sped up; I jerked the Mustang into a small opening. The driver behind me blew his horn. Settled in a rear seat, Bin grabbed the front-seat back for support. "He mad."

Sook let out his breath and settled back in his seat. "Don trying to get us through this tangle."

Mickey, sporting a broad grin, sat beside me in the front seat. "Didn't Roth tell you to investigate the laborers at the uncle's warehouse?"

"Yeah, yeah, I was getting around to checking," I replied.

Bin joined in. "Anyway, my uncle recognized Sang-hun's photograph—a dockhand at his facility."

"We didn't tell Detective Powell?" Sook said. "We have no backup coming?"

I glanced over my shoulder at Sook. "Have to go in alone. If we tell him, we'll lose our licenses and the treasure."

"What if killer's there? What if more than one criminal left?"

The line of vehicles slowed and then stopped altogether. I took my hands off the steering wheel and balled them into fists. "We'll take care of it. Don't worry."

Mickey chuckled. "Three men are dead. We'll have to be careful."

I hit the gas pedal when the vehicles in front of me started moving again. "We don't get to choose when we die. We only get to choose to be careful."

Since our investigation had begun nineteen days earlier, I had been at the rear of the pack, struggling to catch up. The thief showed smarts like the cartoon rabbit, schemed like the coyote, and escaped with impunity like the roadrunner. In the past, I had felt like the goofy guy with the stutter—now I was closing in on the roadrunner. After a minute of standing still, my lane began moving again. "If we're lucky, we'll get to the building before the assassin does. If we're unlucky, he already has the treasure. If the killer gets to the storage facility at the same time as we, then we take back the relics."

I drove in the far-right lane of I-95, a major highway in Maryland, running from the beltway around Washington, D.C. to Baltimore, Maryland, an artery which at this moment was a red parade of brake lights. Ahead of us, the concrete sound barriers terminated, and a shoulder spread out along the side of the road, merging into a forest off to the side. The column of vehicles continued to start and stop.

A sensation of helplessness consumed me. Without conscious control, my open hands banged the rims of the steering wheel. Mickey glanced at me, saying nothing. I shouted, "Hold on," pushed down on the accelerator, steered onto the shoulder of the road, and sped around the mass of vehicles. I heard horns blowing; additionally, I spied hand gestures offered up by the drivers left in my wake.

"You can't do this," Sook shouted.

"Police put you in jail," Bin added.

Mickey remained calm. "Tire blocking shoulder ahead."

I veered toward the lane of cars and avoided the castoff tire, continuing forward on the shoulder of the road.

Sook grasped the back of the front seat with both his hands. "Please stop."

I didn't answer him but concentrated on the shoulder ahead and hoped I wouldn't puncture a tire. Sook and Bin went silent. For a while, I sped along, feeling the Mustang bounce on its shock absorbers.

"Police vehicle ahead," Mickey cautioned. "Better get back on the pavement."

I found a space in the line of cars to my left and nosed my way into the lane. The police didn't see me, focused as they were in moving a broken down vehicle.

I had resumed creeping along. Even with the AC, my body perspired from anxiety. I wiped the sweat from my forehead with the back of my hand.

Bin rang his uncle and turned up the volume on his mobile phone speaker. "Where are you?"

"I-I-I'm at gate with the guard."

So we all could hear, Bin held his mobile phone between the front and rear seats. "Anyone try to enter?"

"No one arrives. Area i-i-is calm."

I leaned closer to the phone. "We're fighting through thick traffic. Stay at the gate until we get there."

"Hurry. If bad man comes, I run." Bin and his uncle disconnected.

As we continued to crawl on four wheels, I felt an opportunity slipping away like touching a greased pig slithering out of my clutches. Why couldn't this line of cars move faster? Vehicles on the two right-most lanes seemed to be moving quicker than those on the left. Finally, up ahead, I saw the cars to my left with right-turn signals flashing. Our obstruction turned out to be a two-vehicle crash that closed two lanes of the I-95 north. Emergency responders were at the scene, taking away the injured. When we got past the hold-up, the column sped up.

"Now, we move," Sook said. "Please! No drive off road!"

"I hope we in time," Bin said.

I pushed down on the gas pedal. "It's not enough to hope. We gotta kill the killers if they're there."

# # #

Pulling into the road fronting the warehouse, I saw both the building and the quay in the gathering dusk. Lights were turned off in the building. No cargo ship stood at the wharf; the mob of Korean workers had disappeared. The uncle and his gatekeeper stood inside the closed entrance.

About the time we stopped at the front gate to the warehouse lot, dusk's concluding darkness descended. Mickey, Sook, Bin, and I got out of our car and met the uncle and night watchman. I scanned the parking lot and saw six parked vehicles. Two belonged to the uncle and the guard. Per the uncle, the other four belonged to workers currently away on one of the uncle's ships. Either we got to the storage facility before the assassin, or he parked somewhere on the street and came through or over the fence. Neither the uncle nor the night watchman had stepped inside the building to inspect for an intruder. We had the building to search. That would pass the time in any case, moving slowly if the building stood empty or rapidly if the killer waited inside.

Mickey and I prepared to enter the facility. I touched my M1911 pistol in its belt holster. I took one of our two flashlights. "I'll go in through the front. The uncle will go with me, behind me, to guide me through the door. Then he'll drop back to Sook and Bin."

Feeling nervous, I brushed down my cowlick and coordinated with Mickey. "Have the night watchman guide you around the facility to the back entrance. After showing you how to get in, he'll rejoin the group at the gate. If the assassin is inside the storage structure, we don't want our clients to get shot."

Mickey nodded. He seemed relaxed.

Mickey and I had turned off the ring volume on our mobile phones. "Once inside, we go to Sang-hun's bunk on the second floor. We have our mobile phones set on vibration mode—to alert us to a call. If either of us finds this facility is empty, we'll let the other know."

"Are we in a hurry?"

"No. We'll take our time going through this warehouse."

"Use our usual mobile-phone code—the number of call vibrations?" Mickey asked.

While we talked, I spread black tape over the hard surfaces of my metal flashlight. "If I call your phone, I'll make it vibrate once and disconnect. If you don't answer, you're in trouble. In other words, I vibrate your phone once, and you vibrate my phone once in return, then I know you're okay."

I brushed my cowlick again and waited for Mickey to respond. "One vibration in return means 'no problem.'"

"Right," I said. "Two vibrations say, 'get out,' and three means 'success.'"

"And for a text message?" Mickey asked.

"I write the text message and send it to you," I said.

Before splitting up to search the building, Mickey said, "I'm the better shot. Let me take the front entrance."

I shook my head. "If we switch, Bruce will badger me unmercifully—endlessly. He'll call me the weak link. I'll take the front."

We synchronized our watches. Mickey went to the rear of the warehouse with the guard.

That night at the uncle's building, a half-moon gave off its soft light in a partially clouded sky, coating the building's surroundings with a blue tint. To my view, the outside of the structure appeared painted half in black and half in blue. On the ground around the warehouse, shadows alternated with the moon's partial illumination, as clouds came and went between the moon and the earth. By the weak light through the few windows, the inside of the storage facility was dark. The high humidity caused me to sweat. I heard a tugboat out on the Patapsco River. The only other sounds were the crickets and an occasional vehicle passing on the road fronting the warehouse.

The uncle and I crept to the front door.

# # #

At the front of the storage facility, I glanced up. The building workers had closed both upper-level doors on the top two floors of the three-story brick structure. At street level, a metal sliding gate—the kind that rolled up and down like a garage door—gave entrance to the facility. Bin's uncle and I stood beside that front door.

"Will this be noisy going up?" I whispered.

"Pus-s-sh door up slowly," the uncle replied. "Force slowly—m-m-make little noise."

I clutched the lower edge of the sliding door and got ready to pull. "What's on the other side of this entrance?"

"Open space—is vast and goes back—a-a-almost to the rear wall."

"When I go through the door, to which side should I move? Don't want to be caught out in the open."

"Go left. Open space to the right. To left crates and pallets—take cover there."

I slowly pulled up the door, sneaking left into the warehouse—when the door was high enough to slip under—leaving the uncle outside. I moved past the battered table and folding chairs. In the partial light from an upper window, I saw a large crate and darted to it, as a bug caught by light scurries to a dark corner. I paused behind the box and listened.

My pulse raced. I breathed in and out slowly, wanting to calm my body. My nose smelled mothballs and a moldy basement. In this portion of the massive structure, the inside was dark as a windowless cellar. A generator—located toward the rear of the building—started, ran for a minute, and then kicked off, breaking the facility's silence. I hoped, *Maybe the assassin hadn't come here. Maybe I got lucky.*

Then, above me, I heard wood sliding on wood, like someone pushing a crate along a floor. The building became silent again. Shortly, I heard a screeching sound, like somebody prying up a nail. Silence.

As my pulse finally slowed, the partly opened door behind me rolled down by itself with a crash—*Bang!*

Stunned, I scrunched down and raised my pistol, searching for a physical threat. Nothing. I listened for several minutes, but the sound of wood scraping on wood—in the interior of the building—had stopped.

It's possible to commit a clumsy mistake—and still succeed. God, I hope Roth will see my blunder that way.

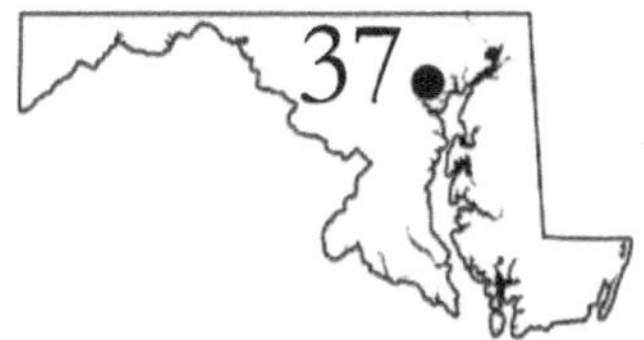

BALTIMORE—4 JULY 2000

With the roll-up door closed behind me, I waited, crouching behind a box covered by a canvas blanket, pressing my body into the cloth to reduce my silhouette. Sweat flowed down my back in a stream. My hearing picked up every rustle around me. Adrenalin pumped into my blood, pushing my heart to beat faster. My brain resisted panic, calling for calm.

My eyes continued adjusting to the darkness inside the warehouse. Slight illumination peeked in by moonlight through a few windows higher along an outside wall, one of the sidewalls. I distinguished hazy forms: an I-beam caught in a moonbeam and patches of the light-colored concrete floor.

Shielding my mobile phone's light with my body and jacket, I slouched down behind the box and pulled up Mickey's mobile number and pressed *send*. After one buzz, I disconnected, which meant his phone vibrated once. In a moment, my mobile phone vibrated once and only once. Nothing had happened, and we continued our search. I placed my cell phone in my rear pants pocket.

In the past, I had learned not to dwell on what might happen next. If I worried about what might be, I would play funny tricks on myself, plant fantasies in my head. I would become nervous, doubt myself, and think up ways to fail. Conversely, when I thought about the gritty details of preparation—going over the mechanics of planning—my mind refocused, my breathing slowed.

Just now, my brain didn't visualize fumbling. My mind fixated on the mechanics of aiming at a target. Don't worry about keeping the gun sight aligned on a single, solitary point in space. Don't stress your body trying not to wobble the pistol.

My cell phone vibrated once in my rear pants pocket. I answered Mickey back with one vibration. I checked for a text message.

"DOOR SLAM," Mickey had texted. "U?"

"YES," I texted back.

"OK," he replied.

I listened and didn't move, letting my eyes adjust further to the slight illumination in this cavernous structure. Back when I had been an MP in the army, we would have sent in a dog to sniff out an intruder. I didn't have a dog, and I would have to do my own sniffing. To stay calm, I refocused my brain back to thinking about the details of targeting.

Don't sight the pistol on a single point in space. I imagined a make-believe box around the center of the target. Put the front sight of the gun somewhere in that miniature box, an imaginary square, and squeeze the trigger.

I hesitated, and then turned toward the building's right side, padding to the sidewall in the dark, toward the stairs, which the uncle had told me went up to the second floor. Taking off my shoes and stuffing them in the outside pockets of my light jacket, I examined the ground for the quietest path, carpet or a rubber mat if possible. In going up the wooden steps, I would put my feet down near a wall and not the middle span of a step.

Using the sparse moonlight from the side windows, I studied my surroundings, being watchful not to brush against boxes or rubbish. I bent my knees to lower my body, so I didn't lock my legs when I stepped down on the floor, edging along the wall to the steps going up to the second story. Always listening for sounds after my movements and searching for the glow of a flashlight, I tried to creep as a stalking cat.

The warehouse remained noiseless. I assumed the intruder—the scraping across the floor meant someone was on an upper level—understood the sudden noise of the front door closing meant people had entered the warehouse. If we had turned the lights on and walked about, then the intruder might assume we worked here. Because we had left the lights off and maintained silence, an intruder would know we stalked him. Also, we weren't the authorities: we hadn't identified ourselves as police and called for any trespasser to come out.

When I reached the first stair, I paused a few minutes.

My mobile phone vibrated once. I called Mickey back with one buzz. He sent a text message, "REAR CLEAR. WHERE U?"

I slumped down behind a packing case, my mobile phone in my lap, covered up by the bottom edges of my jacket. "GOING UP." I sent the text and started up the stairs on all fours.

Nearing the top of the staircase, the beginning of the second floor, I peeked over the top step. Stretching my neck and moving only my eyes, I studied the second floor for a full five minutes—after all, we had all night. The design of the second floor comprised an open space with steel I-beams forming a grid of load-bearing structures. Windows along the walls allowed enough light to illuminate the middle area partially. The partition to my left sat in total darkness.

I crept out of the stairwell onto the second floor, standing close to the left wall. As I paused to scan for the intruder—someone shoved a hard object against the back of my head.

"Oops!" a voice behind me said. "Got yourself in a jam. You move, I shoot."

Startled, I began to turn. The man smacked my head with his gun barrel. I saw just enough to see a pistol. White, flashing light danced before my eyes.

"Stop!" the man said. "Pistol on the floor."

I placed my M1911 on the floor. Damn, there are no second performances in life.

"Two steps forward," the voice said.

I heard him pick up my pistol. "Heavy gun. Better not drop on my toe. I prefer lighter .22 pistol."

The intruder was a comedian. I knew that voice.

"Turn around. Hands up. You need to explain yourself."

I turned and faced a dark splotch in the black area beside the stairway door. It took me a few seconds to comprehend what I saw—the black smudge was a Ninja black cloak covering the intruder.

He dropped his cloak.

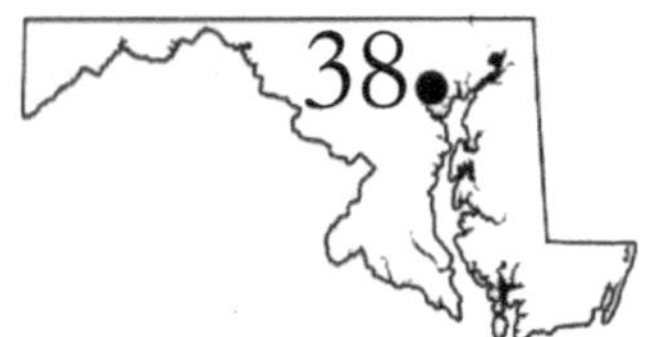

BALTIMORE—5 JULY 2000

Ji-hun Cho, the Korean agent, slipped off his Ninja cloak and tossed it on a nearby cargo box. He wore his stylish black suit but had loosened his black tie, and he held a pistol, its barrel facing me. In the partial light from the windows, I recognized a .22 semi-automatic pistol. My heart and brain raced. My breathing slowed to reduce the pace of the former, and the latter galloped to figure out my options. If Ji-hun were an actual agent of South Korea, he would lower his pistol. Were he the murderer, I needed to talk him into keeping me alive. I had to be calm and come up with a bullshit story.

Ji-hun kept his pistol pointed at my head. "Keep your hands up—get down on both knees."

I quickly obeyed. No need to get killed for obstinate behavior.

"Hands on your head and interlock your fingers."

He had me so I couldn't lunge and tackle him with a single motion. "Ji-hun, where are your FBI colleagues?" I asked.

He stared at me a moment before speaking. "Sook Park had started to send Silla treasure out of the country. I come alone, to stop him."

Sweat continued flowing in a rivulet down my back, sticking my shirt to my skin. I detected a lemon scent emanating from him. He didn't seem to have a backup. Maybe he wanted to get me talking to tell him who else had reached the building. "You're in the warehouse now," I said. "You can call the FBI to back you up."

He had a poker-player face: it wasn't easy to read his thoughts. "I alone search for Sook Park," he said.

I had to guess. Ji-hun had been hunting for the artifacts Sang-hun had hidden. He didn't want to stop the treasure from leaving the country. He wanted the Silla relics for himself. I had to stall. Keep him talking. "Yeah. Why don't you call the FBI?"

Additional light penetrated the side windows when the waxing-crescent moon shown through the clouds. He appeared relaxed, holding the .22 pistol in his right hand and twisting a gold coin back and forth over his fingers with his left. He projected a calm, cocky persona. "No, I look by myself. Where Sook?"

"I could join you in your search."

"I think not. Possibly you helped Park steal Silla treasure."

I shifted my knees a small movement backwards, slowly transferring my body into the limited lighting from the windows. I wanted Mickey to be able to see me, to realize what had happened. Ji-hun kept me at gunpoint but hadn't shot me. He kept talking with me. Why?

"Where is Mr. Park? Is he here with you?"

Keep him talking. "Why do you want Sook?"

"Told you. Park is taking treasure out of the country. Where is he?"

"He's outside." In my back pocket, I felt my mobile phone vibrate once.

"Who else is here?" Ji-hun asked.

I hadn't known Sang-hun worked at the warehouse until the uncle told us. But Ji-hun had arrived here way before I did; only Sang-hun's partner knew he worked here. I had found the mysterious tall man, and he was going to hurt me.

Ji-hun continued twirling his gold coin in his left hand. He showed no emotion, a stone-cold killer. "I am here to reclaim Silla treasure for Korea. How many people here besides you?"

My mobile vibrated once again. I suspected Ji-hun had not yet found the hidden relics. Maybe he wanted to know how many people were at the facility and where they were. He seemed to want to secure the warehouse and resume searching. I had to keep him talking. "What were you searching for when I arrived?"

Ji-hun made a sucking sound with his lips, maybe feeling events moved too slowly. "Let's get everyone together and work this out? How do we get Sook in here?"

"If you planned to return the relics to Korea, you would've

brought the FBI with you. You and Sang-hun were partners, weren't you?"

Other than rotating the coin over the fingers of his left hand, Ji-hun waited motionlessly. "How many people here with you?"

I took half a minute to consider how to answer him. In a single swift action, Ji-hun raised his pistol and slammed it down on the top of my head. I felt dazed and began to suffer blurred vision and ringing ears. Blood flowed down the side of my face. I had to remain calm, feeding him enough information to keep me alive and keep him talking. "Sook Park and Bin Bie are here. You're the brains behind the theft, aren't you?" My mouth was dry as a can of talcum powder. I waited.

"I stole the crown and the other pieces. I asked you, who else is here at the warehouse?"

"Bin Bie's uncle is at the gate. How did you learn about the crown? Why did the theft occur fifty years after the crown left South Korea?"

I thought I heard a slight squeak behind Ji-hun. Then silence returned. My vision and hearing cleared. I fingered the cut on my head, finding it only about half an inch long with smooth edges but still bleeding.

The moon poked through the clouds and shimmered into the second floor. Ji-hun grinned and seemed pleased with himself. "Two years ago, I labored with our archaeologists—exploring Silla tombs near Gyeongju. In my free time, I rummaged around the Korean countryside. Chanced upon the plundered tomb."

I had solved the mystery. Ji-hun, the Korean Agent, had discovered the tomb and started a torrent of kidnapping, killing, and burglary. Unfortunately, my neck stuck out a little just now.

"I found others had removed the artifacts from the tomb," Ji-hun continued. "Exploring around the grave, I found signs of a big battle. I kept knowledge of the tomb from the South Korean authorities."

"But how could no one else in South Korea know about the tomb?" I asked.

Ji-hun appeared to relish telling his tale. "Many of the old Silla tombs remain hidden, covered over with vegetation. Finding an old tomb remains a bit of an art."

Feed his ego. Keep him yakking. "How'd you track down Sook Park and the treasure in Virginia?"

Squeaking sounds continued periodically, reverberations I took as real and not something my frightened brain dreamed.

"I searched through ROK Army records. Read reports on the thousands of soldiers who fought in the area and could have taken artifacts."

Ji-hun observed me as he recounted his tale. I had no chance to rush and surprise him.

"I hunted a soldier who fought at Gyeongju and lived. Eventually, I found him. Gunfire wounded Sang-hun Lee, but he recovered.

"I located him, the old soldier. He had recovered from his injuries and led a grueling life as a laborer after the war. Sang-hun had lost contact with the other members of his old mortar squad."

"How did you know ROK soldiers raided the tomb and not North Korean troops?" I asked.

Ji-hun smiled at me in the limited light and said, "I had access to the ROK Army records but not North Korean records. I talked with Sang-hun. He said his mortar crew had taken the artifacts."

A team had formed: Ji-hun wanted the gold and Sang-hun wanted revenge.

"Using database files and Sang-hun, I identified Seong-gi Kim—living in Seoul—as a living member of old mortar squad. The two of us kidnapped Seong-gi Kim and learned the Silla treasure lay in a room in Northern Virginia. I arranged a tourist visa for Sang-hun and got him a job with the old smuggler, Bin Bie's uncle, in America."

I had heard the slightest squeak of a wood floor off to his right. I hadn't imagined it. Keeping his eyes on me, Ji-hun shifted his head as if he had heard the sound and tried to figure its direction.

At that point, Ji-hun paused and commented, "I was pretty smart, wasn't I?"

I grunted, and Ji-hun resumed his story.

"In early June, I traveled to the United States as a CHA agent and Sang-hun worked at the warehouse. We scouted the Great Falls house, entered through the upper dormer window, used the combination to get into the exhibit room, and escaped with our loot."

Behind Ji-hun, a stooped figure moved through the partial light from a side window. My breath caught, and I steadied myself to keep from swaying.

"And your partner? What happened to him?"

"I misjudged the hatred Sang-hun had for his old mortar squad. He killed Yeong-ho Park. I had to eliminate him before he brought police down on me."

I told myself to relax. "And here we are."

"Funny isn't it," Ji-hun remarked. "I judged nearly everything correctly, but the one: Sang-hun had lost his mind and lashed out with rage to kill the members of his old mortar squad."

Keep him going. "Did you locate the loot upstairs?"

Ji-hun ceased twirling his coin. "I have talked too much. You will help me get the people outside to come inside."

I had run out of a way to play for time.

He moved his pistol closer to my head. "Answer me. I let you live."

Behind Ji-hun, Mickey turned on his flashlight, highlighting the tall man in his dark suit, tie, and white shirt. The light beam caught Ji-hun entirely.

'Freeze!"

As Mickey shouted, the Korean agent turned his head. I vaulted to the side, landing out of the line of fire.

Ji-hun brought his pistol around and shot—*Pop! Pop!*—toward Mickey's flashlight.

Mickey fired—*Pow! Pow!*

His pistol emitted brief flame flashes trailed by an elongated haze cloud of white smoke.

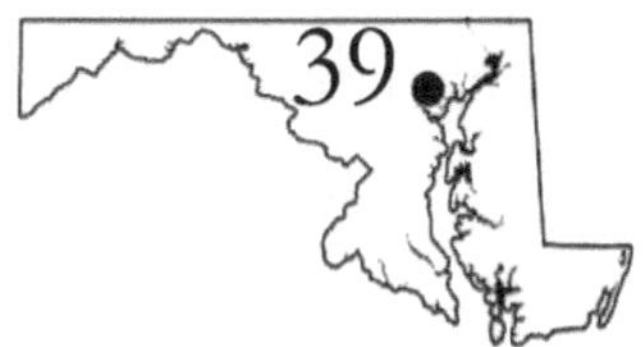

BALTIMORE—5 JULY 2000

The flashlight's blaze had blinded me. The booms of the shots in the warehouse stillness had grated on my hearing. A wooden crate had blocked me from further scrambling away from the firefight. As Ji-hun toppled to the floor, his body had sprawled on my feet and had not budged.

Silence suffused the warehouse, like cold in a refrigerated-storage enclosure.

Mickey stood by himself. "You hit?"

I lay on the floorboards, a pleasant sensation pumping through my body: I lived. I pulled my feet free from Ji-hun's weight and glanced up at Mickey. "What took you so long?"

Mickey's flashlight illuminated the body on the floor. "Thought you were going to talk him to death before I got to him."

"I improvised."

"That another word for 'whined?'"

I sat up, experiencing an urge to vomit. It passed. "You hit?"

"His shots missed me. He looks bad."

Ji-hun's stylish suit seemed fine, but blood had soaked through the front of his white shirt. In death, his hair was thick, his body slender, and his age still appeared mid-thirties. A .22 semi-automatic pistol, a Ruger Mark II, lay beside him on the floor. The South Korean agent would never again interrogate Sook.

"Who's he?" Mickey asked.

"The CHA agent . . . Ji-hun," I said. "Worked with Detective Powell and the FBI."

"What's he doing here?"

"Looking for treasure."

I prodded the figure on the ground for a pulse, listened for breathing, and held the flashlight on his eyes watching for his pupils to constrict. Ji-hun had two sizeable holes in his chest. Sure looked dead.

I regarded my partner with approval. "For a big man, you were stealthy getting here."

He emitted a snorting chuckle. "Little known fact—donuts make you light-footed."

My legs wobbled as I stood up with Mickey's help. I found my pistol and flashlight. I phoned Sook at the front gate and told him to bring Bin and the uncle.

Mickey went to search the rest of the structure, checking no one else was present, turning on overhead lights as he went along. The uncle arrived, saw what had happened, and phoned his night watchman to stay at the gate—admit no one.

"It's Ji-hun Cho," I said. "He played the lawful government agent, but he stole and killed."

Neither Sook nor Bin seemed shaken by the dead South Korean. I recalled they'd seen corpses in heaps—fifty years ago in the Korean War. I placed a blanket over the dead man's face. "I figure he shot Seong-gi in South Korea. Many secrets died with Ji-hun."

Sook searched near the dead man. "Where is our treasure?"

I could see Ji-hun had no relics with him. "Ji-hun had a flashlight, a small-caliber pistol, and a pair of shoes in his pockets."

Sook shot me a puzzled glance. "Shoes in pockets?"

I brushed my cowlick, thinking how Ji-hun had outsmarted me. "He took off his shoes, so he wouldn't make noise."

It took a moment for Sook to understand, but then he said, "Where are relics?"

"Not here."

Sook held his head as if in pain. "You put us in bad place. You killed man but did not gain Silla artifacts." He shouted, losing his usual calm.

My shoes were still in my jacket. I took them out, sat down on the floor, and put them on. "Let's search where Sang-hun had his bunk."

Sook and Bin frowned. They appeared to blame me for not locating the treasure with Ji-hun. We went to an alcove on the second floor.

"He-r-r-re is Sang-hun's bed," the uncle said in a stutter.

In his search for the treasure, Ji-hun had tossed and jumbled the objects near Sang-hun's bunk. I walked over the area, peering into the corners. "Maybe Ji-hun searched here, and—not finding what he wanted—moved to other areas."

I led the way into the cargo space next over from Sang-hun's bed. Our intruder had ripped open crates in this storage area. The ripped-open boxes held no Silla artifacts.

We moved to the next storage space. Finding nothing near the bunk or in the first storage area, our intruder had started opening crates in this second storage area.

I saw two opened crates and many he hadn't torn open. "Probably Ji-hun had gotten this far when we interrupted him by entering the building."

Sook studied this second region overflowing with boxes. "Searching for Silla artifacts among all these crates will be difficult, like seeking for polar bear in a snowstorm."

The uncle found crowbars for Mickey and me.

"Suggest big men open box-e-e-es," he stuttered. "Then Sook and Bin search box-e-e-es by hand."

We tore open boxes in the second alcove. After an hour, I found two medium-size wooden crates with shipping labels back to South Korea. "Let's open these two crates."

When we had the tops off, I stepped back to allow Sook and Bin room to paw through the contents. I spied bubble-wrapped objects of different sizes inside the two crates. I told myself, "Be patient." Roth's advice—"Don't expect a winner every time, or disappointment will make you miserable"—burst unbidden into my brain.

Sook held up the prize, a Silla crown of worked gold. "Eureka!" I shouted.

The top of the imposing object extended upwards, shaped like deer antlers, with strands of smaller, interlocked gold pieces hanging down from the sides. Sook grinned at me.

I grinned back. "Hell's bells. We did it."

From the first crate, Sook took a pair of earrings, of bright gold in three parts: a top designed to attach to the ear, a middle section with a ball-like shape, and a bottom section comprised of small gold bells.

From the second crate, Bin pulled out a little box containing rings of gold. Bin had a list of the entire collection of artifacts, placing a check mark beside each item as they extracted a piece. They covered the floor with objects. We had all the Silla pieces.

After a period of grinning and shouting, Sook turned glum again. "What we do? We killed an agent of South Korean government. Do we have to tell police?"

I didn't know how to answer Sook, but at least he seemed to have stopped blaming me for our troubles.

"Hold on," Bin said, pointing at Ji-hun. "He is responsible for killing two dear friends, Seong-gi and Yeong-ho. He stole our treasure. He had .22 pistol to kill more people." Bin's arm shook, pointing at the body. Not moving, Sook seemed to listen to Bin.

"I agree with Bin," I said. "Ji-hun said he sought the artifacts for himself."

Sook and Bin stopped their discussion and listened to me. "Ji-hun's partner, Sang-hun, had stashed the treasure in this warehouse, for shipment back to Korea. All along, Ji-hun killed, stole, and covered his tracks."

Sook and Bin stood over the rows of relics. The uncle sat on a crate with an index finger against his cheek. Mickey gazed at me, maybe waiting to hear what I planned to do.

My thinking raced, analyzing our situation. "We have a body, someone we killed. As soon as we tell the police, Sook and Bin will lose the Silla treasure and may go to jail for stealing it from South Korea. Probably, Mickey and I will lose our license for withholding information from the police."

"Ji-hun responsible for three deaths," the uncle stammered. "He evil man. He shot at Mickey, h-e-e-ere in my building."

"This murderer, Ji-hun, has been punished for killing my friends," Bin said. "Nothing more would be gained by telling police. All we would do is dot i's and cross t's. No good gained."

The room grew still, like naptime in a preschool. Mickey said nothing, standing with his arms crossed. The uncle remained calm, his head slightly swaying up and down. I drew back to a corner. All eyes stayed on me as if expecting me to light the way out. My brain roiled in turmoil, uncertain what to do.

When the uncle finally spoke, his speech was quiet, slow, and stumbling. "B-a-a-altimore running 300 homicides a year. Wh-a-a-at is one more? Get rid of evil man's body.

"Have s-s-shipment going to South Korea in two days. When s-s-ship two days out, my crew drop him into the deep."

Sook bit his lower lip. "I agree with Bin's uncle."

"Me, too," Bin said.

Mickey just stared at me.

I pondered how my ethics covered our difficulty. The killers of Seong-gi and Yeong-ho had paid an awful price, loss of their lives. I had been taught to do the *right thing*. The right thing meant I had to report Ji-hun's death to the police. Turning the body over to the police wouldn't bring anyone back to life. Sang-hun and Ji-hun had gotten what they deserved.

If I dump the body in the ocean, I serve the greater good.

What about Roth? She—the essential person for me to be concerned about—would figure out what happened. But would she want me to let treasure slip through her fingers?

Dropping a body in the deep is what outlaws do. Thoughts of *Macbeth* popped up in my head: "Fair is foul, and foul is fair."

I lowered my head. "Drop the body in the sea."

Forgive me, for I do wrong.

#

Mickey and I ditched Ji-hun's rental car, along with its keys, in an impoverished section of Baltimore. Sook and Bin hid the relics. Bin's uncle cleaned up the warehouse mess. I never again saw the body.

To split up our salvage, Sook and Bin agreed to meet Roth in Asheville in early July. As our clients had no further need of us, Mickey and I announced we would return to Asheville Wednesday afternoon.

We packed Mickey's Explorer, turned in the rented Mustang, and checked out of our hotel.

I called Carla, who spoke in a sad tone. "Heard you were leaving. Are you coming over to say 'Goodbye' to me?"

I felt a little intimidated by Carla. She was sexy, witty, and thought like me, like a gumshoe. We'd spent an enjoyable time together. "Could I come by now?"

"I'll wait outside my building."

I disconnected and located Mickey lingering by his SUV. "I want to see Carla before I leave."

"I'll wait here."

Carla, in her short shorts and a tight tee shirt, sat on a child's swing beside her building. She appeared lovely. She rolled out of the swing, her ponytail flying, pulled my head down and kissed me on the lips. "When do you leave?"

"I'm going now. I'll miss you."

She peered up at me with those brown eyes. I remembered telling her she was full of chocolate. "We got close. Can't you stay longer?"

"You take my breath away," I answered. "You're stimulating, but I thought you detested me after the fire drill."

"I've forgiven you. I do remember we were getting undressed. We might develop a warmer relationship . . . if you'd give it a chance."

I had had fun with this woman. She had talked about things I liked discussing—why people did what they did, who was lying, and what caused an event. I had a major lust for this beautiful female. Despite my feelings for her, I had to return to North Carolina, and she would be returning to Ohio. No opportunity for growing an intense passion.

"Carla, I'm finished in Northern Virginia. You'll be gone soon. Time for me to leave."

She stood close and hugged me. "Thank you . . . for good food and good times. Somehow, we never could finish the evening in a normal way."

"I apologize for embarrassing you—the night of the fire drill," I replied.

"I told you I forgave you."

"Well, goodbye." I turned to go.

"Wait!" Carla grabbed my shoulders, pulled my torso and head down, and kissed me. I kissed her. She released me with a hungry expression and stepped back.

As I walked away, I peeked and saw Carla following me with her eyes and waving her right hand at me.

Mickey waited in the shade beside our vehicle. "How'd your goodbye go?"

"She forgave me for the fire-alarm episode."

"Is this a never-see-you-again goodbye or will you stay in touch?" my partner asked.

"I think she's fun."

As Mickey got in the driver's seat, he glanced at me but didn't speak.

After a little time had passed on our drive to Asheville, he turned to me. "My wife thinks you're a mess with women."

"Taylor thinks I'm a mess with women?"

"She does."

"I love women."

"Taylor says you don't know what the hell you want."

"I don't know what I want?"

"That's what she said."

I didn't respond. Mickey drove for a few minutes longer and then said, "Pass me a donut."

We continued down I-81 for home.

ASHEVILLE—5 JULY 2000

That night in Asheville, Mickey and I narrated to Roth how we recovered the Silla treasure at the warehouse. We sat facing her desk, as she stood to water the plants around her fireplace. I tried to compose myself with a glass of Chianti. Roth stopped to pick up her glass of wine, sipped, and said, "Report." While she watered and picked leaves, I described what happened, omitting the death of Ji-hun Cho in the firefight.

When I finished, she put down her watering pot, sat at her desk, and seemed to ponder what I had related. "The uncle knowing the man in the picture wasn't a coincidence. It was a matter of time until you would have distributed Sang-hun's pictures around Baltimore. Or you would have investigated the uncle's workers, as I instructed, and found Sang-hun, the man you sought."

I fidgeted with the crease in my pants and waited.

Roth began tapping on her desk. "Let me visualize what happened. Did you reach the warehouse before or after darkness fell?"

"After."

"Was the building dark or lit up?"

I had often gone through deep questioning by Roth. She rarely left the mansion and customarily used my eyes to investigate outside events. Mickey and I had agreed to present a misleading story to Roth: the one where he didn't shoot and kill Ji-hun, the Korean agent. Maybe she had detected a change, a tell, in my voice and had begun asking questions to check my narrative's truth. In asking about the light in the warehouse, she wanted to see if I would give a lengthy explanation about light conditions, which might mean I felt nervous about telling a lie.

I didn't elaborate. "Dark."

She observed me with a resolute expression. "Where did you find Ji-hun Cho, that night in the warehouse?"

"On the second floor. Found him ripping open boxes. We exchanged gunfire—he escaped."

She tapped some more. "Who got to the building first?"

"He did."

"And you found each other after bumping around in the dark? No one happened to get ambushed?" she asked.

"We ran into each other by chance."

Roth paused, swallowed a little of her wine, and turned to Mickey. "You agree?"

"Yes, Ms. Roth."

She turned back to me. "You got close enough to recognize Ji-hun?"

I concentrated on showing my confident expression. "Yes, ma'am."

She pursed her lips. "I have difficulty believing the action happened as you described. You and Mickey are crack shots. Was Ji-hun injured?"

I had been lying to Roth, the smartest person I knew. "Mickey winged him."

"Where did he hit Ji-hun?"

Roth stared at me unceasingly, maybe trying to catch hesitation on my face. "Think the arm."

"What happened then?"

"He ran."

"He vacated the building on his own two legs?" she asked.

I drank a little wine. "Yeah."

"That's not the way it happened," she said.

A confrontation with Roth was what I dreaded. I kept my mouth shut.

She stopped tapping. "Ji-hun would have gone to the FBI. You had no proof he was anything other than a CHA agent. The FBI and the police would have arrived at the warehouse in crowds."

I told myself to give her *the short answer.* "Maybe Ji-hun panicked?"

"The police didn't question you? You just upped and departed Northern Virginia?"

"They didn't. We left this afternoon."

Roth waited and appeared to consider her next question. "Did you cancel the security for Sook and Bin?"

I begged my body to calm, but my temperature rose, like a fever coming on. I had continued the services of the bodyguards. I reasoned Detective Powell would deduce a link between the disappearance of the Korean agent and a cancellation of the guards. Separately, Roth would have understood withdrawal of the bodyguards meant Ji-hun had died, ceased to be a threat.

"The guards protect Sook and Bin," I answered.

"Did you search for Ji-hun or his car?" Roth asked.

I sipped wine. "Mickey and I didn't."

She continued tapping on her desk and stared knives at me. "Why not?"

"We salvaged the stolen crown and kept a tight lid on rumors about the artifacts," I responded.

She took the last swallow from her glass. "Did you perform an illegal act? Tell me. Now!"

Mickey and I said nothing.

"You salvaged the artifacts and kept Sook and Bin from being killed—at what cost?"

The room seemed to grow warmer. I sweated. I wasn't going to get Roth in trouble. What she didn't know, she wouldn't have to tell the police. "I told you everything you need to know."

Over the next half a minute, her face turned from her milky-white complexion to red. I guessed she didn't like my impudence. "I am not a simpleton. Tell me what you did."

"What you don't know can't be held against you," I said. "After the shooting, Ji-hun dashed from the warehouse into the night."

She stopped tapping, and whacked objects, propelling them off her desk: book and paper-clip dish to the right, phone to the left, and the flower vase with flowers to the right. She rose to her full five-foot-eight-inch height in her burgundy tunic dress and spoke in a steely voice. "What haven't you told me? Speak! This moment!"

Sitting with my head bowed like a scolded first grader, I didn't respond. Mickey sat beside me like a burly, silent sphinx.

Taylor opened the door to the office, glanced around the room.

"Do you need me, Ms. Roth?"

"Get out!"

Taylor left, closing the door.

"Answer me!" she shouted.

Roth could be gloomy and enigmatic, but now she was pissed off. I knew this about her: she was now my adversary. My shirt stuck to my back. I avoided her eyes and studied the fireplace mantle. "I gave you a full report."

"Did you hear me, Mickey?" she asked.

"Yes, ma'am."

"Are you going to answer me?"

"Don gave a full report, Ms. Roth."

Roth appeared to fume and stared at me. "You can't play Starskey and Hutch with everyone all the time! There are ethical and legal rules you must follow. What have you done?"

Mickey and I remained still as granite blocks. Roth glowed an unhealthful red and visibly trembled.

"I no longer trust you. You're burglarizing homes and shooting people. You're out of control." She appeared infuriated as she left the office.

"Taken a dislike to us," Mickey said.

"Give her time," I said. "We recovered the Silla treasure for her and stopped the killings. She'll calm down."

"Wonder if she fired us?"

I walked to the bar cart, grabbed the half-empty Chianti bottle, and filled my glass. "Don't know. Have to wait and see."

ASHEVILLE—19 JULY 2000

Wednesday morning at the Asheville airport: the sun's rays streamed out of a pale blue sky, warming my face. I stood surrounded by a bright, summer day—not the other frequent choice, an overcast, pouring-down-rain day. Nothing could be finer. Mickey and I hung around outside the main concourse a little after ten o'clock. I defended the sartorial honor of Roth Security by wearing a white seersucker suit with a tan shirt and light-brown tie.

Sook Park and Bin Bie came through the concourse's front doors. They displayed taut facial muscles with dull eyes, seemed forlorn; indeed, they had experienced and suffered much in recent weeks. Both—wearing suits as if they dressed for a board meeting—gave me a weak handshake. They didn't seem pleased to see me, their old colleague. Their bearing and behavior struck me as odd, a tune off-pitch.

Once they sat in the rear of Mickey's Explorer, I opened the passenger door to climb inside. My vision happened to sweep back over the row of clear-glass doors leading into the main hall of the airport building. Clear as a crisp spring morning, Wang Gang and his bodyguard walked into and out of my line of sight, heading toward the rental-car area at the left side of the airport. Gang led the way, dressed in a white wide-brimmed hat and a white linen suit. Big Guy, in white slacks and blue blazer, trailed him. I hesitated, decided not to chase them, and then sat and closed the door. Maybe Roth had arranged for Gang to be here. Our gathering boded to be more complicated than I had imagined.

At the mansion, I ushered our guests into Roth's office. She put down her current book and leaned forward in the chair behind her desk.

I walked to her and whispered in her ear, "Gang and his bodyguard were at the airport."

She bobbed her head slightly. "I know. They're coming here."

Our two clients sat in chairs, which Roth had placed in front of her desk. Taylor Ploughman served tea and coffee. The doorbell rang, and Taylor went to see who chimed. She reappeared with Wang Gang and Big Guy.

I strode to Big Guy. "We're not armed. Are you carrying?"

"I am."

"May we leave your pistol in the hallway?"

We went back to the front hall, left his pistol in a belt holster on a table next to a bouquet of Roth's picked roses, and returned to the office. Gang took a chair near the windows to the right of her desk. His guard stood with his back toward the windows. Mickey stood against the wall to the left. Sook and Bin glanced at Gang, bowed their heads slightly at him, and appeared stunned to see him.

"Today another beautiful day in Asheville," Sook began.

"Our summers are gorgeous," Roth replied. She tapped her fingers on the desk and changed subjects abruptly. "Did we salvage the Silla crown and deal with the culprits to your approval?"

Our two clients nodded and then leaned forward in their chairs, with their heads bent toward Roth. "We wish to alter our agreement about recovered items," Sook began. "You fulfilled your part—finding artifacts without telling authorities—and salvaged them."

Sook paused and sat up straight in his chair. "I know you were to get half the recovered treasure. Bin and I have decided to return the crown and all relics to our native country."

Roth ceased tapping and stiffened, maybe studying Sook's temperament. "Did I overvalue your pledge? Are you more scoundrel than I thought?"

Sook closed his eyes and shook his head violently. "Bin and I are returning all the Silla artifacts to South Korea."

What ho! Was he serious? I had been taut keeping an eye on Big Guy. Sook drove me into the tightness of a groom at his wedding.

"This sounds to me like a catharsis," Roth said. "Tell me what caused you to change your thinking."

"Taking golden crown and artifacts killed friends, Seong-gi and Yeong-ho. If we hadn't stolen relics, they be alive.

"If we continue to keep Silla treasure, we would have to hide the crown, and people in South Korea wouldn't see it. The curse of the crown would continue to haunt us. We will return gold crown and all the relics to museum in Korea."

Roth seemed to consider what Sook had said. "You sought me out and pledged your honor in exchange for our services. Now you do a bait and switch, taking off on a new cause."

I glanced around the office. Sook had gone back to closing his eyes and shaking his head. Roth had her hands flat on her desk and stayed motionless. Gang crossed his hands in his lap and seemed tranquil.

"Without love, without a cause, I am nothing," Sook said. "I cannot live without my love of friends and country."

Maybe the intensity of the search and the deaths had overwhelmed Sook? He had blown a gasket. There was no curse on the Silla crown. Because he had taken a national treasure from his native country, he seemed to have jumped on a crusade to atone for the deaths of his friends. Roth wasn't going to talk him into changing his mind once more. He had decided to ship the salvage to a museum in South Korea, and he could not care less if we threatened to tell the police he stole national relics.

She commenced tapping on her desk. "You feel you caused Seong-gi and Yeong-ho's death by stealing from the Silla mound?"

"I cannot keep the pieces. The blood of my friends covers them. You got the salvage, but I must send the artifacts back."

Roth's complexion hadn't turned rose. She remained calm. "Half the salvage belongs to me. Send your part to your newfound cause. Let me keep my part."

Sook didn't speak. Roth switched to Bin Bie. "You agree with reneging on our agreement?"

Bin didn't answer. No one spoke. Roth wasn't going to shame or spook Sook or Bin into changing their minds. They had plunged off an abyss, disbursing homage to their lost friends. I saw little we could do. We couldn't pistol-whip them. Or could we?

Wang Gang tapped his porcelain teacup onto the saucer in his left hand, giving off rings echoing across the office. I had been watching

Roth and Sook, but I had the impression Gang hadn't stirred for several minutes. Now he fixed his half-closed eyes on Roth. "You're at a stalemate with Mr. Park. Let me try my hand?"

Roth pressed the intercom on her desk; Taylor entered the office and refreshed the drinks. Gang handed his empty teacup to her. "Mr. Park, I have a personal stake in half the salvaged pieces. Negotiating through Isaac Hunter, the antique dealer, Ms. Roth agreed to sell her share to me at a reasonable price. When our discussions conclude, she will contact you with details about the delivery of my Silla pieces to me."

She interrupted Gang to fill me in on what she had done. "Mr. Gang stated he has video evidence you invaded his home—and damaged the power grid in Leesburg, Virginia. He threatened to present proof of your guilt to the police."

"I don't think the videos are irrefutable proof of anything," I said.

She glared at me like an angry primary school teacher. Before responding, she drank coffee and put down the cup. "I am cognizant of the limitation of Mr. Gang's statements. After negotiating with him, I agreed to give him the Silla artifacts we salvaged. In return, he shall provide us with cash and a notarized document stating he commissioned you to break into his house to test his home-security system."

"Our half of the salvage goes to Mr. Gang?" I said.

Sook glanced from Roth to Gang. "Ms. Roth does not have the pieces. I am returning them to their home."

Everyone watched Gang. "You must do what your heart tells you. I too shall do what my heart tells me."

Sook stared at Gang with wide-opened eyes and mouth. "Follow your heart?"

"My heart."

To face Gang, Sook rotated further in his chair. "What your heart say?"

Gang's lips slightly turned up at the edges. "If you steal my Silla relics. Get ready to die."

Noise in the office ended. Sook uttered a weak chuckle. Gang didn't laugh. A hush fell. Gang faced Sook without emotion, like a sleeper whose eyelids drooped. I didn't know if he would do what he said, but I wouldn't gamble my life.

"Tell him he cannot make threat like that," Sook said to me.

I didn't help him. Sook had turned on us by his bizarre and sudden decision to give away our Silla pieces to a museum.

"Do not ask Mr. Gannon to help you," Gang said. "Help yourself. Do you have a list of the Silla pieces?"

Roth seized her copy and passed it to Sook. She watched him and impatiently tapped on her desk again.

"Divide the list into roughly equal portions," Gang said to Sook. "If Ms. Roth agrees with your division, send your half to a museum and my half to Ms. Roth. Then, my heart tells me you and your family live."

Sook scribbled on the sheets Roth had handed him. Then he rose, leaned over my boss's desk, and gave the sheaf of papers back to her. "Pages are catalog of salvaged Silla treasures, in two groups roughly equal value. Will you take proposed split? Or make a different offer?"

Roth ceased tapping her desk, spread out the papers, and read each page. She reread the pages and sometimes stared at the ceiling while she appeared to think. After about five minutes, she spoke.

"I accept. In summary, you and Mr. Bie would keep the crown, the biggest piece, and we will take many of the remaining pieces. These artifacts are priceless, which precludes a division that is perfectly even, but your proposed split is fair."

Sook concluded his discussion with Gang. "Then we agree with Ms. Roth. Where we send your pieces?"

Roth resumed talking with Sook and Bin. "I'll send instruction. When will you send the crown to the museum?"

"Tomorrow," Sook replied.

We had finished the negotiations. South Korea got half the Silla relics, and Wang Gang the other half. Roth got her money, a hefty sum.

#

West Asheville has the shape of a triangle: it lies between the French Broad River to the east and south and Route 26 on the west. Haywood Road is a commercial artery through the middle of the triangle. Its residents are often reliable manual workers. Roth chose this afternoon to treat her team to a celebration marking the close of the Silla crown case. Roth had invited me; I took this as a sign she had forgiven me for what she called my rogue behavior during the recent investigation.

We sat in chairs on a wood-like deck outside the Urban Orchard Cider Company on Haywood Road. To drink cider with her staff, Roth had left the mansion on one of her rare outings. Mickey, Bruce, and I each selected a flight, a sampling of four different flavors of ciders, an alcoholic drink produced from fruit like an apple.

Unwisely, I had relaxed, thinking I had escaped Roth's payback because I got her the salvage. Repeatedly, I had refused to tell her about my actions in Baltimore. She had decided not to fire me, but she had an intricate, devious method of tit for tat.

"I answered the house phone yesterday," Roth said. "I've meant to ask—who is Carla Diaz?"

I paused imbibing my hard cider. I kept my head down and hoped the moment would pass unnoticed.

Three seconds passed without comment, and then my friend, Mickey, torpedoed me. "She's Don's friend."

The dike had cracked: I had to plug the leak. "She is one of the professionals who happened to stay at the hotel where I lodged in Herndon."

"Did you take other professionals to taverns?" Mickey asked.

"She's brilliant," Roth said. "She has always been interested in the detective profession. A Nancy Drew fan. I could work with her."

"Got along well with Don," Mickey said. "Often checked to make sure he enjoyed his stay in Herndon."

"Guys, it would be good for Don to have a friend here in Asheville," Bruce said. "He follows Mickey and me around all the time. We try to help him learn to socialize with others."

Roth pursed her lips and faced Mickey. "Did Don take Ms. Diaz along on his investigation?"

"Yes, Ms. Roth."

She sipped her cider. "And what did Don say about her ability?"

"Took to an investigation like a duck to water," Mickey replied.

Roth studied Mickey. "Is she resourceful?"

Mickey nodded. "She helped us investigate our recent case."

"Perhaps we could find her a position at the mansion?" Roth said. "She told me she's interested in what we do."

"A lady would help mature Don," Taylor added. "Just now, he needs a compass to aid him in finding his path in life."

I thought this was a clear case of piling on and not at all

sportsmanlike. Based on the width of Bruce's grin, I sensed he looked forward to needling me in days to come.

"I think it would be fun to have another female around," Taylor mused. "The mansion tends to be male-centric at times. Ma'am, do you have her number?"

Roth could not be trusted. She had found a way to get even with me for lying to her. Mickey and I had recovered the treasure where Sang-hun had hidden it in the warehouse, but I had disobeyed her. Now she had found a way to control me better. I wondered how her approach would work out in the next case we got?

EPILOGUE

Weeks later, Roth and I worked on office invoices and payments at her desk. When we finished for the night, she signaled the meeting was over by picking up her book and beginning to read, dismissing me.

As I reached the door, she said, "I know you won't tell me what happened in Baltimore, at the warehouse. Whatever you did, I don't hold you in disapproval. You performed satisfactorily. Good night."

I turned and found Roth again reading her book.

Like a deity atop Mount Olympus, she had spoken, and never another word on that subject did she utter.

ABOUT THE AUTHOR

R. M. Morgan worked as an engineer in both the U.S. government and academia. In his job, he investigated mysteries like a detective, unraveling the physics of car crashes to establish how to save drivers and passengers. After years of writing articles in that world, R. M. Morgan discovered the joy of writing mystery novels. Currently, he lives in Southern California and is writing the third book in the Roth/Gannon series.

He writes for the reader's delight, seeking to ease their frustration with daily snags and tribulations. The perfect read entails curling up in a comfortable chair with a mystery, solving a puzzle, identifying and running down a cunning villain. A good mystery challenges the reader: can they solve the enigma before the detective?

Further information about R. M. Morgan is on his website, www.rmmorgan.com.